The
SICK FOX

The
SICK FOX

PAUL BRODEUR

An Atlantic Monthly Press Book

LITTLE, BROWN AND COMPANY · BOSTON · TORONTO

ATLANTIC–LITTLE, BROWN BOOKS
ARE PUBLISHED BY
LITTLE, BROWN AND COMPANY
IN ASSOCIATION WITH
THE ATLANTIC MONTHLY PRESS

Published simultaneously in Canada
by Little, Brown & Company (Canada) Limited

PRINTED IN THE UNITED STATES OF AMERICA

To Malabar

A portion of this book originally appeared, in *The New Yorker*, in different form.

Contents

PART I

The Sick Fox

1

PART II

A Sanctuary Shared

51

PART III

Vulpicide and Vection

99

PART IV

All Manner of Venery

175

PART V

Fog Behind the Moon

229

PART I

The Sick Fox

1

IF IT HAD NOT been for the sun, Harry Brace would not have seen the fox to begin with, but the sun was still high above the mountain at the western end of the valley, and the foliage on saplings and bushes had already begun to wither so that the stream no longer flowed in the leaf-covered twilight of summer. The stream entered the valley from the Pfalzer hill country, to the west, ran past the American military post where Brace had his office, and fed into a larger stream in the flatland near the Rhine. The fox lay by the water's edge at the bottom of the bank, and at first Brace thought it was a garment someone had thrown away. Then he saw it move. (He did not really see it move, he saw it breathing.) The fox was rust-colored in the sun and lay curled into a ball, so when Brace squinted down through the bushes lining the bank, he saw a pair of pointed ears sticking from its loins. He laid his fly rod in the grass of the meadow, and moved closer for a better look. It's a fox all right, he thought, but it's a careless fox to get caught sleeping in a place like that.

Brace picked up a stick and threw it over the edge of the bank, toward the fox. The animal did not stir. It's deaf, Brace thought, or the stream is making too much noise on the gravel. He threw a larger stick, and this time the fox jerked its head from its loins and looked into the water.

"Hey!" Brace said.

The fox twisted its head toward the man standing above it.

"Hey!" Brace said.

The fox got to its feet and, without looking at the man again, crept upstream and hid behind a stump. Brace could see the tip of its tail through the bushes. This fox is an ostrich, he thought, or a remarkably intelligent fox who knows I'm not carrying a gun and that if I start down the bank he has only a couple of yards to jump to reach the other side. "You're a damned insolent fox," Brace said, aloud, and went off into the forest bordering the meadow to find a branch.

When he returned, Brace was carrying a length of sapling. He knelt in the grass at the top of the bank, pushed the branch down through the bushes, and drove it against the stump. The fox left its cover and loped along the edge of the water, watching the man, who was running now along the top of the bank.

"Hey!" shouted Brace again.

The fox crouched, jumped, and landed with a splash in midstream; then it scrambled to the farther bank, paused to shake itself, and climbed slowly through the bushes to the meadow on the other side.

He's sick, Brace thought. No fox in his right mind lets himself get wet.

The fox was moving downstream, and Brace followed, paralleling it until the brook cut through a thicket of scrub. At this point, the animal lowered itself in a patch of sunlight by a marmot hole and regarded the man on the other side.

Brace squatted on his heels and stared back. There were several possible courses of action. He could cross the stream at some shallows, and approach the animal by creeping beneath the lip of the bank; or he could try to come up behind it by cutting through the thickets from the meadow; or he could return to his office for his revolver. He rejected the first two alternatives at once. The sapling isn't thick enough to serve as a club, he thought, and if I should miss with a stone . . . Brace shuddered involuntarily as he imagined the diseased fox lunging down upon him from the top of the bank, or outflanking him in the tangle of brush. Then, knowing that if he returned for his revolver, he would lose twenty minutes of fishing, he lost interest and got to his feet. The fox blinked, lowered its head, and gazed somnolently at him.

"Old sport," said Brace, "that's a face full of wisdom you've got. I hope you dry off and get better."

Ahead of him now, Brace could see part of the military post, a former *Wehrmacht Kaserne*, which lay at the eastern end of the valley, where the forest gave way to gentle hills that were treeless and covered with grain stubble and the green leaves of sugar beet plants. He could see the white flagpole, and the slate roofs of the cement barracks, where the soldiers of the resident ordnance battalion were writing Sunday letters and listening to radio music beamed from the Armed Forces Network stations in Frankfurt, Stuttgart, and Berlin. In the second story of the Headquarters Building the windows of his office were shining yellow in the sun of late afternoon. For a moment, Brace pictured the telephone sitting on his desk and wondered, as he often did when not in his office, if his chief at Area Command Intelligence was trying to reach him, or if some new problem of security had arisen at the nuclear storage site which the battalion maintained in the middle of the forest. Putting business from his mind, he turned and retraced his steps to the place where he had left his fly rod; then he continued upstream, keeping an eye on the brook and knowing that he would hear the *Kaserne* bugler summoning the soldiers to mess at evening.

Half an hour later, Brace was crouching against the bank at the head of a pool and watching his line sweep downstream with the current. When the line reached the tail of the pool, he drew up on the rod tip, felt a trout, and lifted it quickly to the bank. It was a brown trout, colored dark, like the shale at the bottom of the brook. Brace cut a forked stick from an alder, threaded it through the gills, and laid the trout in the grass. He lit a cigarette and sat with his back against the bank, watching the pool. At the western end of the valley, the mountain was blue in the evening, and Sunday strollers were singing as they returned from the *Gasthaus* at the summit to the town below. Brace baited his line, flicked it into the pool, and caught another trout. Then he heard sheep.

The sheep were moving down the opposite side of the valley in a solid wall stretching across the meadow from the stream to the woods. A pair of mongrel dogs paced up and down at the edge of the woods to keep them from the trees. Behind the flock, a shepherd walked slowly along the bank. The shepherd was a sun-browned old man who carried a staff, and wore a green cape and felt hat; a pair of binoculars was slung around his neck, a rucksack was strapped to his back, and in the crook of his arm he held a lamb. When he saw Brace on the opposite bank, he stopped. The sheep moved on down the valley, and the two mongrels came running across the meadow to his side.

"*Wie viele Fische haben Sie?*" shouted the old man.

"*Ich habe zwei,*" Brace answered, holding up two fingers of his right hand.

The shepherd laid the lamb on its side in the meadow and moved closer to the bank, squinting in Brace's direction. "You're an American!" he shouted, and started down the bank. The mongrels preceded him across the stream, milled around Brace's legs, and sniffed at the trout. The old man jumped across the shallows at the head of the pool and labored up the incline. "I speak English!" he said.

"You speak good English," Brace replied. All Germans speak English, he thought.

"I speak English," the shepherd shouted, "but in one ear am I deaf!"

"You speak good English!" Brace shouted back.

"Listen!" said the old man. "One, two, three, four, five, six, seven, eight, nine, ten!"

Brace grinned.

"Listen! Ten, twenty, thirty, forty, fifty . . . sixty, seventy, eighty, ninety, one hundred!"

"Very good," Brace said.

"One thousand!" shouted the old man. "Ten thousand! One hundred thousand! *One million!*"

"*Ein, zwei, drei, vier, fünf*"—Brace began.

"Listen!" the shepherd shouted. "I can count French and Yiddish and Polish!" He began to count, throwing a finger toward Brace's chest with each number, and when he had finished he grinned happily and closed his eyes as if tired from a great effort. When he opened them, he looked at Brace and grinned again. The eyes were blue and set deep in his head, and were triangular, like gabled windows.

"Where did you learn English?" Brace asked.

"From a long time," said the old man. "At the end of the war I am the only one in Grumbach who can speak it. Every morning and night I went to the Americans and translated for them their difficulties."

"Grumbach is a long way from here."

"I follow my sheep. They lead me everywhere."

"Where do they lead you now?"

"Who knows?" said the old man with a shrug. "I'm looking for a place to spend the fall and winter."

"What kind of place?"

"Any kind! Before the first cold weather I must mate my ewes so they will have lambs in the spring. Then I must keep them warm. Do you know of an empty barn?"

Brace shook his head.

"No matter," said the shepherd. "If there are none, I can sleep in the open."

Brace looked at the binoculars slung around the old man's neck. I wonder why the shepherd carries binoculars, he thought. "You have a fine-looking pair of glasses," he said.

"The ears grow old first and then the eyes," replied

the shepherd. "If it were not for the glasses I would certainly lose some lambs in the trees and bushes."

"Are they Zeiss?" Brace asked.

"No, not Zeiss. But they are German." The old man pulled the strap over his head and handed the binoculars to Brace. "After the war they were valuable!" he shouted. "All the Americans wanted them!"

Brace studied the binoculars, noting the mark of the German manufacturer stamped on the crosspiece, and thought about the glasses with which the guards at the storage site constantly surveyed the surrounding woods. Why is it, he wondered, you can never completely forget business — even out here? "They're a fine pair," he said, returning them.

"Until my eyes grew weak, they were not a necessity," the old man replied. He looked at the trout lying on the grass. "How do you catch them?"

"With worms," Brace answered.

The old man shook his head. "The trout are under the rocks." He made a scooping motion with his hands. "You must reach under the rocks and take them with your hands."

"The proprietor of the stream won't allow it," Brace said, grinning.

"With your hands!" said the old man.

"It's *verboten!*" Brace shouted.

The old man laughed. "Who owns this stream?"

"Herr Saul of Weiersheim."

"I don't know of him. How much have you to pay?"

"Twenty marks for the season."

"It's too much. Take them with your hands!" The shepherd laughed and watched Brace toss his cigarette butt into the water. "After the war I smoked a lot of them!" he shouted. "The Americans gave them to everybody! Five years ago, I stopped smoking. Now I feel better. I am seventy-three and I have brought my sheep forty kilometers in four days. The ears and the eyes have grown old but I have never been stronger in my life!" The old man held his elbows out from his sides when he said this, and started down the bank with his mongrels.

Brace saw the lamb stir in the meadow on the other side of the stream. "There's a sick fox nearby," he said.

The shepherd jumped the brook and turned around. *"Ein Fuchs?"*

Brace pointed downstream. "About three hundred meters."

"The dogs will have him," said the old man.

"He might have rabies."

"Rabies?"

"A sickness. It could be dangerous if he bit one of your lambs."

"Rabies . . ." the shepherd said. "Why didn't you kill him?"

"Live and let live," said Brace with a shrug.

The old man shook his head. "It's a faulty principle. If you make yourself a lamb, the wolf will have you."

"In this case, a fox," replied Brace, laughing. "But perhaps I should notify the proprietor."

"Never mind!" the old man shouted. "I myself will look at the fox, and when he don't get well I will kill him!"

"If he has rabies, he could be dangerous," Brace said. "Don't worry. When he don't get well, I will kill him!" The old man picked up the lamb, waved, and set off down the valley after his flock.

At evening, Brace followed the brook downstream to the forester's road where he had left his jeep. The sun was dropping behind some spruce at the top of the mountain, and a shadow was rising in the valley, like tide in an estuary. Tendrils of mist were curling over the edges of the meadow, and the woods were dark on either side and filled with the dankness of old rain. When he came in sight of the *Kaserne,* Brace looked for the fox, and found it curled beside the hole. The fox had buried its nose beneath its tail, and the fur along the ridge of its back was being ruffled by a wind that crept through the valley. Now an ear folded next to the ground picked up the tremor of footsteps pulsing from the soft earth, and an eye blinked open in the ravaged face that was no longer cunning, but gaunt. Lifting his head, the fox gathered his failing senses and projected himself into the surrounding thickets. The nostrils of his fevered snout expanded with the reception of an excruciating and overwhelming scent; for a second, every nerve stretched with anguish to leave the body. Then the fox lowered his head upon his tail and lay perfectly still. Only the sleepless eye gave sign of life as, rolling upward, it fixed itself upon the shadow of the man who stood at the edge of the meadow.

The shepherd has forgotten, Brace thought. I must remember to mention it when I stop at Saul's on my way home.

[11]

The fox blinked. The bright and outraged eye grew veiled, as if hooded with fatigue. Now it opened wide, focusing upon Brace in a final assault; then it closed slowly, opened halfway, and closed again.

Brace was filled with a grave and tender pity. "Sleep, fox," he said aloud. "Here's your chance to recover."

When he reached the jeep, he dismantled his rod and laid it and the trout on the floorboards; then he drove up over the ridge and out of the forest past a deserted military training area on the hill above Weiersheim. The forest to the west of the training area was a hunting preserve traversed by parallel shooters' lanes that tunneled through the woods like gloomy corridors. At the edge of the forest stood half a dozen *Hochsitze* — high chairs with fir trunk legs that afforded hunters a vantage point, twenty feet above the ground, from which to ambush roebuck. The training area itself, built by an engineer outfit from Kaiserslautern, had not been used for years. As recompense for some favor performed by the engineer commandant, Brace's superiors had designated him as a kind of caretaker. A storage shack (for which he carried a set of keys) and some dilapidated sheds, once used to shelter vehicles, sat near the edge of the woods. In the center of the field was a prisoner-of-war compound that had been constructed during some long-forgotten maneuver. The compound was square-shaped and fenced with barbed wire strung on heavy cedar posts. On one side, there was a broken gate with a badly defaced sign that had once warned off trespassers in three languages. Now some rickety guard towers, weakened by the depredations of wood-seeking peasants, stood tilting at each corner, and in the center of the compound, raised on stilts, there was a cylindrical wooden water tower. To the east of the training area, there was a plateau that was carpeted with the broad green leaves of sugar beet plants; beyond these the road descended a steep hill to the village of Weiersheim, which lay in a deep hollow between the plateau and an escarpment that was stitched with vineyards and topped by the ruins of an old castle.

Brace left his jeep in the cobblestoned market square and, carrying the two trout he had caught, walked to the end of an alley where he found Herr Saul repairing his motorcycle in the yard behind his cottage.

"*Guten Abend*, Herr Saul."

"*Guten Abend*, Herr Brace!" Saul leaned the motorcycle against the fence surrounding a hen coop and advanced, extending his hand. He was a short, stocky man who worked as a clerk in the County Administration Offices in Gerberstadt, and he wore thick glasses that magnified his eyes out of all proportion. As if to mitigate the effect of oversized scrutiny, he always smiled, and now, as he saw the trout, he bent forward and smiled broadly. "*Petri Heil!*" he said, pronouncing the invocation to the patron saint of fishing.

"*Petri Dank!*" Brace replied.

Saul fingered the larger trout. "It will weigh four hundred grams!" He spoke in German, and Brace, who had a good command of the language, answered him in German.

"I brought them as a gift," he said.

"I thank you. They'll make a fine breakfast."

Saul took the trout and peered into Brace's face, still smiling.

"Today I've seen a sick fox," Brace said. "He is three hundred meters below the big pool."

"A fox," Saul repeated. "Yes, there are many of them in the woods."

"The one I saw is sick, perhaps with what we call rabies."

"Rabies? You will have to show me this word in the book." Saul led Brace into the cottage and then into a small living room, where he stooped to search a shelf for his dictionary. When he found it, he switched on a light and handed the book to Brace, who leafed through the pages.

"*Tollwut*," Brace said. "*Der Fuchs hat Tollwut, glaub' ich*."

"*Tollwut*," Saul echoed, peering at the dictionary. "Rabies . . . yes," he said in English. "That's very dangerous."

"Of course I'm not sure of this. It's only possible the fox has *Tollwut*."

"Rabies," Saul repeated. "One moment please, and I will write this word." He took a notebook from the shelf and looked again at the dictionary.

When Brace glanced at the notebook, he saw rows of English words with their German meanings listed in neat columns beside them. "So you're studying English," he said.

Saul looked up from the notebook with an embarrassed smile. "Each word I write I will remember," he replied, tapping his head.

Brace nodded, and went on in German. "I met a shepherd by the stream who told me he would kill the fox if it didn't get well."

"Was the shepherd an old man?"

"An old man with two dogs."

"Yes, I've heard of him. There is reason to believe he's a poacher, that one. If the fox has rabies, it cannot be left to him to kill it. The situation would be serious if this fox should bite a child."

"I didn't think of that," Brace replied. "I told the shepherd because of his sheep."

"Very serious, this rabies. Since the land belongs to the town, I shall report it to Town Secretary Vogt, but it is also a matter for the authorities of the county. The *Kreisjäger* has jurisdiction over the wild animals. Yes, I must report it to the Secretary and the *Jäger* in the morning. Perhaps the *Kreisveterinär* should be informed as well, and also Herr Zabern who leases the forest for hunting."

"By all means," said Brace, who was amused.

"You know Herr Zabern?"

"I've met him at the tennis courts in Gerberstadt."

"Ah yes! A sportsman through and through, Herr Zabern. They say his wife's an excellent player."

"Excellent," Brace repeated. And beautiful, he thought.

Saul drew himself up and accompanied Brace to the door. "So, I thank you for bringing this to my attention, Herr Brace. *Auf Wiedersehen!*"

"*Auf Wiedersehen,*" Brace replied. He was thinking of Greta Zabern and he nearly forgot to shake Saul's hand.

2

༄༄༄༄༄༄

IT WAS DARK when Brace returned to the *Kaserne*. Flood-
lights had been turned on to illuminate the chain link
perimeter fence, and the guard mount was being
changed at the sentry gate. Brace waved to the ser-
geant-in-charge and drove through the gate and into a
walled courtyard, where he parked his jeep. Then,
carrying his fly rod, he walked across the courtyard to
the Headquarters Building, listening to the clicking of
bolts as the guards presented their carbines for inspection. He knew that at the storage site, deep within the
forest behind Weiersheim, a similar scene was taking
place, and that the first heavily armed patrols of nocturnal probers were being sent into the gloom beyond
the glare of searchlights that restlessly swept the en-
circling woods. When he entered the Headquarters
Building, he stopped by the telephone switchboard room
to see if he had any messages.

"Nothing for you," said the duty operator with a
yawn. He looked at Brace's fishing rod, and grinned.
"Been out catching spies?"

"Yes," Brace replied. "With hook and line."

Upstairs, in his office, he put his fishing gear away,
opened a steel cabinet safe that stood against the wall

beside his desk, and took out a report he had finished typing the day before. The report was a routine monthly security survey of Alpha Site, and was due at Army Headquarters, in Stuttgart, the following week. It was eight pages long, and there were seven onionskin carbons. Brace arranged the manuscript on the desk before him in eight neat piles, and carefully stapled the pages of each pile together. Then he started the long process of signing his name in the bottom right-hand corner of each page. Afterwards, he would ink in the logbook code number in the top left-hand corner, and after that he would stamp each sheet at top and bottom center with the appropriate classification — "Secret," in this case, because the report dealt with the storage site. "Secret" times one hundred and twenty-eight, Brace thought. No, counting the times he would punch the rubber stamp into its red inkpad, it would come to "Secret" times two hundred and fifty-six, plus sixty-four times the logbook code number, plus another sixty-four times his signature . . .

He leaned back in his swivel chair and lit a cigarette. How simple life had become here in the Pfalz! When he had been sent up from Stuttgart, the previous winter, he had expected to be hounded by his superiors, but no one had come to visit him, and even Moran, the Chief of Area Counter Intelligence, was so occupied with his own bailiwick in Kaiserslautern, forty miles away, that he always relied on the telephone.

Brace remembered that he had been lonely and restless for the first several weeks. Then, in March, he had been marooned for ten days by a series of heavy, late-season snows. The roads had become impassable, and only by throwing his jeep into four-wheel drive had he been able to get about. Suddenly he was truly alone — a vassal lord in a remote province, a latter-day palatine, enchanted with the brilliance of his solitude and already disaffected with the Empire. He had gone skiing on the mountain, breaking out a slalom course through the trees that covered the steep eastern face, and pausing from time to time to gaze out over the motionless landscape that only he could traverse in freedom. In May, he had leased the trout stream from Saul. And, gradually, he began to sever relations with headquarters. His method was simple: he stopped writing the kind of reports that, like delayed seedlings, sprouted curiosity and query, and blossomed into such consequences as the desire for further clarifications and, finally, more reports. He did not, however, cut off all correspondence. At regular intervals, he telephoned Moran, in Kaiserslautern, and sent down a few routine surveys and inspections to Stuttgart — seasonal plantings to reassure the gardeners who tended the master files that the district of their tenant was still fertile. By thus controlling the echoes of his activity, he ensured his freedom, assuring his superiors and telling himself at the same time, as if to satisfy a flagging sense of duty, that he was "keeping an eye on things." Now he glanced at the recommendations he had made on the last page of the report. They were suitably modest, entailing nothing that might alarm the analysts at Headquarters, who were forever sticking red pins into huge wall maps and nodding solemnly at one another in recognition of the vast patterns of conspiracy that were obviously unfolding before them. Brace looked at his own wall map, and shivered involuntarily. Even the *thought* of another man poring over a map of his district filled him with anguish! He had become jealous of his domain and his solitude — as if of an uncertain mistress.

He resumed his work until, some minutes later, he heard the slamming of car doors and loud voices from the courtyard below. Glancing through his window, he saw half a dozen lieutenants of the battalion walking unsteadily toward the Bachelor Officer's Quarters, and found himself straining to hear the end of a ribald tale that was provoking immoderate laughter. The junior officers were, for the most part, electrical engineers who spent their weekdays sealed beneath the earth's surface in the great igloo storage vaults at Alpha Site, and their weekends with high-priced whores in Frankfurt, Mannheim, and Mainz. Though Brace occasionally envied them their camaraderie, he rarely sought to join them. The ordnance battalion had been formed as a special weapons unit two years before, in New Mexico, during which time its personnel had been under a strict surveillance conducted by agents of the FBI. The memory of this had lingered, with the result that Brace's presence inevitably imposed a certain restraint on any gathering. For a time, he regretted this; then, unwilling to render himself sufficiently familiar to cultivate their trust, he began to avoid them. As he stood by his window, he was, moreover, a little contemptuous of their need to escape the rural isolation with organized urban philandering on the weekends. But their confident garrulity and laughter also provoked him to imagine the adventures from which they were returning, and now he experienced a familiar stirring within him — a diffuse animation which soon became an ambition that must be appeased. Returning to his desk, he finished marking the report. Then he put the manuscript in a large compartment at the bottom of the safe, where there was also a revolver, a Thompson submachine gun, ammunition for both, and some incendiary devices for destroying documents in the event of emergency. Afterwards he locked the door of the safe, left his office, and stopped by the Charge-of-Quarters Room on the ground floor to inform the duty sergeant that he would not return until after midnight.

The air was cool and filled with the sweetish odor of grapes fermenting in the neighboring vineyards. As Brace drove up the hill to Weiersheim, he could see in his rearview mirror the reflection of the *Kaserne* which sat bathed in its own light at the mouth of the valley. At the top of the hill, he switched off the engine and allowed the jeep to coast through the cobblestoned street that descended to the market square. On either side, a solid façade of darkened, tightly shuttered houses formed a sluiceway that was filled with the smell of an Augean stable and the stench of human manure collected in the farmers' "honey wagons." Toward the end, the street plunged steeply like a chute, and the vehicle, silent as an owl on nocturnal wing, dropped into the bottom of the town and swept across the market place. Brace brought it to a halt before the *Gasthof Post* and climbed out. The sound of his heel striking the cobblestones was suddenly ominous, like the click of a rifle bolt in a remote region of the forest. Almost as a reflex, he glanced around him, but nothing stirred behind the shuttered windows. These hamlets that nestled in the hollows of the Pfalz slept soundly, inaudibly, as if night were a blanket they pulled over their heads. There was a stale, heavy odor of sleep in the air, and the cobblestones beneath his feet glistened with a slippery film, as if the breath of some slumbering animal were condensing into rime and falling back upon its nocturnal lair. Before him, thin slivers of light showed through shutters on the first and second floors of the inn. The innkeeper and his wife, refugees from Königsberg, never went to bed at the rural hour.

Inside the *Gasthof*, Brace stood in a hallway at the foot of a staircase that led up to the guest rooms and the keeper's lodgings. The kitchen was closed by now, he knew, which meant that Lisl was probably in her room, reading in bed, with her head propped on her elbow, her feet tangled in the eider-down puff, and her white flanks exposed to the door. For a moment, he debated whether to risk the stairway — his caution wavering with the knowledge that she preferred to be surprised. A slender barrier, the stairway, a mere twelve steps. All the more slender for the fact that once he gained her room, there would be little risk. Lisl lived separately — a condition she had imposed when her husband had been repatriated from Russia, and which had given rise, inevitably, to rumors that he had been wounded in some special manner. Brace did not believe the rumors, but the alternative — that Weber did not care to assert himself — seemed equally improbable. Surely when he saw her undressing, or caught sight of her padding about in her brazen and habitual nudity, he must be aroused. That large, proportioned body which did not invite caresses so much as it seemed to challenge them, even to render them superfluous, would give anyone ideas. It must kill him, Brace thought. He tried to imagine the man's torture by dissecting the image of Lisl into a series of erotic tableaux — an immobile, sculptured face with green eyes and red mane of hair; nipples in relief against their paler rosettes; the russet-colored wedge beneath her belly . . . "Idiot!" he muttered. He was merely torturing himself. Taking a deep breath, he pushed abruptly through a door and entered the restaurant, where he found Weber watching television.

"— *'n Abend*," he said.

"*Guten Abend*, Herr Brace." Weber got to his feet and extended his hand across a table strewn with papers. He was a small, gaunt man whose movements, like his pronunciation, had a certain Prussian precision, but lacked the usual Prussian stamina. As if to counteract this deficiency (which Brace ascribed to a sense of inferiority caused by his refugee status) Weber invariably affected cynicism. Now, as he saw Brace looking about the empty room, he pointed with a grimace to the television set that was tuned to some wrestling matches from Düsseldorf.

"One of your American morality plays," he said scornfully. "The villain always loses."

Brace smiled, knowing that like most refugees Weber had been violently anti-American since the abortive Hungarian uprising, and glanced at the screen, where two flabby performers were tugging and pulling each other around a ring. Another indication of Weber's deficiency, he thought. Men who watched such spectacles usually read physical culture magazines as well. An interesting clue, the wrestling. A form of escape. Perhaps Weber was impotent after all.

Brace sat at the table while the innkeeper gathered up

his papers, and looked up at the ceiling where there was a metal grate designed to facilitate the rise of heat from the restaurant into the upstairs lodgings. Even as he did so, he saw a glimmer of light appear from the room above. Lisl . . . She had heard his voice and pulled back the carpet. Brace averted his eyes but the thought of her crouching over the grate above them made him hold his breath. He turned to Weber, who was stacking his papers in a neat pile.

"A bottle of Würzburger, please," he said, aware of the strain in his voice. "And some bread with ham."

The innkeeper pushed the pile of papers to one side of the table, and disappeared into the kitchen. Once again, Brace looked about the room. Nailed to the top of the window frames were the prongs of several dozen roebuck, and over the center of the room, casting shadows like those of branches upon the ceiling, hung a chandelier fashioned from the interlocked antlers of *Hirsche*. The inn with its heavy beams and tiny windows — through which, even on bright days, only the faintest light filtered — was somehow emblematic of the forest itself, where heavy stands of trees stood guard against all but the most slender rays of the sun. There was a certain austere imagination, something intensely traditional, virile, and German in the room. It's almost feudal, Brace thought with pleasure. Here, he felt himself a kind of seigneur — a baronial lord descended from his castle.

The inn had been in existence since the Napoleonic era, at which time it had been a way station for coaches and couriers traveling between Paris and Frankfurt. Long ago, however, a highway had been constructed to the east, bypassing the village, so that now the several rooms upstairs were rented only during the hunting season, or in the winter months when a rare storm forced automobiles off the road. To survive the dearth of guests, the inn had become a restaurant specializing in wild game, and, largely because of the hunting preserve, it enjoyed a modest reputation in the district, although not with the soldiers at the *Kaserne*, who found the *Post* too quiet, and who invariably referred to the town as "Sleepy Hollow." Rabbit, hare, venison, and wild boar were served during the autumn and winter, and trout appeared on the menu all year round. For the benefit of tourists, the trout were kept in a large tank by the front window, and were fed liver scraps until they became fat and soft and tasteless.

From the voluminous reports of his predecessors (which filled an entire file drawer of his safe) Brace knew that Heinz Weber had arrived in Weiersheim three years before, having spent more than a decade as a Russian prisoner. His wife, Lisl, had come to the town as an expellee from Königsberg shortly after the end of the war. Endowed with a stunning body, she went to work in the *Post* as a barmaid and soon became the mistress of the owner, a widower with a bad heart, who willed her the establishment when he died (in her bed, the townspeople claimed) a few months later. Her subsequent exploits with officers and men of both the French and American Occupation Forces had become a legend in County Gerberstadt by the time her husband arrived on the scene. Emaciated and exhausted from his long incarceration in a Soviet labor camp near the Arctic Circle, poor Weber gained his freedom only to find that the Russians had taken his house and land in Königsberg, and that a whole army of men had taken his wife. Almost without protest, he allowed himself to be reduced to the role of her employee. In his spare time, he immersed himself in refugee politics, hopeful that one day he might at least regain his land.

Brace glanced at the pile of papers the innkeeper had stacked on the table. On top was a letter addressed to the Minister of Refugees in Bonn. It was the usual diatribe; filled with the hopeless sense of outrage and recrimination that motivated all the active refugee groups, it demanded a firm policy to regain the lost territories east of the Oder-Neisse. The stationery carried the official inscription of the BHE Party — the "All-German Block of the Homeless and those Deprived of their Rights" — and listed Weber as a district leader. Beneath this was the party's official slogan: *From the Saar to the Memel!* How absurd, Brace thought. As if people cared any longer for the return of a river on the Lithuanian border!

In the last election, Weber had pasted up BHE posters in the surrounding villages. The posters showed a strong pair of hands fitting together pieces depicting the now divided parts of Germany, including the Polish Corridor and Prussia. But the Catholic farmers of County Gerberstadt had voted overwhelmingly as always, for the Christian Democrats. The BHE failed to win even a single seat in the Bundestag. Now the party was virtually finished. Depleted by wholesale defections caused by the continuing economic boom, and weakened by the cunning of Adenauer, who had enticed two of its most prominent leaders into his cabinet, the BHE had ceased to be a political force. But Weber continued to write his letters. A die-hard. A fool obsessed with what was irretrievably lost. Still, the innkeeper's political hatred and his central location made him an ideal source of information. And, of course, there was Lisl . . .

Now Weber returned to the room, carrying two bottles of beer, two glasses, and a plate with the ham and bread Brace had ordered. When he had poured the beer, he sat down opposite Brace and lifted his glass.

"Königsberg," he said, and drank.

It was a toast without variation, and Weber always uttered it like a blessing, or a superstition.

Without reply, Brace raised his own glass and took a sip. He started to look toward the ceiling but saw that Weber was watching him. To Königsberg, he thought, a Russian city now called Kaliningrad.

"I've come across some interesting news lately," Weber said, leaning forward and lowering his voice.

Brace recognized the lowering of the voice. "News" for the innkeeper was always some vague international development in which he could interpret the chance of returning to Prussia. Brace found the incessant self-delusion boring, but he was resigned to it. He sat back and stole a glance at the grate in the ceiling. The light in Lisl's bedroom had been extinguished. Did that mean she was already waiting for him outside?

"The government's trying to keep it a secret, of course," Weber said. "But it's no use. A trade commission has come back from Danzig with word that certain relaxations may be possible. The Silesians are even hopeful of returning to their homes."

"Why should the Poles allow them to do that?"

The innkeeper shrugged mysteriously. "History proves these unnatural ethnic divisions never heal. Look at the Balkans! Now if those birds in Bonn would apply the necessary pressures —"

"You're forgetting the last election," Brace said.

"Elections are meaningless, Herr Brace. What matters now is to merge the Federal and Democratic Republics. Once the political differences between ethnic Germans have been neutralized, pressures can be brought to bear against the Czechs and the Poles for the return of the Sudetenland and Silesia."

"But can the Soviets be pressured into returning Prussia?" Brace asked with weary malice.

Weber ignored the thrust. "Once the political boundaries move eastward, there'll be no stopping us," he said.

Brace nodded without comment. As usual, the innkeeper was parroting the pamphlets of professional émigré intellectuals. Whatever the latest variations of policy, the basic thesis always remained the same: the refugees were innocent because they had been unlawfully deprived. Therefore, any form of redress was valid. "You people have become strategists," Brace said with a smile. "For years you wanted war with the Reds. Now you're toying with the idea of a Socialist neutrality which even the Socialists have given up."

"In the end, Herr Brace, nationalism will prevail over socialism. It's a question of practicality. Just as for the individual the safeguarding of property is the first consideration, so for the state the regaining of lost territories will supersede idealism. History bears me out. Except in captivity, what nation has ever gone over to the Communists when it had outstanding territorial claims against its neighbors?"

So you're willing to risk war after all, Brace thought. He studied the innkeeper's face. It was still the face of a prisoner — deprived, yet full of hope and cunning, especially around the eyes, which glittered like those of a ferret. Brace finished his beer quickly, and got to his feet.

Disappointed, Weber raised a hand as if to stay him. "I hear you've seen a sick fox," he said.

Gossip is like water, Brace thought. It seeks the lowest level. "Where did you hear that?"

The innkeeper shrugged. "The village elders, Herr Brace. They heard it from Saul. D'you really think the fox has rabies?"

"Who knows?" Brace replied. "When I saw him, the fox was almost too weak to move."

"In any case," Weber persisted hopefully, "the possibility exists."

The innkeeper is a true anarchist, Brace thought. "Yes, it exists," he said. "*Gute Nacht*, Herr Weber."

When he emerged from the *Post*, he saw Lisl sitting in the jeep. Through the windshield, clouded with mist, her pale face seemed soft and indistinct, like the disembodied marble heads seen at night in the gardens of châteaux. Brace quickened his step, climbed into the jeep, and started the engine. Then, without a word, he wheeled the vehicle around in the square, and raced up the road leading into the forest. Even when he turned and looked at her across the seat, he said nothing, for he knew that she would not speak or change her expression until they were clear of the town. It was this very stolidity of hers that excited him. The mask she wore was another challenge, like the one of her body. He would animate the first as he would arouse the second. He often thought that her secret façades and her almost kaleidoscopic capacity for changing them would make her a perfect subject for photography. (Sometimes he even imagined himself posing her, despite the fact that he took a kind of counter-military pleasure in not owning a camera.) When she was working in the kitchen of the inn, Lisl wore blouses buttoned severely to the top, and her hair done up in a bun with pins; when the kitchen closed, she went upstairs to her room, took the pins from her hair, and sat in the nude, brushing it. He wondered if she knew that these transformations were a source of secret delight for him, if she understood that it was the metamorphosis of her features from stolidity to carnality which intrigued him.

Now they passed the last drab houses, and plunged across the plateau toward the forest. The first stand of trees loomed ahead — scrub birch and oak, bent and withered by the constant wind that swept eastward across the open hill country — a frail and ragged breastwork for the deeper forest beyond. The cobblestones gave way to gravel which splattered against the insides of the fenders, and the trees on either side grew denser, crowding the passageway. In some places, their branches met overhead, obliterating the stars. Then, suddenly, they opened into the clearing that contained the prisoner-of-war compound and the shacks of the training area.

Lisl had closed her eyes and tipped her head back against the seat.

"Hey, redhead," Brace said softly. "We're here. We're in the forest."

"Yes," she replied. "I can smell it."

There was a huskiness, a weary satisfaction in her voice which touched him, for he knew that behind the mask lay melancholy. When he had first taken up with her, three months before, there had been bitterness. Time had blunted that. Yet there was no placing Lisl in time. Too vital to live in the past (and thus incapable of sharing Heinz's obsession with retrieving it) she derived all joy and sadness from the present. Did the future exist? No, she never spoke of it. Nor could his ego conceive of it. He liked to think of her as a day to day dependency — his mistress.

Lisl had opened her eyes. "Will you build a fire in the stove tonight?"

"Certainly."

"Before . . . or after?"

He smiled. "Whenever you wish."

"Ah, then you're going to be gentle." She tucked her feet beneath her, and wrenched herself around to face him. "So gentle."

He looked at her and saw a faint smile of amusement and disdain on her face. In turning, the coat she had merely wrapped around her by knotting the belt had come open at the throat and chest.

"So gentle," Lisl repeated softly.

Was she goading him? He never knew with Lisl. Her face, in transformation now between the bored, indifferent countenance with which she faced the daily world and the frantic, nocturnal animation he would

soon summon up, was always mysterious. It was, therefore, in transition that she seemed farthest from him.
He disliked his inability to comprehend the very grada-
tions of feeling which so fascinated him. Or was it an
unwillingness to investigate — a fear that by doing so
he might somehow alter the pleasurable sequence he
was accustomed to experience with her? Brace was
aware of his own question only in the vaguest sense —
as all men perceive their shortcomings. Lacking the natural intuition to understand women, and distrustful of
intuition as a focus for judgment, he had always been
accustomed to rely upon experience. Now he found
himself remembering the first days of their affair. She
had just given up a German lover, a wealthy vintner
from Bad Dürkheim, who drove a Mercedes. Flattered
and curious, Brace had asked her why, and she had
smiled the same goading smile.

"Because you are stronger, my dear," she had said.

Now they were skirting the edge of the barbed wire
compound. Beyond the shack and the sheds, the trees
of the hunting preserve loomed above them like a
breaker about to crash upon an open beach. Here the
anarchy of the forest commenced, boiling over the corrugated contours like surf over rocks, unbroken save
for the street lamps of a small town that nestled against
the side of the distant mountain — another town of
farmers, with lights that twinkled in the darkness like
those of some coastal ship moving cautiously on the
edge of the vast sea. Brace stopped the jeep and turned
off the engine. Was there any soul awake to wonder at
his headlights against the dark horizon? Or was his the

only drama being played out on this lonely shore? These beet farmers stuck into the earth like posts — was there not some equivalent mystery in their slow tempo? Ah, but were they even living, the peasants who crept into their fields at dawn, and who returned at dusk behind their plodding oxen?

"Because you are stronger, my dear," Lisl had said.

He took her roughly in his arms, recognizing in the image of his grasp the sense of tyranny that she found indispensable.

Smiling, Lisl raised herself upon her knees, and, half straddling him, her back touching the steering wheel, undid the belt that closed her coat. Glimpsing the effect of her nakedness on his face, she leaned confidently back on her haunches as he slipped the coat from her shoulders. Then, feeling the weight of it imprisoning movement, and the sudden strength in his hands that held her arms against her sides, she moved against him, shifting her body with slow rhythm as she delivered first one and then the other nipple of her breasts between his lips.

When he had built a fire in the stove of the hut, he dragged a mattress and pillow from a cot and tossed them on the floor. Afterwards, he started to undress. As he finished, Lisl let her coat drop and kicked it aside with her foot. For a moment, she warmed herself before the fire; then, sensing his approach, she knelt quickly on the mattress, leaning forward on her elbows and touching her forehead to the pillow.

He stood above her, profoundly content. Within the tiny hut, shadows flickered on the walls; outside, the night and the forest conspired together with mist and murmuring; at his feet, this woman kneeling in submission, who preferred him because he was stronger. For a moment longer he savored the vulnerable symmetry of her flanks. Then, quickly, he bent over her.

3

〰〰〰〰〰〰

THE FOX HAD come awake. Twitching his ears, he listened to the stream gurgling over pebbles at the bottom
of the bank; then he lifted himself on his forelegs and
stared at the tail and hindquarters curled limply beneath
his body, raising one paw and then the other as if to test
his strength. The sound of running water came to him
as an agonizing reminder of a thirst that was too painful to slake, but his fevered nostrils were assuaged by
the cool respiration of the valley which had filled the
trough of the stream with mist. The fox brought himself
erect, wriggled his stiff joints, and crept along the stream
bank to the shallows; there he paused, poised himself,
and leaped across the water to the other side. Then,
taking in all the rich smells of night, he slithered through
the tall wet grass toward the forest.

When he emerged from the trees, the fox found himself at the edge of a field that rolled up from the meadow
to the beet fields on the plateau above the town. Here
his nostrils quivered at the strong stench of oily wool
which was mingled with a fainter but still dread canine
odor and the sweat of man. Without pause, the fox trotted into the open and sat upon a knoll, a vantage point

from which, unabashed, he looked down into a hollow where the old man's flock of sheep lay huddled in sleep. The warm smell of them excited his emboldened spirit, and heedless of the constriction in his throat, he lifted his head toward the night sky, and barked.

Below, in the hollow, the shepherd's dogs sat up and growled. The old man, who was sleeping in his cloak, awakened instantly, raised himself on an elbow, and scanned the rim of the higher ground around him. Seeing nothing, he watched the cocked and restless ears of his mongrel auditors until the dogs relaxed and lowered their heads upon their paws. Then he lay back in the grass. It's probably a marmot, he thought.

Once awake, however, the old man was unable to return to sleep, and so he thought about the enemies that had conspired to deprive him of it in the past. Cold was his worst enemy, but he had many others. In addition to cold, there were poisonous plants such as pennywort, belladonna, and fermented pasture; sicknesses such as smallpox, liver rot, and cachexia; and nervous ailments of all sorts. In his youth, there had been wolves in the Alps and great hawks that soared above river valleys in the springtime, when floods drove rodents and small animals into the open, but now his enemies were not so exciting. Cold, sickness, and fatigue were the foes of his old age, but especially the cold — a nasty, ignoble enemy against which he plotted constantly. This year, for the first time, he had left extra wool on his animals at shearing time, so they might be able to endure a longer outdoor season. Now he reminded himself, hopefully, that his sheep were Saxony merinos, carefully bred to withstand humidity and chill. They can endure anything, he thought proudly. They are tough, as I am.

Tough as you are, he reflected. But if you're so tough, old man, why did you not kill the fox which the American pointed out to you this evening?

The fox was rabid and I was tired from the day's trek, he answered himself. I'll kill it tomorrow when my strength returns.

Tomorrow! Then why did you tell the American today that you had never been stronger? Are you looking for excuses, old man? Are you becoming decrepit? Can you no longer carry a lamb without croaking?

Listen, it's never wise to admit weakness to strangers, and the fox had all the symptoms of the madness called hydrophobia. You saw yourself the lassitude, the lack of fear in the eye, and the longing to lie near water. You know as well as I that victims of the madness are unpredictable, and that if you had failed to strike true, the fox might have become enraged and dashed into the midst of the flock.

Yes, I saw everything. And I know that you were filled with the prudence and fear of senility. Why don't you admit you were afraid, old man, and that your arms were trembling even as you thought of lifting the staff?

Listen, I was fatigued. I was looking at a dying, witless fox, that's all. Don't make a fable of it. Go to sleep . . .

But the shepherd was too agitated to fall asleep, and so he got to his feet and inspected his sheep. The animals were resting quietly and he knew that they, too, were tired from the day's trek. With the approach of the mating season, he had tied pieces of linen around the bellies of the rams so they would not top the ewes prematurely. The rams, sullen and ill-tempered because of the linen, often turned upon the dogs, but now fatigue had even made them docile. The shepherd reached down and felt the grass with the palm of his hand. Dampness was one of his great enemies because it caused cachexia in his sheep, but the day had been warm, and the hollow was higher than the meadow and still dry.

Now, satisfied that his flock was secure, the old man climbed a knoll and looked down into the valley. In the distance, the *Kaserne* sat blinking like a sentinel's gatehouse at the edge of night, and beyond the *Kaserne* the bare, stubble-covered hills rolled on like a diminishing sea swell toward an invisible horizon. In his mind, the old man made a journey past the hills to the Rhine-Graben — that enormous sunken trench where the river flowed through the coils of its discarded meanders. Then he crossed the river into the Odenwald. From there he went south through the Black Forest, and then east, into the Alps. The shepherd had spent the summers of his youth in the Alps, but since the war he had grown too old to undertake long transmigrations, and had spent his summers in the Eifel, a range of hills to the north, above the Moselle. The only real treks he undertook now were those of his dreams. Once, during the war, a Basque prisoner working by the roadside had told him that giant fern grew in the Pyrenees and that because of the fern the mountains seemed to ripple in the wind. The old man often dreamed of going to the Pyrenees, but he knew that he never would, and that he would never return to the Alps. He would remain in the

Pfalz — a migrant who had returned to gentler hills. But since the gentler hills evoked cruelly for him his descent into age, and since his dreams of real mountains served to remind him of his infirmities, he often chose to dream of the sea. He had never seen the sea. He dreamed of it frequently, however, and of the shepherds in the South of France, who pastured their flocks in the mountains during the summer and spent their winters in the windswept hills behind the Mediterranean.

When the old man came back from all the places he would never see or return to, he looked up at the dark sky. Listen, you old fool, he told himself. You are daydreaming and it is night. Forget the fatigue of your old age and don't fear the madness of the fox which you must kill tomorrow. Be afraid instead of your dreams for they perform nothing except to make you lose time and courage when you have none of either to lose. Soon the nights will be too cold and damp for outdoor folding, and you will have to find a permanent shelter for your sheep. The rains will start at the end of October, the pasturage will die off in November, and in December the first snow will come. Then, in the spring —

"Don't let yourself think about spring," the old man muttered. "There's a full winter to be endured before spring."

Now he descended again into the hollow, where he stood watching his sleeping flock. Could Spanish sheep endure such cold as mine can? he wondered.

Probably not, he answered himself. But could your sheep withstand the heat of Spain?

For some moments, the shepherd pondered this question; then he lay down in the grass and shut his eyes.

Go to sleep, old man, he told himself. You have enough problems without imagining new ones.

The fox was climbing slowly through the forest. When he emerged from the trees a second time, he was at the edge of the training area. Panting, he sat down in the grass and surveyed the field surrounding the barbed wire compound and the storage sheds. Then he heard a hare.

The hare was somewhere in the tall grass between the gate of the compound and Brace's jeep, which was parked beside the sheds. Though he could not see it, the fox could hear the unmistakable *thump-thump* of its progress from one tender clump of shoots to the next. The fox lifted his head, sniffed, and caught an aroma that tightened the muscles of his famished stomach. Then, belly to the ground, he started forward.

The hare brushed against some tall blades of grass and froze, ears erect, all fear and trembling.

The fox moved quickly, with legs splayed out and tail dragging limply behind him.

The hare took a series of tiny hops and paused, whiskers twitching, to nibble at the bark of a small bush.

The fox parted the last barrier of grass with his snout, shrank back, and gathered all his remaining strength. Then he bounded forward — the white tip of his tail soaring after him — struck the ground, bounded again, and missed.

With a squeal of terror, the hare fled. The grass quivered in its wake. Bouncing, the hare fled on — bouncing, bouncing, reappearing an instant, bouncing, gone . . .

The fox lay spread-eagled against the earth, dizzy

with the effort of his stalk, and shaking his head savagely as if to clear his fevered brain of the viruses swarming through it. Then, in fury and frustration, he leaped high into the air, twisting as he did to snap at his long, graceful tail. And, suddenly, there was a noise from the shack. The fox searched the gloom with eyes and ears and nose but there was no sound or smell, just a flickering glow in a windowpane. For a moment longer, he crouched, tense and undecided; then he vanished in the direction of the fields above the town, where pheasants sometimes hid in sleep beneath the leaves of the sugar beet plants.

The fox sat at the edge of the bowl that held the village, his gaunt snout swaying gently to and fro with rhythmic pleasure at the heavy mixtures wafted up to him in their base ingredient of mist. An almost unbearable olfactory anguish rose from the cluster of cement and stone houses that sat like blocks of pumice soaking up the moisture and the color of the earth — the scent of hens and geese and ducks; the stink of cows and goats and dung; and the fetid odor of dank masonry and outside plumbing. With a sudden fit of twitching, the fox bared his teeth. The layers of muscle and sinew quivered beneath his once sleek coat. Then he started creeping down through the yards of the first cottages. Down and down he slithered, traversing the steep slope in a great concentric circle, edging ever lower toward the pit of the village which was steeped with smells that enticed his dying senses, and that filled his riddled brain with an excruciating torment of fear, exhilaration, rage and despair.

A noise . . . The fox, suddenly sly, shrank into a bed

of turnips and peered out across the rooftops of the lower houses. Light flickered on the wet cobblestones of the road leading down to the square from the opposite hill, and a coughing, sputtering sound floated up on the mist — the motorcycle of the town policeman returning from a nocturnal ramble. The fox lay perfectly still. There was a scraping of metal against the pavement followed by the clump of a boot and the click of a door closing; then, stillness again.

The fox resumed his journey and came to the escarpment that dropped away from the crumbling ruins of the *Schloss* which sat upon the heights above the town. Now he began wending his way through an intricate network of trellised vines until he reached a steep staircase that descended perilously toward the stone conglomerate of the village. The steps were cool to touch and the animal, exhausted from his arduous circuit, lay down to rest. A thick, tenacious stream of saliva had begun to spill from his jaws, and suddenly he was racked by a series of violent convulsions. For some moments he lay writhing on the stone; then the convulsions passed, the spasms of breathing grew measured, and the terror inspired by the seizure subsided only to be replaced by another terror as, from the steps below, came the smell of a man. With a supreme effort, the fox crawled behind a vine, coiled himself, and waited. Now, as he heard his enemy ascending, fear filled him with a maniacal rage. He saw the dark mass of the man's torso rising through and above the vines; then he saw the legs. He tensed, clawing gently at the earth, and measured the distance to the movement that would pass directly before him. But even as he edged forward to strike, the man's foot bumped against the post of a trellis and brushed past his snout. Distracted, the fox shrank back, and the man continued up the steps.

When his enemy had passed from sight and sound, the fox started off again, avoiding the steps but continuing his descent by jumping over a series of low retaining walls that divided the vineyard terraces. Below the last terraces were several small vegetable gardens, and just below and beyond these sat a row of houses — all dark save one. The fox crept through the gardens and paused at the edge of a pale reflection cast by a lamp in the study of Town Secretary Vogt. He had reached the village proper, and for a long time he sat blinking at the light, fascinated by the sight of a human he could not scent.

The Town Secretary looked up from his book and yawned. Rheumy-eyed and rotund, he had retired from schoolteaching to write history, more than a decade before, but had been persuaded by the Occupation authorities to take a position in the postwar civil administration. Since then, he had labored conscientiously to maintain the usual records concerning property, expenditures, births, and deaths, and had been reappointed to his post, first by a succession of military commanders, and later by a succession of German county administrators. Now he pushed a pair of ancient, steel-rimmed spectacles up over his forehead, and, placing both palms upon the top of his desk, lifted himself heavily to his feet. Moving to the window, he looked out at the dark mass of the escarpment that towered above his cottage.

At the summit, in rubble, sat the remnants of the *Schloss* — the symbol of his highest aspirations.

For many years, Town Secretary Vogt had investigated a local myth that followers of Adolph of Nassau — an obscure Rhenish count who, in 1298, was defeated and slain outside the neighboring town of Göllheim — had taken refuge in the castle from which they had later tried to escape by digging a tunnel beneath the ridges overlooking the Pfrimm Valley. It had been an elusive quest, for the story was without extant documentation — Adolph's vanquisher, Duke Albrecht of Austria, having been murdered soon thereafter by his nephew — and it had been interrupted by the war and by the Town Secretary's official duties. According to the myth, however, the besiegers of the castle had stormed the walls only to find their quarry vanished, seemingly from the face of the earth. An incurable romantic, Herr Vogt had long ago accepted the myth as fact. He had, moreover, studied the topography of the ground that sloped away from the ruined *Schloss*, and, after careful analysis, come to the conclusion (based upon the declivity of the land and sightings he had taken from the crumbling walls) that the tunnel must have passed beneath the military post at the mouth of the valley. The Town Secretary was certain that if his theory proved to be correct, it would constitute an historical find of proportions sufficient to ensure the proper reception of his *History of the Pfalz* by those in authority at Mainz. Consequently, when he was not doing research for, or laboring over, his manuscript, he daydreamed about the tunnel. He imagined the stale odor of long imprisoned air; he envisaged petrified relics, human bones . . .

Now he turned away from the window, sat down at his desk, and plunged into an account of the final breaching of the Rhine in the year 406, when the Asdingian and Silingian Vandals, together with the Alani and the Suebi, crossed over the ice at Mainz, during a bitter winter, and then looted Gaul and invaded Spain. And soon he was deep in concentration, his spirit soaring above forgotten battlefields from which rose wild, barbaric war cries and the clash of spear on shield. When, a few moments later, the lid of his garbage can clattered upon the stones outside his door, he did not stir. But when the can itself tipped over, he straightened up and gave an audible chuckle at his powers of imagination. The Town Secretary went to the door, opened it, and looked out into the yard.

He was just in time to see a shadow disappear behind the wall of his garden.

The fox fled until his legs would carry him no farther, at which point he found himself in the yard of Herr Saul, where he could hear the throaty, nocturnal cluck of dozing chickens. For a moment, he remained absolutely motionless, torn between fear of pursuit and the possibility of feast. Then he crept to the wire mesh fence surrounding the hen coop, and sniffed along its edge until he came to a tiny gate that was propped closed with a stick. Beneath the gate there was a slender space, and for some time he scratched at the hard earth, trying to dig a hole that would permit passage. Giving up, he sat before the gate, pawing tentatively at the wire mesh. The mesh stretched slightly, the stick fell, and the gate swung open. The nearest hen sat in the opening of the coop, swaying in sleep with her head tucked beneath her wing. The fox raised himself on his hind legs, twisted his neck for leverage, and, with a fierce snap of his jaws, plucked her neatly from the perch. There was a muffled squawk, a frantic beating of wings within the coop, and then a loud, distraught commotion. And, once again, the fox was running — this time with plunder between his teeth — a dark, rust-colored streak racing for the higher ground across streets, over walls, beneath fences, and up alleys where lean cats fled on quick, silent pads. Then, at the village outskirts, he cut across a yard in which, sleeping fitfully, sprawled the dog of Jakob Huy.

The Huy dog spent the days dozing in the sun and the nights lying close to the wall of the barn. Called "Bismarck" because of a certain heavy, gray-muzzled resemblance to the first chancellor, it possessed neither courage nor character, but merely a surfeit of the irritability common to the very aged. At Huy's insistence, however, it was accorded the privileges of rank and time-in-grade, for the farmer saw in the dog the incarnation of his own longevity. Jakob Huy was a charter member of the village elders, called "Ganders" by their fellow townsmen but never within earshot, for nearly all of them were retired beet farmers who still owned the land now tilled by sons and sons-in-law, and who — such is the power of the male hierarchy in rural Germany — still commanded the sentimental respect of their neighbors and the fear of their children, who, in turn, waited patiently for them to die. Wearing black-visored forage caps and black cloth jackets, the Ganders appeared in the market square each morning, as soon as the sun had warmed the cobblestones. They came singly and in pairs, like crows settling into a hollow. They sat on a large stone watering trough that stood before the *Post* and watched everything that happened in the square, in the entrances of the buildings and houses that lined the square, and in the fields and vineyards that surrounded the town. From their vantage point, which was the lowest part of the village, they scrutinized everything and approved of nothing. They found the children saucy, the women lacking in industry, the fields badly managed, the vineyards ill-tended, the buses behind time, the hunting not what it used to be, and the Americans incredibly noisy, wasteful, and unsoldierly. In the evenings, they returned to their homes where, after supper, they sat puffing curved stem pipes with pewter caps, and pondering ancient and long forgotten triumphs and insults. Thus did they stoke the fires that still flickered within their breasts.

Like its master, the Huy dog was senile. And so it was that, disturbed in the sanctity of its lair, it came awake with all the outrage of a proprietor against whom the most blatant trespass has been attempted. With a snarl of anger and fear, old Bismarck bared his worn and broken teeth, and flung himself upon the intruder. The fox dodged easily to one side, dropped the chicken, and promptly sank his teeth into the dog's neck. Then he twisted free, fled from the yard, and thence through an adjacent field to the top of the hill.

The dog's mournful howling brought lights on in

the house, and in a few moments Huy and his daughter-in-law hurried out into the barnyard in their night-shirts.

"Hey, what's this?" the farmer exclaimed. "The dog has scared off a chicken thief."

"It's not one of our chickens," the woman replied.

"What does that matter? It's a dinner, isn't it?"

"Agh!" said the woman, grimacing at the chicken's torn breast and blood-clotted feathers.

"Take it inside," commanded Huy. "Since when are we rich enough to ignore chickens that drop from the sky?"

Holding the bird at arm's length by a claw, the woman disappeared into the house.

Whimpering, Bismarck lapped his master's hand.

"Good boy," Huy said, patting the old dog's griz-zled head.

The dog whimpered again, but the man mistook its pain for affection.

"Good boy," he said.

The fox was hiding in some weeds that grew beside the roadway at the top of the hill, all the frustration of his abortive foray focused upon a vehicle that sat parked on the other side of the macadam. Too exhausted to make another circuit, the animal was content now to watch, with an eye that opened and closed in slow rhythm, the glowing and then diminishing end of a cigarette that was being smoked by the night's last enemy — Harry Brace, who had stopped on his way home to look out across the hills of his district.

To the northeast, beyond Gerberstadt, Brace could

see headlights flickering over the highway that crossed the plateau to Alzey which, like all the surrounding towns, lay buried in a deep hollow. Alzey — the old Altaia of the Romans — where Julius Caesar had camped on his way to the Rhine, and where, fifty years later, just before the birth of Christ, Drusus, the stepson of Augustus, had built a fort before pushing on to Mainz. Brace wondered if the legionnaires had been bored with the tedium of garrison duty. Yes, he decided, as bored as we are, and probably just as prone to diverting themselves with hunting, drinking, and sporadic conquering of Alamanni women. Nothing has changed . . . Slipping over two thousand years had a momentarily powerful and calming effect on him; life seemed cyclical and full of meaning in the sweep of history. For some moments, he found himself picturing the stockade of Drusus — a stone tower, perhaps, filled with spears and shields and those short, heavy Roman swords that had carved a path through the rough Teutonic lair. But when, inevitably, he compared that ancient stockpile with the one at Alpha Site, his glib mastery of twenty centuries slipped away. Suddenly he felt cheated and left alone, as if he were pausing not at the edge of a plateau worn with history and erosion, but on the brink of an immense void. He looked up at the night sky filled with stars — the mystery from which as child and man he had so often flinched — and found it still mysterious, still inscrutable, profoundly calm. No wonder man was suddenly engrossed with shooting off his puny Roman candles into the universe! If there was an impasse on earth, where else to turn but space? Everyone detours in his own fashion, Brace thought. Now he looked out over the hills again and watched the earth twinkling and whispering into the night through soft coils of vapor. The rich smells of autumn filled him with an exhilarating melancholy. His district was still enchanting. Perhaps he would be snow-bound again in the coming winter. I could stay here and watch the seasons change forever, he thought.

PART II
A Sanctuary Shared

4
ᛏᛏᛏᛏᛏᛏ

IN THE MORNING, Brace picked up his mail and messages at the Battalion Classified Message Center, on the ground floor of the *Kaserne* Headquarters Building. The corporal behind the desk always called him Mr. Brace, but although Brace wore civilian clothes and worked alone, he was not a civilian. He was, in reality, a military officer, who had been given civilian status for the performance of his mission. This fact, however, was known only to his superiors at Counter Intelligence Headquarters; to the military personnel of the ordnance battalion quartered at the *Kaserne*, and to German officials of the towns and the *Kreise* that made up his district, he was simply the Resident Intelligence Agent.

Upstairs, in his office, he read the mail and the morning newspaper, and started leafing through the messages; there were the usual bulletins, some reports of demonstrations against rockets and atomic cannon in the town of Kusel, and a letter of information from Counter Intelligence Headquarters. At first glance, it seemed to be a typed form similar to the thousands of descriptions and summaries that filled the files. Brace scanned the letter and tossed it into the basket on his desk. Then, frowning, he picked it up again. At the top were two words of title: "Possible Subversive." Beneath was a slender column of type describing "Subject" — a man named Pucher, whose first name and place of birth were unknown, who was a shepherd, and whose last known address was listed in capitals as "GRUMBACH." Brace read the letter once more, reached for his telephone, and dialed his chief at headquarters.

"Moran, this is Brace speaking. I have a letter here on a shepherd. You know anything about it?"

"What's the file number?"

Brace read off a series of digits from the top right-hand corner of the letter. There was a short pause, during which he could hear the clacking of typewriters, and then Moran spoke again. "It's by way of an office memo Coolidge sent in last week."

"What's the alleged activity?"

"It seems the shepherd's been seen wandering near a few of the *Kasernes*. Coolidge heard a rumble he might be political, but there's nothing definite."

"That's not much to go on," Brace said. "Is he supposed to be political because he's been seen near some *Kasernes?*"

Moran laughed. "Coolidge turned it in as a matter of routine. He picked up the rumble in a *Gasthaus* and thought he'd pass it on just in case. Yours is the next district, so I forwarded you an information summary, in the event the shepherd shows up."

"He's here," Brace said. "I saw him yesterday in a meadow. Nothing there but grass and sheep."

There was another laugh at the end of the line. "It's routine, Harry. It's a precaution. Frankly, I don't think it'll amount to anything, but we have to check it out."

"Look, Moran, I talked with the old guy. He follows a flock of sheep around the countryside. The sheep eat grass, and grass grows in the valleys, which is where you find the towns and where the Germans built the *Kasernes* — it's as simple as that. Besides, the shepherd couldn't leave his animals untended ten minutes, let alone —"

"Harry, you've been in the business too long to forget we go by the book." Moran's voice was friendly but cool.

"I know," said Brace. "And the book says you double-check everything and everybody. What'll I do — interrogate the old guy?"

Moran chuckled. "Stop giving me a hard time on Monday morning, Harry. You know damn well we haven't the right to interrogate civilians on our own these days. Now, look, I realize you're busy, so don't go to a lot of trouble. Follow it up with the local police when you get the chance. I'll put through a records check and have Coolidge pin down the rumor at his end. If we get a cross-fix and the shepherd comes out clean, we can strike him off the casebook. But since Coolidge put him on paper to begin with, we'll have to get the machinery in motion and check him out."

Brace hung up the phone and glanced again at the letter. You're getting careless, he thought. The book is always right — that's been proved before — and you know from experience the business can crop up anywhere and any time. Besides, why run the risk of antagonizing Moran, who leaves you alone up here? The trouble with you is you want that fishing stream to be some kind of sanctuary . . . Brace remembered the binoculars slung around the old man's neck, and felt annoyed with himself for remembering them.

At coffee call, Brace sat with the *Kaserne* doctor, a pale, red-eyed captain who had been drafted eighteen months previously, upon completion of medical school, and who had recently made his captaincy but had not yet forgiven the Department of the Army for delaying his career. "Here's one for you," the captain said. "I met a girl in Mannheim over the weekend. She asked me where I was stationed, and when I told her, you know what she said? She said I was 'behind the moon'!"

"*Hinter dem Mond.*" Brace grinned. "That's how city Germans describe the farm districts."

"Which is poetic for boondocks behind the sticks! By the way, Brace, what do you do for kicks out here in the boondocks?"

"I go fishing," Brace replied.

"Well," said the doctor, "not being a fisherman, I've put in a request for transfer. If it gets by the major at Area Command, I should be able to go into one of the hospitals."

"Who'll stay up here to save lives?"

"You mean who'll stay up here twenty-four hours a day to tell dependent wives there's no known cure for the common cold!"

"You're a great reassurance to them," Brace said, smiling. "In the event of plague, you'll be a hero."

The doctor pushed his cup and saucer impatiently to one side. "There hasn't been anything more than a strep throat since I came here."

"Wait until the dependent kids get mumps."

"It's a diagnosis my replacement will make blind-folded."

"How about rabies?"

"Altogether different," said the doctor. "That's a disease usually transmitted by dogs. They used to call it hydrophobia. You seen a sick dog or something?"

"I saw a sick fox in the valley yesterday."

"A sick fox, hanh?" The captain leaned forward and dropped his voice. "I guess you know a rabid animal of any sort can be sheer poison!"

Brace noted the confidential lowering of the captain's voice. Like everyone else up here, the captain is bored, he thought. He's going to start impressing me with his medical knowledge.

"How far away was this fox?" the doctor asked.

"A mile or so," Brace said.

"What made you think he was sick? You notice any particular symptoms?"

Brace laughed. "He wasn't foaming around the mouth, if that's what you mean, but he didn't run away. He acted as if he were fed up with everything."

The captain continued in his serious vein. "If he should become a vector by infecting one of the dogs around here, we'd be in a bad way. There's a vaccine for rabies, but it should be administered quickly."

"I don't know if the fox has rabies or not," Brace said. "All I know is he's sick."

After lunch, Brace drove up the hill to the Gendarmerie Station in Weiersheim. When he entered the dark hallway, he rapped on the door marked *POLIZEIAMT* and walked inside. Polizeiwachtmeister Brausch, who was sitting at his desk talking into the telephone, looked up and pointed to a chair. Brace sat, lit a cigarette, and gazed at the wall before him, which was covered with carefully wrought diagrams of traffic accidents showing the precise position of vehicles at the point of impact, the direction in which they were originally traveling, the distance and direction traveled after impact, and the exact position of the slightly injured, the disabled, and the dead. Then his glance fell, as it always did, upon the wall above the heating stove, where there was a photograph showing Brausch in his Wehrmacht tunic and officer's peaked hat. Brace looked at the desk where Brausch's automatic pistol lay hidden in its shining black holster and, finally, at Brausch himself, who, in his policeman's green uniform, sat leaning over the desk and barking into the telephone. Except for what Brace knew to be a difference in color, the uniform was nearly identical with the one in the photograph. Brace examined Brausch's long black boots, shuffling in irritation on the floor beneath the desk, and the tiny, well-oiled folds where the leather creased above the ankles. Then Brausch hung the receiver on a wall hook and turned the crank handle to cut off the call. The two men stood and shook hands.

"So, Herr Brace . . ."

"I stopped in a moment to ask you about a shepherd whom I've seen in the valley," Brace said. With the Wachtmeister, he always spoke German.

"In the Weiersheim Valley?"

"An old man who comes from Grumbach."

"Ah, that one! That one comes through twice a year. He comes once in the spring and once again early in the autumn after the last hay is cut."

"What do you know of him?"

The Wachtmeister shrugged, smiling. "He is solitary like all shepherds. At night, he leaves his sheep in someone's barn, and occasionally he is seen in a *Gasthaus*, drinking beer."

Brace took a package of cigarettes from his shirt pocket and proffered the open end to Brausch, who selected a cigarette and held it carefully between his lips as he applied the match flame. All right, use the direct approach, Brace thought. This Brausch is not a diplomat from Bonn. "Does the shepherd have a criminal record?" he asked.

"The shepherd has no criminal record in this district," replied Brausch, "but who knows what record he may have elsewhere? You would have to visit every village in the Pfalz! Once, a long time ago, some farmers claimed he had not obtained the proper grazing permits, and another time he was suspected of snaring rabbits — but nothing was proved." The policeman shrugged. "Who can tell about shepherds? They are always moving from one place to another."

"What do you know of his politics?"

"Ah!" Brausch smiled. "His politics . . . Who knows about the politics of a shepherd? They are always alone. This one is sometimes seen in a *Gasthaus*, but I have never heard of his discussing politics. Who knows about the politics of a shepherd? His dogs, the sheep perhaps . . ." Brausch laughed through the smoke of the cigarette.

The Wachtmeister is having a fine time, Brace thought, and it is your own damn fault. Coolidge is a fool for having written up a report on the basis of hearsay, and you are a fool for coming here with these stupid questions. I'll be damned if you're going to give Police Sergeant Brausch the pleasure of telling you why it is the shepherd carries binoculars.

"Does the shepherd have any physical defects?" Brace asked.

"Defects?" Brausch repeated, shrugging. "His ears, perhaps. People shout at him to make themselves understood."

"And the eyes?"

"*Ja*, also the eyes! Once, during the rabbit business, I demanded his papers and found an administrative mistake in his identity card. When I brought this to the shepherd's attention, he had difficulty in seeing it." Brausch was smiling again. "You have some suspicion, *nicht?*"

This time it was Brace who shrugged. "Nothing important," he said. "A few rumors." The shepherd was telling the truth, he thought.

"You know the shepherd's name?" asked Brausch.

"Pucher."

"*Ja*, I remember it now. Perhaps he has come over from the East. As I say, there is no telling about these shepherds. When there are no barns, they sleep in the woods."

"It is undoubtedly a rumor," Brace said. "Have you heard of the demonstrations in Kusel?"

Brausch was at the window, looking into the street. "These shepherds are like animals," he muttered. "They are never of any one town or place, so it is entirely possible the rumors are correct. I will make some inquiries. Perhaps I will find the shepherd has failed to obtain the proper grazing rights." He turned and smiled at Brace, who had risen.

"I'm sure it's a rumor," Brace said. You can't beat this Brausch's thought processes, he told himself. Now that the bastard thinks you know something he doesn't know, he's willing to nail the shepherd with anything he can lay his hands on. "With the autumn maneuvers approaching, the disturbances in Kusel have particular significance," he said. "Please let me know if you hear of any demonstrations that are scheduled locally."

The Wachtmeister laughed harshly and pointed out the window. "Have you looked at the *Schloss* today, Herr Brace? *There's* a local demonstration for you!"

Brace walked to the window and squinted through the sun's glare toward the ruins that topped the vineyard. On one of the crumbling walls, splashed boldly in red letters three feet high, were the initials of the outlawed *Kommunistische Partei Deutschlands* — "K.P.D."

"Herr Sekretär Vogt noticed it this morning when he first awakened," said the policeman with a smile. "The Secretary believes the castle is of great historical significance. You can't imagine how upset he was."

Brace looked at the letters again. "Have you been up there?" he asked.

"I went at once, Herr Brace, but as in the case of the railroad bridge, there wasn't a clue."

"I'm beginning to think it's the work of a practical joker," said Brace, turning from the window.

"*Ja*, I agree," Brausch replied. "A little joke at our expense. But the author will have some explaining to do when I catch him, *nicht?*"

"Let me know if you find out anything," Brace said.

"I will telephone you, Herr Brace, and I will mention our shepherd to the authorities. One must keep a constant eye on such wanderers."

The Wachtmeister came outside and stood on the stoop as Brace went down to the street. When Brace turned to say good-by, he saw the black boots on a level with his eyes, at the top of the steps. Polizeiwachtmeister Brausch was smiling down at him from the same height as that from which Brace had first looked down at the fox. The boots were immaculate in the sunlight.

5

By MAKING INQUIRIES at several farmhouses on the village outskirts, Brace learned that the shepherd had been seen, earlier in the day, returning up the meadow with his flock. Accordingly, he drove west on the road leading to Alpha Site until he reached the far side of the hunting preserve, at which point he turned south on another road that dropped into the valley before the mountain. Here he parked his jeep by a small bridge that spanned the upper reaches of his trout stream, and walked along both sides of the roadway, looking for tracks and droppings. Finding none, he got into the jeep again and turned off on a cart track that followed the stream down through the meadow. At the first bend, he came into the midst of the sheep.

The flock divided immediately, and the sheep pressed around either side of the vehicle. Caught in the crush, some of the lambs began to bleat. The ewes from whom they had become separated also bleated, and soon the entire flock, driven by the mongrels, was in full cry. Imprisoned in the jeep that was filled now with a rank, animal scent, Brace lit a cigarette and watched the shepherd, who was still some distance away. The old man was carrying a lamb in his left arm, and a yearling in a sling that he had fashioned from his cape and hung from his shoulder. To support the weight of the yearling, he was leaning heavily on his staff which he held with his free hand. He was walking slowly, but when he looked ahead and saw the jeep, he hitched the sling higher on his shoulder, and came on quickly.

"That's quite a load you've got!" Brace called.

The old man slipped the sling from his shoulder and eased it to the ground. Then he sat on the fender of the jeep. "It's nothing," he said. "I used to carry three at a time — one around the neck and one in each of the hands."

"What's wrong with them?"

"They're lame! The little one picked up a stone and the larger one has hoof rot."

"Where are you off to?"

The old man squinted at the mountain, and shrugged. "Who knows? Somewhere I must find a barn."

"I thought you might be staying near the town for a while."

"There were no empty barns," replied the shepherd. "It's an old story."

"What about the fox? Did you see him?"

"Yes, I saw him, but there were not the right conditions for me to kill him, and when I went back this morning he has gone away."

"Perhaps he's on the mend," Brace said.

"Mend . . . ?"

"Getting better!"

"No," the old man replied. "The fox has *Tollwut*. He will not get better. His is an affliction that always ends in death."

"He's probably gone off into the woods to die."

"Perhaps, but when I did not see him today, I am sorry that I did not kill him yesterday. It's deadly — *Tollwut.*"

"So everybody says," said Brace.

"Listen, I am sure of it! We should have killed him yesterday."

"Don't worry," Brace said with a smile. "I told Herr Saul, the proprietor, and he's telling everybody."

"We should have killed him yesterday," the shepherd repeated. "We should kill them when we have the chance."

"At that rate, there wouldn't be many foxes left," replied Brace, laughing.

The old man gave him a baleful look. "Be quiet," he said. "*Tollwut* is nothing to laugh at."

Brace nodded seriously. The old fellow's a regular patriarch, he thought.

Now he remembered his conversation with Wacht-meister Brausch. "Where do you obtain your grazing permits?" he asked.

"What foolishness is that? When the last hay is cut, the grass is free."

Brace grinned. "But I thought that when you moved from one district to another —"

"Listen, I am of no one district. I am always of the district in which I find myself!"

Brace grinned again.

"Nor am I one of these tenant shepherds. The sheep are mine, and I come and go as I wish."

"Without permits," Brace observed.

"Certainly without permits! D'you think I am going

to ask every idiot with a field for permission to use his grass?"

"I've been talking with the village policeman," Brace said. "I'm afraid he intends to make trouble for you."

The shepherd's blue eyes narrowed with suspicion. "What d'you have to do with policemen? I understood you were a soldier — an American."

"I am," said Brace with a laugh, "but I'm not one of these tenant soldiers. Like you, I come and go as I wish."

"What kind of soldier is that?"

"A special kind," Brace replied. "I'm responsible for the guarding of certain installations in the district."

The old man indicated his sheep. "I, too, am a guard," he said proudly. "But I don't remain in one place or one district. The guarding of stationary objects would have no satisfaction for me."

Brace nodded. "In any case, since you're moving on, the policeman is of no consequence."

"None," the shepherd replied, "and none if I chose to stay!"

Brace was amused. Proud, stubborn old bastard, he thought. "The policeman also suspects you of poaching," he said.

The old man reached into the pocket of his trousers and drew out a pair of large trout wrapped in ferns. "I don't worry about the police. All of them look the same to me."

Brace admired the trout. "Where'd you get them?"

"From beneath the rocks."

"Some day you'll get into trouble for that."

"Listen, I am seventy-three years old and I have taken

trout with my hands long before you were born and I have never been in trouble for it!"

Brace laughed. What an old renegade, he thought.

The shepherd spat contemptuously. "The police, the Jägers, and their peasant allies — I'm too clever for them," he boasted.

Laughing, Brace leaned against the jeep.

"You don't believe me?" the old man shouted.

"Calm down, Methuselah," Brace said. "I'm on your side. I even know a place where you can winter your flock."

With a scowl, the old man bent down and lifted the sling that held the yearling.

Brace restrained an impulse to seize him by the arm. "Wait a minute," he said. "I'm serious about this. You can stay in a field over which I have jurisdiction. There's a shack for you to live in and some sheds you could fix up to make a stable for the sheep. There's even a fenced area to keep them penned up at night!"

The shepherd lowered the lame sheep to the ground. "What kind of soldier has fields and stables to give to strangers?" he asked suspiciously.

"I told you before — a special kind."

"But I'm a stranger," the old man insisted.

"Take it or leave it," said Brace with a shrug. If he takes it, Lisl and I will have to find another trysting place, he thought.

The old man was shaking his head. "You must have some reason."

"Reason?" Brace echoed. Reason, indeed, he reflected. Was it out of animosity for Brausch? Was it annoyance with Coolidge for his ridiculous suspicion, or with Moran for meddling in his district? Or was it something about the shepherd himself — this old man with such a sense of his own omniscience, who felt he was of whatever district in which he found himself? "Listen, this is *my* district," Brace said with a sudden, expansive sweep of his arm. "I don't have to give reasons for what I do here any more than you do for poaching trout or grazing without permits." The arrogance of his words caught up with him as soon as he had spoken them. "Perhaps you and I have something in common," he went on, suppressing a smile. What're you trying to prove? he wondered. The only thing you and the old man have in common is a romantic notion about the land beneath your feet. Beyond that, he has ten times your confidence . . . Brace suddenly realized that he was staring at the shepherd with almost hostile envy. He averted his eyes. Yes, ten times the confidence of ten men! he thought ruefully. Ah, but could the old boy possibly imagine what lay buried beneath the ground at Alpha Site?

"I'll look at this field of yours," said the shepherd with reluctance, "but it probably won't be suitable."

"Fine," Brace answered. "D'you want to carry the lame sheep back, or shall we put him in the jeep?"

Without reply, the old man knelt on the ground and drew two lengths of cloth from his pocket. Then he tied the legs of the yearling afflicted with hoof rot, and lifted the animal into the rear seat of the jeep. Afterwards, with a series of whistles and waves, he sent his mongrels to turn the flock, and when the sheep had begun to move, he picked up the lamb and started off.

"What happens if we meet your friend, the policeman?" he shouted.

"We'll tell him you've lost your way," Brace said jovially, and switched on the engine of the jeep.

"I've *never* lost my way!"

"We'll tell him you've lost a lamb!"

"What kind of shepherd loses a lamb?"

Brace shrugged. "Hell," he said, "we'll tell him you've lost your binoculars!"

As a reflex, the old man lifted his hand to touch the glasses hanging around his neck. Then he laughed and started back down the valley with his flock.

Brace drove on ahead to the training area. As always, he was struck with the ugliness of the place. The dilapidated sheds and storage shack sat cringing and derelict at the edge of the forest. The tottering water tank and the leaning guard towers of the prisoner-of-war compound seemed on the verge of being brought down by weeds that grew in choking profusion around their foundations. For a moment, Brace found himself wishing that he had some time to clean the place up. He wandered along the edge of the barbed wire fence, aimlessly plucking some of the weeds; then he went over to examine the vehicle sheds — a series of connected wood frame bays that were enclosed on three sides and covered with a corrugated tin roof. Afterwards, he sat down to wait for the shepherd.

When the old man arrived, he inspected the entire area with great care, starting with the vehicle sheds and the shack, and then moving on to the POW compound.

Filled with impatience, Brace followed in his footsteps. "Well, what d'you think?" he asked, pointing to the shack. "There's a stove for heat, and I'll bring you some tarpaulins so you can close off the open side of the sheds."

"The sheds are no problem," the shepherd replied. "Happily, the open side faces south and will be warmed by the morning sun. But how much water is in the tank behind the wire? I have forty-five animals, and each of them drinks three liters of water a day!"

"There's a well and a hand pump beneath the tank," Brace said. "It's hidden by the weeds."

The old man nodded without enthusiasm. "What kind of place is this?"

"It's a prisoner-of-war compound."

The old man frowned at the tilting guard towers. "I've seen these places before," he said. "In Bavaria, I saw camps filled with Ukrainians."

"This one has never been used. It was built after the war — for practice."

"Nevertheless, I don't like it."

"Nor do I," Brace replied. "Would you prefer a hotel, perhaps?"

The old man laughed. "Don't misunderstand with jokes. It's just that I don't like the wire and the towers. They remind me of the camps."

"The wire will serve to hold your sheep while you fix up the sheds."

"Yes?" said the old man. For a second, he wore a puzzled expression; then, abruptly, he sat down in the grass. "I will stay here," he went on. "I will stay here because I am very tired, but I will need many things."

"I'll bring you everything you need," Brace replied.

The old man nodded slowly. "Listen," he said, "I lied

to you yesterday when I told you I had never been stronger. The fact is I am old and very tired. I will undoubtedly die this winter."

"Nonsense!" Brace said. "I'll bring you everything you need. I'll even bring you food." The idea filled him with pleasure. For a moment, he imagined himself churning across the plateau through deep snow, his jeep laden to the rooftop with supplies.

The old man patted the bulge in his pocket made by the trout. "You won't have to bring me food," he said.

"Don't plan on poaching," Brace warned. "The forest here is a hunting preserve. There's a Jäger who watches it closely."

"Yes, and I will watch the Jäger. It's an old game."

"You've got no respect for other people's land," said Brace, shaking his head.

"Yes, I have a great respect for land. I've spent a lifetime walking over it."

"Without permits . . ."

"Certainly without permits! Why should I ask these beet diggers for permission? The peasants are like cabbages. They spend their lifetime in the dirt. What do they know of the world?"

"What d'you know of the world, old man?"

"Listen, we shepherds know it. We have to walk over it."

Brace lit a cigarette. "The peasants work hard," he said. "They tend their fields and they also tend livestock."

"Oxen!" the shepherd scoffed. "Oxen made that way by professional gelders."

"What of it?"

"What of it?" the shepherd repeated softly. "Listen, before the end of this month I will give my ewes to the ram. In March, the ewes will have lambs, and in April I will have to castrate the male lambs. How will you like to help me with this?"

"Why not?" said Brace, sitting down in the grass.

"Why not?" the old man chuckled. "Listen, I will tell you about it. First, you will take the lamb between your knees so that the legs are apart and in the air. Then, holding the scrotum in your hand, you will press apart the sacs of the testicles, and make a small cut with a knife. When this is accomplished, you will push down upon the sacs until the testicles pop out. Then you will twist and knot the connecting cords. Afterwards, you will sever the ends with your teeth, which is better than the knife because it avoids infection." The old man looked carefully at Brace, and grinned. "Well, special soldier," he said, "can I count on you in April?"

Brace closed his eyes with an involuntary shudder. "Jesus," he said. "An old man who castrates lambs with his teeth. You must be touched in the head."

The shepherd laughed gleefully. "After the biting, you will cauterize the knife cut with a little wine," he went on. "Then you will start with another lamb."

"The cups are rattling in your cupboard," said Brace, inhaling on his cigarette. "And I am crazy myself to sit here listening to an old man who bites off the balls of sheep."

"Be quiet, I haven't finished. In May, the lambs that have not developed favorably into rams will also be castrated. But these we'll do without cutting or biting. First, we'll tie the legs together. Then we'll slip the testicles through the noose of a cord that has been smeared with grease. At each end of the cord is tied a piece of wood large enough to be gripped firmly in the hand. In this way the greased twine will not slip through our fingers when we tighten the knot around the testicles. Do you follow me?"

"I follow you, all right," said Brace. "And the hell with it."

The shepherd smiled. "When the knot is in place, each of us will take an end of the cord and face the other, one knee on the ground, and the other leg foot against foot for force. Then we'll begin to pull upon the cord, evenly and equally, until the twine no longer yields."

The old man paused, noting Brace's blanched but disciplined face, and the inner constriction that had caused him to shift position so that his knees were drawn tightly together.

"When the noose cannot be drawn further," he continued, "we'll pass the twine several times around the circumference of the testicles, and make a single knot in back and a double knot in front. Then we'll cut off both ends of the twine and paint the affected area with tar. After five or six days, the testicles will atrophy, at which time one or the other of us will cut them off without difficulty."

When the shepherd had finished, Brace ground out his cigarette and got to his feet. "Well, have I passed the test?" he said.

"You did very well," the old man replied. "Better than I expected. You were a bit nervous for a while, but you controlled it."

"What's your name?" Brace asked.

"Mathias."

"And your surname?"

"Pucher."

At least he has told the truth, Brace reflected, and extended his hand. "Well, Mathias, I'm glad you've decided to stay here," he said.

But as he watched the old man lead his flock behind the barbed wire, he was assailed by a mixture of elation and doubt. On the one hand, he was filled with a profound satisfaction, which he recognized as having come from "tidying up," from putting everything in place. He felt that somehow he had strengthened his hold on the district. The shepherd's in his fold, all's right with the world, he thought. Ah, but was this feeling of accomplishment any different from that of the custodians who locked the hydraulic doors of Alpha Site each night? As he drove through the beet fields, Brace remembered the expression that had clouded the old man's face when he learned the significance of the barbed wire and the gun towers; then, vaguely troubled, he started down the cobblestoned street toward the town square which, though the sun still hung at mid-afternoon height, was already in shadow.

When Brace returned to the *Kaserne*, he found a note tacked to his door requesting his presence in the office of the battalion commander, Colonel MacIntyre. The colonel was an ordnance specialist who had spent the better part of the postwar decade isolated from the world at a vast special weapons development redoubt in the desert of New Mexico. Now, having been transferred bag, baggage, bombs and battalion to Germany, he found himself shuttling daily from *Kaserne* to storage site through the gloom of a forest. The change of geography — the sudden and oppressive encirclement of trees — and the enormous responsibility of guarding his cache in a foreign land had made him a furtive caretaker; there was a piercing cunning in his expression, but behind the nervousness — the fits and starts of a squirrel burying acorns in the forest floor — there was also a squirrel's ability to withdraw instantly into watchful immobility. Distrustful, conscientious, and curious, the colonel took considerable pride in knowing every facet and characteristic of his *Kaserne* and command; hence he rarely summoned the resident intelligence agent except when something turned up in the latter's field that made this knowledge appear incomplete. During such interviews, Brace always revolved in ever-diminishing circles around the subject, leaving innumerable loopholes to afford the colonel an opportunity of claiming prior knowledge at some convenient point. It was an old military game, in which each participant was fully aware of the other's intentions, and it was played without rancor.

Brace went to the colonel's office and waited outside until the adjutant asked him to step in. The colonel, a small, severe man, sat dwarfed behind an immense mahogany desk with two 75-millimeter-shell book ends before him and a pair of crossed flags at his back. He pressed his lips together as Brace came over the carpet, and Brace recognized the pressing of the lips as an unfavorable sign.

"You wanted to see me, sir?"

"Yes, Brace," said the colonel. "I received a telephone call this afternoon from the commander of the Area Medical Detachment. He's sending an inspection team out here at zero-eight hundred hours tomorrow morning. It seems our good doctor phoned in some damned nonsense about you seeing an animal with rabies."

Brace smiled. "I told the doctor I'd seen a sick fox."

"Well the medics have made the usual flap out of it." The colonel cast a humorless glance at Brace and rustled through some forms lying on his desk. "Group sent instructions by courier an hour ago. First of all, I'm supposed to furnish someone who'll lead the inspection team to the fox. Then I have to corral all dog owners in my command and determine whether all dogs are properly registered. And finally" — the colonel said this reproachfully, looking Brace in the face — "I've got to prepare a list showing dog owners, kind of dogs owned, and date of last rabies injection."

"My God!" said Brace. "I only mentioned it in passing!"

"So did the doctor," the colonel observed dryly. "It's how flaps get started. Since you're the one who indirectly got the ball rolling, I'd appreciate it if you'd be at the gate at zero-eight hundred to meet the inspection team. I'll furnish some men, and you can lead the expedition out to wherever it is you saw this animal while I have the list made up." The ghost of a smile appeared on the colonel's face.

"I'm sorry about the trouble, sir, and I'll do what I can to help," Brace said. "I want to assure you, however, that my official functions have nothing to do with diseased foxes."

"I know that," the colonel replied. "Mine have nothing to do with canine injections. I'm not a veterinarian, Brace. I'm trying to ready this battalion for the Inspector General's visit tomorrow."

Upstairs, as Brace unlocked the door to his office, he heard his telephone ring. He went in, moved quickly across the room, and picked up the receiver.

"*Ja*, Herr Brace," a voice said. "Here is Saul. I have been trying to reach you this afternoon for I have important news of the fox."

Brace swung the phone cord around the corner of his desk and sat heavily in his swivel chair.

"I have spoken with the Town Secretary and the Jäger, Herr Brace. Our Secretary is much interested and has written a proclamation ordering children to stay out of the forest until the matter is settled. He has asked me to tell you that he would be pleased for you to meet the Jäger and Wachtmeister Brausch tomorrow morning. They would like to see this fox and shoot it. The Town Secretary also believes the *Kommandant* of the *Kaserne* should be notified, but as I do not have his telephone number, I thought perhaps . . ."

"The *Kommandant* already knows of the fox," Brace replied. "At what time does the Jäger wish me to meet him?"

"At your convenience, Herr Brace."

"Tell him I'll be in the square shortly after eight o'clock," Brace said, and hung up the phone.

The sun was falling behind a barracks building, and a

final ray of light slanted through the window, striking
Brace on the small of the back. For some minutes after
he hung up the phone, he sat in his swivel chair and
thought of the fox recuperating in the warm afternoon.

6

"IT IS THE TIME of evening," Konrad Zabern was saying, "when everything is still and the slightest movements are visible." He was sitting in an elevated umpire's chair at the racket club in Gerberstadt, casually calling service and baseline shots of a practice match between his wife, Greta, and Frau Kemp, the wife of the County Administrator. Below him and to his right, Brace sat at a table, sipping a bottle of *Apfelsaft*. In the dusk, the white costumes of the two women seemed to float above the red clay surface of the court. They were playing intently and in silence; the only sounds were the scudding of shoes, the snap of the ball rebounding from the rackets, and the heavy panting that accompanies female exertion.

"It's the absence of glare," said Brace, without looking at the man above him.

"Yes, but not entirely," Zabern replied. "There's a special reflection in the sky, almost an illusion. I've noticed it often."

Brace did not answer. He was watching Greta, a slim, hollow-eyed blond who wore a pleated skirt and a white jersey with starched collar. She had parted her hair in the middle, and made two short braids that she had tied with white ribbon, and that snapped against her neck as she ran forward now, toward the net. She was holding her racket elbow high and close to her body, and, just before she swung at the return, she took a series of tiny steps, up on her toes, in ballerina style.

"Do you hunt, Herr Brace?"

"No," said Brace, absently. "That is, not for some time."

"*Aus!*" Zabern called. (Greta was serving.) "We hunters anticipate this light," he continued. "It comes just as the roebuck leave their beds."

Brace looked up and saw that Zabern had tilted his head back and was following the play with the merest flicker of his eyes. There was a strange intensity in his posture, as if he were sitting in ambush atop one of the *Hochsitze* that lined the edges of his preserve. He was a powerfully built man in his middle forties, with long sandy hair combed flat and straight back in the popular coiffure that sets off the grave and chiseled immobility of Teutonic faces.

Brace noticed that he was examining Greta's opponent, a large brunette with solid thighs and rounded buttocks that were creased by the hems of a snug pair of shorts. Frau Kemp ran slowly, heavily, but with fetching awkwardness. She swung viciously at the ball, twisting her torso as she did. Brace liked her style. He wondered if she was wearing a brassiere beneath her shirt, and decided after a moment's scrutiny that she was.

"*Gut gespielt!*" Zabern called out.

Frau Kemp had slammed a hard cross-court forehand for the point. In doing so, she had run close to the sidelines. As she turned away, Brace noted that she was

perspiring; her thighs were damp, and her shirt, transparent with sweat, clung to the hollow of her back, just
above the rump. I'd like to see you exerting yourself in
bed, he thought.

As if reading Brace's mind, Zabern looked down from
his perch, and smiled. "I've always enjoyed watching
the tennis played by women. More exhibition than
sport."

"But at this time of night hunters must prefer the
cavorting of roebuck," Brace replied.

Zabern laughed softly. "One should not be forced to
choose between distinct and separate pleasures."

"Bravo!" he shouted. The point had been taken by
his wife, who was a deft and delicate volleyer.

Now he climbed down from the umpire's chair. Brace
stood, and the two men shook hands. (When Brace had
arrived, they had also shaken hands, with Zabern leaning
over the side of the chair, and Brace reaching up from
the ground.)

"We don't see you here any more," Zabern said.
"You've stopped playing?"

"Yes," Brace replied. "I've been too busy."

It was not true that he had been too busy. During the
summer, he had played a great deal. A steady retriever,
he had managed to beat the club's fourth-ranked player,
but some unpleasantness had followed. As if to salvage a
nettled pride, his opponent had insisted that Brace's
name replace his own on the ladder. Brace protested that
he did not wish to compete, but to no avail. His name
was dutifully inserted, and remained for some time,
strangely out of place, while he deliberately stayed away
from the Saturday ladder matches. Now he looked at the

glass case which enclosed the neatly lettered listings, and saw that it was gone.

"I didn't take up tennis until after the war," Zabern said with a shrug. "It seemed the thing to do, perhaps because at first it wasn't possible. During the early years of the Occupation, the French banned civilians from the courts and played volleyball on them. Then you Americans arrived and we reclaimed the club, and now" — Zabern laughed pleasantly — "we're pleased to have you as our guest."

"An evolution that parallels history," Brace said dryly.

"I stopped playing several years ago," Zabern went on. "Frankly, the local players offered little competition, and it seemed too much trouble to travel all the way to Ludwigshafen or Kaiserslautern for satisfaction."

"Satisfaction . . . ?"

"Why do you play tennis, Herr Brace?"

"Why . . . for relaxation, I suppose."

Zabern smiled and shook his head. "There's more to sport than that. In life a man must compel others to do his will. Thus at all levels, he is coercing and being coerced. Naturally he seeks an escape from this by engaging in some activity where the primary objective is not to overwhelm, or to avoid being overwhelmed, but nonetheless to test himself severely. That is why man evolved games, and why games are called sport."

A curious definition, Brace thought. "We Americans are not so purposeful," he said.

"You will come to it, Herr Brace. One hesitates to judge you on the basis of the Occupation because it has been so generous. Yet I think your altruism rests upon an image you have evolved of yourselves. If, slowly, your presence here begins to have purpose and definition, that is because you have begun to be afraid, and because, sooner or later, after power is consolidated, it is always maintained through fear."

Brace was aware that Zabern had deliberately shifted the focus of conversation. "Do you mean coercion?" he asked.

"No," Zabern replied. "I mean fear that you may lose this power. Coercion and terror are often corollaries of such fear, but do not think that we Germans must necessarily reflect our previous involvement in a police state. For centuries, Europeans have had to live with delicate balances of power achieved and maintained. And now, so will you. But remember, it is easy to be, or to try to be, supreme. It is something else to connive for the maintenance of power parity between more or less equal blocs of power."

For some moments, Brace pondered this in silence. He believed that the political philosophies of men were largely derived from personality, but that only rarely were they practically applied in action, and as he considered the man opposite him, he realized once again that statements of abstract thinking could be connected with experience and reality only by tenuous links. Konrad Zabern was one of two men in the district who were called *Chef* — the other being the County Administrator, Herr Kemp. Zabern was called *Chef* because of his holdings which included a sawmill and a small leather tannery in Gerberstadt, some vineyards on the terraced Schlossberg above Weiersheim, a stone and gravel quarry a few kilometers to the north, and — most important of all — two thousand acres of forest which he rented from the State of Rheinland-Pfalz as a hunting preserve. For a man of such influence, a title of some sort was inevitable. The Germans were inordinately fond of titles, Brace reflected.

The two men applauded in a perfunctory manner the conclusion of a game won at love by Greta, who was playing with her usual grace. Now, glancing at the women's tennis ladder posted on the fence behind him, Brace saw that her name was still at the top. He wondered if Zabern was pleased that she excelled.

Because Zabern's control of the district was rooted in the livelihood of the inhabitants, it nourished strange offshoots, tentacles as secret and subterranean in origin as the mushrooms that sprouted in the forest. His hunts were attended by state cabinet ministers from Mainz, officials of such firms as the Badische Anilin- und Sodafabrik of Ludwigshafen, and various judges and others of similar rank, whose presence lent style and status to the entire district, and whose effect on the local peasantry, gathered four or five times a year into a small army of beaters and gunbearers, was immense. Opportunists by nature, the peasants of County Gerberstadt were quick to seize the attendant portion of fame to which they felt their association with sportsmen entitled them. Thus had Konrad Zabern reawakened the dormant germ of Merovingian forest virility in a strain of obscure farmers who had been growing sugar beets for centuries.

The beets were a story in themselves. The red clay soil of County Gerberstadt supported them admirably, but the only route to the sugar refineries in Hesse was a railroad spur that came down from Mainz to the county seat. Before the war, the railroad had continued south and joined the east-west line between Kaiserslautern and Worms, but a Panzer Division, retreating toward the Rhine in the spring of 1945, had blown up the trestle across the Pfrimm Valley, and the postwar economists of the *Deutsche Bundesbahn*, loath to expend funds to link the booming infant Republic with a district behind the moon, had not yet seen fit to rebuild it. Consequently, no middle men came into County Gerberstadt to buy beets, and the farmers became desperate. It remained for Zabern to step in and form a consortium of beet growers. Using his prestige as vintner, tanner, and quarrier, he arranged freight delivery to Mainz at the end of each harvest season. He was, of course, president of the consortium, and if the profits he extracted from the arrangement prevented the beet growers from prospering, at least they continued to exist. For this they were eternally grateful. They tipped their black-visored forage caps when Zabern passed, and murmured, "Good day, *Chef*." There was no limit to the gratitude of the German peasantry, Brace thought.

Frau Kemp was trying to rally, but she was no longer hitting the ball with confidence. Brace saw that she had begun to play Greta's game. A fatal mistake. The end was inevitable now . . .

The vineyard had been in Zabern's family for generations. Weiersheimer-Schlossberg the wine was called. Like most wines of interior Rheinhessen, it had body, but little flavor. Invariably, it had to be sugared. No matter. It was a wine of the district, and the fact that it did not approach the *Spätlese* of Nierstein, or Oppenheim, or of the famous vineyards of Rüdesheim and the Rheingau meant little to the inhabitants of County Gerberstadt, who could not have afforded the better wines to begin with. Weiersheimer-Schlossberg was a good-bodied wine of the district; it was, moreover, picked in the vineyard, pressed in the press, and stored in the cellar of Konrad Zabern. Drinking it was a duty, an affirmation of loyalty — the loyalty of German peasantry, which, as Brace knew, was equally limitless.

The sawmill and tannery in Gerberstadt were also inherited. Since the war, state law had drastically curtailed logging, and the sawmill had been converted gradually into a small furniture factory, where a few elder artisans spent long hours whittling bedposts and chairbacks, and deploring the decline of their craft. The reason for the decline was well known — *"die verdammten Franzosen"* — those damned French, who had done their best to denude the Rhineland forests during two occupations. And not only forests, but the fishing as well, for the French had thrown hand grenades into the streams, killing the trout by concussion and then feeding them to the populace during the famine winter of 1946. Between the denudation of forests and the massacre of *Forellen*, the French would not soon be forgiven, for the old men never tired of reiterating their ancient complaint — proving once again that the capacity of the German lower caste for bearing grudges is considerable.

The tannery had been founded by Zabern's father, and, with the exception of logging and wine pressing, was the oldest industry in the district, depending on the proximity of birch and oak forests which provided bark for the dyes. Before the war, hides had come to the tannery by train from Saxony; then they were shipped south by rail to the shoe factories in Pirmasens. But since the war there had been no railroad to the south; there had been a curtailment in logging (and, therefore, dye-making) because of the denudation of forests by the French; and there had been a shortage of hides because of the lack of trade behind the Iron Curtain. Consequently, most of the tannery workers had drifted off to Mannheim and Ludwigshafen to work in the chemical factories. The remaining handful were mostly old men and young boys, who pedaled to work on bicycles from outlying villages, and who toiled incredibly long hours with outmoded equipment. Brace had never ceased to be amazed at the capacity of German workers for toil.

Greta was running out the match. She had taken the last four games in a row. How poised she was! As he watched her stretching to serve, Brace decided that tennis was a game for lean women.

Zabern had purchased the stone and gravel quarry from the *Kreisleiter* of the Nazi Party, late in the winter of 1945. (The transaction was mentioned in a French intelligence report that still remained in Brace's files.) The Allies were pounding against the Siegfried Line, below Zweibrücken, and the German High Command was planning to make a final stand behind the Rhine. The Nazi county leader, a provincial idiot, was preparing to flee to a supposedly "impregnable" redoubt that was being prepared in Bavaria. Panicky and desperately in need of cash, he had sold the quarry for practically nothing. For Zabern it was a stroke of luck. The quarry was taken over by the French, after the surrender, but transport and machinery remained in such terrible state that little rock was extracted. By the time the French relinquished control, the Cold War had set in, and the

Americans were building enormous supply depots in the vicinity of Kaiserslautern, and handing out generous contracts for material as part of the recovery program to "help the Germans help themselves." Zabern began to sell them crushed rock for their roadways. He had been the sole provider of rock for the storage site in the forest behind Weiersheim — a top priority project for which the Americans spared no expense. Miles of roadway had already been built, and there was more in the offing; in the spring, alternate routes would be constructed to connect the site with the main highway leading south to Kaiserslautern, the Sub-Area Headquarters. The Army's engineers were, for the most part, bored and anxious to return to civilian life, but with unlimited funds to expend in the meantime. Speaking no German, they staffed their offices with German civilians, who spoke English, and to whom they entrusted a major portion of contracting. Consequently, the Sub-Area Engineer Office was a hotbed of intrigue: affability for the Americans and bribery for their civilian administrators — such was the secret of success of Zabern's *Pfälzische Hartsteinfabrik*. His quarry was working full blast. He was becoming rich. Soon he would be able to lease the largest hunting preserve in the state. There was no limit to the gullibility of amateur conquerors, Brace had decided long before.

Frau Kemp was demoralized. Brace could hear her panting and see her breasts heaving as she set herself to receive service in the near court. On her flushed face there was fatigue and resignation, which he found provocative as he did all vestiges of female surrender.

Now Zabern was speaking again, deliberately and

carefully, as if he had chosen the words during his long silence. "Naturally, Herr Brace, all the world hopes that you Americans will succeed in maintaining the balance of power. I have only wished to indicate that it will be enormously difficult."

"I've heard similar expressions before," Brace replied shortly. "I don't doubt their validity, but I've noticed that the difficulty of our new prospect invariably seems to evoke a certain . . . relish."

"But a very human reaction, *nicht?* Partly it is because of your previously abundant confidence, and partly it is a certain relief that now the burden is upon someone else."

Brace was momentarily astonished. "Someone else!" he said. "When did Germany assume such a burden in the past?"

Zabern laughed. "I'm speaking as a European, Herr Brace. No offense was intended."

"None taken," Brace replied, but as he watched Zabern's faintly condescending smile, he was annoyed in spite of himself. The Germans always like to sit in the umpire's chair, he thought.

"Examples of national purpose are everywhere to be seen, these days," Zabern went on. "It's the strength of the Soviet Union, and of France under de Gaulle. The lack of it is the weakness of England since the war."

"Or because of the war," said Brace, who was fond of the English.

"Very well, Herr Brace, but remember that it's no good to base judgments upon emotion. We also admire the English because they refused to quit. It's an irony we share in common, you know. By 1943, we knew the war was lost — Stalingrad, of course, and the landings in Italy, and" — here Zabern smiled fleetingly — "the indiscriminate bombing of the homeland cities."

I ought to call him on that, Brace thought. I ought to shove Warsaw, Rotterdam, and Coventry down his throat.

Instead, he looked out across the court where Frau Kemp, lunging vainly for a soft placement, shouted "*Ja, ja,*" in weary tribute.

"Purpose comes from the willingness of people to recognize leadership even when they do not fully understand it," Zabern continued. "One is told that workers and farmers in America are motivated by the possibility of prospering, and those of the Soviet Union by the promised goals of a state-sponsored panacea. Their German counterparts, however, are largely guided by a set of traditional loyalties — to the nation, to cities and towns, and to leaders, local and national. As history has proven, it is at the same time our great strength and our great weakness. But if there is a man in Germany who will understand this fount of loyalty, who will hold himself aloof and in readiness, awaiting the proper moment —" Zabern broke off to watch a spirited rally on the court as Frau Kemp fought to avoid match point.

The tenuous link, Brace reflected. Was this why Zabern chose to remain in the Pfalz, this microcosm behind the moon, where, each autumn, the age-old rituals of rank and privilege were perpetuated, and where he, lessee of forests, could thus affirm the very foundations of national culture? Sport is an escape from coercion, he had said. Perhaps it was not such a curious definition after all. Brace remembered reading an account of the Emperor

Maximilian, who had pointed out to his son and heir that the advantage of hunting as a sport for the ruler was the opportunity it gave his subjects to come into close yet well-ordered contact with him. But Zabern had no real power. Power resided in the Federal Government by consent of the industrialists one saw in the casinos and in the black Mercedes that pounded over cobblestone highways connecting the Rhineland spa towns. Perhaps that was why Zabern included them as hunting guests. Brace was struck by the incredible romanticism of such a notion, yet was it not a strange combination of romanticism and domination to which Zabern aspired? Brace could not help feeling envious of the possibilities the man's rooted influence afforded him. Not since he had come to the Pfalz had he realized so keenly how transitory was his own stay. Suddenly Zabern appeared as a rival — a formidable antagonist. Brace wondered how many others there were like him in Germany. He recalled the private armies of the Bavarian aristocrats and landowners who had plagued the postwar era of the Weimar Republic. Absurd? No, even now Zabern could probably recruit two or three hundred followers. If, in some future crisis with the East, the Federal Government should falter, and the industrialists began casting about for a new alliance . . .

Greta was serving match point. Brace watched her as she skipped toward the net, stooped gracefully for a low ball, and stroked it deftly into the corner past Frau Kemp. The match was over, and he got to his feet as the two women came off the court.

Although he had seen the County Administrator's wife at the club before, Brace had never been introduced to her. "*Sehr erfreut*," he murmured, stiffening in spite of himself, and bobbing his head as she offered him her hand. You're getting Germanized, he thought grimly. Give it another year and they'll see you in boots and a leather trench coat. "You played very well," he said.

"No, no — only in the first set." Frau Kemp smiled and showed a set of unfortunately oversized and discolored teeth. "I should practice more," she said. "I should discipline myself like Frau Zabern."

Brace turned to Greta. "You're still playing every day?"

"Of course!" she replied gaily, ordering a citronade from the caretaker.

He had known it without asking. She played with an almost frenzied regularity — two matches a day, three, sometimes four — as if she hoped to achieve a total exhaustion of mind and body.

Zabern smiled. "You see, Herr Brace, my wife has purpose."

"Yes," Brace said, looking at Greta. "One of these days she'll be champion of the Pfalz."

"Champion of the Pfalz," Greta echoed sadly. "I don't think so."

He began to question her about a recent tournament she had won at Bad Kreuznach, but her gaze had moved restlessly around the table, and then off across the court. In this mood, the shallow, slightly darkened hollows beneath her eyes lent the spare beauty of her face an appealing gravity.

Zabern was explaining the intricacies of hunting to Frau Kemp, and Brace saw that Greta was receptive to echoes of the conversation. He looked carefully at Zabern, noting the sports jacket and brown breeches that disappeared without the trace of a wrinkle into a pair of slender cavalry boots. The breeches and boots were his agricultural habit — he wore them in his vineyard and when he visited the beet fields. At the sawmill and tannery, he wore business suits; at the stone quarry, a trench coat for protection against the dust; and in the forest, the inevitable green velours garb of the huntsman. So many roles, Brace thought, and a change of costume for each. How convenient. Every day, a fresh image, another projection. Did this not explain his arrogance, the pride of a soldier for his various uniforms, and the actor's insatiable ego for each new part?

"Every man is assigned a lane to traverse," Zabern was saying, "and one or two gunbearers, depending on whether he wishes to use several weapons in rotation. The beaters are spread out in the interval of woods between the lanes. At a signal from myself or the Jäger —"

"The whole skirmish line moves ahead like a dragnet," Brace said abruptly. He had seen it often. Even farmers hunting rabbits in open fields moved in tight formation.

"You don't approve, Herr Brace?" Zabern was looking at him with amusement.

"It's a system that has merit if the purpose of hunting is to ensure the largest possible kill," Brace replied.

"But that's precisely the purpose! Our forests are carefully regulated in Germany, so we are invariably faced with overpopulation of game. If the animals are not thinned out by hunting, they become stunted and diseased. This is something we do not allow."

Brace was provoked by the absolute assurance in Zabern's tone. "You haven't sufficiently decimated the fox population," he said dryly. "Yesterday I saw one that was sick. Probably with rabies."

"Then it's *you* whom my Jäger is meeting tomorrow morning in the square!"

Brace nodded and grinned, pleased at the surprise on Zabern's face.

"You will find yourself mistaken," Zabern went on stiffly. "This fox may be wounded, or dying of old age, but rabies has never been seen in this district. It is unknown here."

"The diagnosis was not mine alone," Brace replied. "It was confirmed by a friend of mine — an old shepherd who has undoubtedly seen many rabid animals."

"This friend of yours is a poacher. According to the Jäger, he has made trouble here before."

Brace smiled. "I think you're mistaken. The old man is really quite harmless."

"Nevertheless, he would be well advised to move on," Zabern said evenly. "Poaching is a most serious offense, Herr Brace. It is something we do not allow." He turned to Frau Kemp. "The hunters are allowed to shoot only straight ahead at game flushed across their lanes," he went on. "By listening to the calls of the Jäger's horn, they and the beaters are able to keep themselves in alignment. Thus there is no danger of accident."

Brace struck up a conversation with Greta, but his attempts were awkward for he could sense in her a measure of his own embarrassment. He was about to make some excuse and leave, when suddenly he saw that Zabern and Frau Kemp were standing and looking down at them.

"I must be off to supper," said Frau Kemp, whose large

teeth gave a nervous quality to her smile. "It's nearly dark."

Zabern had already picked up her racket. "I shall be glad to drive you home, of course." He nodded at Brace and Greta. "Enjoy your citronade," he said.

"Really, I don't mind the walk," Frau Kemp was saying.

Brace was on his feet, watching her tug at the edges of her shorts. He imagined her tugging at them after she had slid into the Mercedes, her shoulders braced against the back of the seat, her body arched, and her bottom lifted.

"Good-by," he called.

"*Auf Wiedersehen*, Herr Brace! *Auf Wiedersehen*, Greta!"

Brace stood until the Mercedes disapppeared into the street. Then he sat down again. "Do you also hunt, Frau Zabern?" he asked.

She smiled quickly at him. "No, I detest it."

Brace looked at the fields on the hills surrounding the town. The hills had turned yellow and then brown, as the hills do in the Pfalz, where autumn comes slowly and the wrinkled land changes hue in the way of old newspaper. "The tennis will soon be over," he observed. "Summer has ended."

Greta was staring across the court, and for a moment it seemed to Brace that she had forgotten he was there. But then she turned to him, and nodded somberly. "Yes, like a sad refrain," she said, as if she had heard his words in the context of her own thoughts. "*Das Lied ist aus.* Now one must stay more at home."

He had passed the house only once, but he had seen it

from a distance many times. It was a large baroque manor which sat close to the edge of the forest beneath a clump of shade trees on an otherwise denuded ridge.

"Of course I shall take long walks," Greta said. "Autumn is the best season for hiking."

He thought of her confined within the big house, listening to the sound of gunfire from the forest — detesting it. "Perhaps we could play a set or two before the season ends," he said.

"Yes, that would be very nice."

"Tomorrow . . . ?"

Greta hesitated. Then, "Yes, tomorrow. In the afternoon."

"I probably won't give you a very good match. I'm out of practice."

"You forget I've seen you play," she replied, looking at him coolly, evenly. "You are a very good player . . . very graceful."

Brace was holding his breath. What is she saying? he thought with wonder. He gave his head a tiny, incredulous shake. You're crazy, he told himself. You're imagining things. You've been stuck away in the boondocks too long.

But when he looked at her again, he nearly suffocated. "D'you like it here," he gasped, "in the Pfalz?"

"It is very bleak."

In the darkness, Brace could scarcely see her.

"There's a carp pool before our house," Greta said. "Each winter it freezes to the bottom. The carp freeze inside the ice and mud, and in the spring, when everything melts, they come alive again. Some of the fish are not affected but others swim on their sides in circles.

After a few days, they die and the gardener must take them out. So the pool goes on — winter to winter, freeze to freeze, and thaw to thaw."

"The cycle of life and death," Brace said huskily.

They were suddenly bathed in the brilliance of Zabern's headlights, and now Brace saw that she was smiling, with tears in her eyes, in the insistent glare which had already lifted them to their feet.

"*Ja*," said Greta, softly. "But to survive, one must endure."

PART III

Vulpicide and Vection

7

㘈㘈㘈㘈㘈

THE MORNING WAS COOL and hazy, as autumn mornings are in the Rhineland, where night slips off the open fields, leaving a wake of mist. Brace sat in his jeep at the front gate of the *Kaserne*, watching two white-helmeted M.P.s check the passes of incoming personnel and wave on outgoing cars filled with dependent wives bound for the shopping centers at Mannheim and Kaiserslautern. Across the roadway, some manure wagons were passing out to the fields, the men sitting in the wagons and holding the reins of oxen, the women wearing kerchiefs and plodding in the road behind, and the cargoes steaming in the morning chill. Presently, a jeep turned off the highway and started down the hill toward the *Kaserne*. When Brace made out the white circle and red cross emblazoned on the canvas top, he stepped into the road and signaled the vehicle to a halt; a lieutenant in field uniform and sunglasses opened the door.

"Good morning," Brace said. "Are you the veterinarian?"

"I'm a physician," the lieutenant replied unhappily. "The vet is checking cows today."

Brace looked at the unhappy lieutenant and suppressed a smile. Then he turned and waved toward the parking

lot inside the gate, where a sergeant and two soldiers —
the men the colonel had promised him — were waiting
by a three-quarter-ton truck. "All right," he said to the
lieutenant. "Tell your driver to follow me and we'll get
this over with as quickly as possible."

When the three military vehicles ground to a halt on
the cobblestones of the square in Weiersheim, Brace saw
the Jäger and Polizeiwachtmeister Brausch sitting side by
side on motorcycles. As Brace got out of his jeep, the two
men kicked the stands beneath their cycles and dismounted. The Jäger wore green breeches, and the green
jacket and hat of his profession, and carried a shotgun
slung over his back. A large, confident Airedale sat patiently in a carrier attached to his motorcycle. Brace
glanced at the two pairs of immaculate boots and shook
hands with both the Jäger and Wachtmeister Brausch.

"We must wait for the Town Secretary," Brausch said,
grinning and rubbing his hands in the morning chill.
"Our Secretary has undoubtedly prepared a speech for
the occasion."

As the policeman spoke, Brace saw Herr Saul and Secretary Vogt emerge from the Secretary's office across the
square. Saul was also wearing boots — not the high, tight-
fitting boots of the policeman or the Jäger but the heavy
kind worn by peasants in the fields. Brausch grinned
again and repeated his joke about the Secretary's speech,
but Brace pretended not to understand. Behind him, he
heard the door of the truck slam shut, and turned to see
the sergeant and the soldiers lean their carbines against a
fender and light cigarettes.

"*Guten Morgen*, Herr Brace," said Saul, out of breath
from walking across the cobblestones.

"*Guten Morgen*," Brace replied, and shook hands with Saul and the Secretary.

"And why do the soldiers carry weapons?" the Jäger demanded. His lean face had flushed, and he directed the question not to Brace but to Secretary Vogt. The Secretary, who had been on the verge of speaking, minimized the soldiers with an impatient wave of his hand, and smiled.

"No doubt because the *Kommandant* has ordered them to do so," Brace said to Saul.

The Jäger's gray eyes narrowed. He turned again to the Secretary. "It is not necessary that the soldiers carry weapons. I myself will dispose of the fox — if, indeed, there is any fox to be disposed of."

A point well made, Brace thought. If there is no fox to be disposed of, the game warden is not going to be disappointed. That's a military face, the warden's; it's the face of a man who has counted tanks in his day and who now counts hares and roebuck and who isn't any happier about your finding a sick fox in his territory than the colonel was when you . . . "It is customary for soldiers to carry weapons, is it not?" Brace said, addressing Saul again.

"Yes, certainly," Brausch said. "But the Herr Jäger must do the killing. This is also customary, Herr Brace."

"Naturally," Brace replied.

"You may be interested to know that we've found something about the shepherd," Brausch went on, his voice faintly placating. "Our shepherd has indeed failed to obtain the proper grazing permissions this season, so we shall have the opportunity now to question him."

"I am no longer interested in the shepherd," Brace said.

"It appears to me the rumors against him have no foundation."

"I will require the soldiers to leave their weapons in the truck," the Jäger announced, and then said something that Brace did not understand.

"The soldiers are under the orders of the *Kaserne Kommandant*," Brace replied. "Let's get going." He climbed into his jeep, opened the door for Saul, and started the engine.

"*Gute Jagd!*" the Town Secretary shouted.

Brace waved to the Secretary, wheeled the jeep around, and started up the hill out of town. Yes, it'll be a good hunt, he thought. It's going to be one hell of a pleasant safari. At this point, the clients would like to substitute the White Hunter for the fox. The doctor is offended because you mistook him for a veterinarian; the Jäger was offended when the fox was reported in the first place, and now his professional pride is outraged because the soldiers have brought along their weapons; to top it off, the Wachtmeister appears honor bound to prove something derogatory against the shepherd. The fox may be a loser, too, but by this time he's probably taking his rest cure in another county. It's your own damn fault for not having left him alone to begin with . . .

Saul and Brace arrived first at the meadow and waited for the others. It was cold and quiet in the valley, and steam was rising from the hollow of the brook. The motorcycles of the Jäger and the policeman appeared at the edge of the forest and slithered across the wet grass, leaving serpentine trails in the dew. When the party had assembled, Brace walked to the truck and told the sergeant to keep his men in the background and to allow the Jäger to do the shooting if there was any shooting to be done. Then he started upsteam, followed by the Jäger and the dog, who was sniffing eagerly at the bushes, and the others strung out behind like a column on patrol. When he drew opposite the point where he had last seen the fox, he descended the bank and jumped the brook. The others came after him, except for the sergeant and the soldiers, who remained on the bank smoking cigarettes. For several minutes, Brace searched through the scrub; then he stopped in puzzlement and pointed to the place where the marmot hole had been but where there was now a mound of red earth and a cleared area showing the scars of fresh digging. Turning, he noted the serious face of the lieutenant from the medical detachment, the disappointed face of Saul, and the disdainful faces of the Jäger and Brausch. Whining, the Jäger's dog began to paw the ground at his feet.

Upon a quiet command from its master, the dog went to the edge of the meadow and lay down, watching the assemblage that had gathered in a semicircle around the clearing. The Jäger took up a stick from the brush and prodded the pile of dirt; then he removed the shotgun from his shoulder, stood it against a tree, and, with both hands on the stick, began to scoop the earth backward between his legs. Below the surface he uncovered traces of fur and, after more digging, unearthed the fox sprawled forlornly in a shallow grave, with mud caking its wet and matted pelt.

"But you were right, it is certainly a fox!" said Saul, clapping Brace on the back as if to reaffirm a confidence that had begun to waver.

"The shepherd has done as he promised," Brace replied.

"Our instructions are to take the animal to the *Kreisveterinär* for examination," said Brausch, glancing at the lieutenant from the medical detachment. "Naturally, Herr Brace, the results of this examination will be made known to the American authorities."

The Jäger had taken a length of leather thong from his pocket and passed it carefully beneath the corpse. Now he drew it about the forelegs and knotted it tightly. Then, leading the way, he descended to the stream, swung the fox to the farther side, and jumped across. The soldiers cast indifferent glances at the dead animal as he dragged it through the brush. Brausch hurried to his side. "Our shepherd has killed and buried the fox, Herr Jäger, but perhaps his mongrels have engaged the animal! Perhaps it has bitten one of the sheep!"

The Jäger deposited his burden beside the motorcycles and nodded. Brausch began to speak in a torrent of dialect, which Brace could not understand.

"What the Wachtmeister thinks may be true," said Saul. "If some of the animals of the shepherd have come in contact with the fox, they may indeed be infected. We are back where we began, Herr Brace!"

"Who knows if the fox had rabies or not?" Brace replied. "How will anyone know until the veterinarian has examined the animal and given his report?"

"But, Herr Brace, that the fox had rabies was your opinion in the beginning."

"So it was," said Brace, wearily.

The Jäger and Brausch were conversing with slurred German vehemence when the latter suddenly stepped aside and pointed up the valley. The sun, mounting in the east, had cast a long corridor of light toward the mountain, and far away, where the meadow diminished into the woods, Brace saw the shepherd and his flock outlined like a miniscule crèche against the grass. Saul rushed to Brausch's side and squinted along his outstretched arm.

"Our shepherd has not moved on fast enough this time!" Brausch shouted. He smiled at Brace.

"Wait!" Brace said. "When the fox was first discovered, the shepherd stated he would kill it if it did not become well. What justice can there be in troubling him now, when he has only carried out his promise and thereby saved us trouble?"

"But, Herr Brace, certain elements of the situation remain to be determined, and the finding of the fox *dead* merely brings new complications to light . . ." The voice of Polizeiwachtmeister Brausch was soothing, and the smile was still on his face. "To begin with, there is the matter of grazing permits that the shepherd has failed to obtain. Secondly, there is a question as to whether the animals of the old man have come in contact with the fox. Then, there is serious doubt whether the shepherd had the right to dispose of the fox without consulting the proper authorities." Here Brausch looked significantly at the Jäger. "And, finally, Herr Brace, is there not some doubt remaining as to your own suspicions? Would it not benefit you professionally to interrogate the shepherd at this time?"

"I am convinced that any professional suspicions concerning the shepherd have been unwarranted," replied Brace.

Polizeiwachtmeister Brausch was smiling politely. "Naturally, you must do as you think best, Herr Brace. I merely thought you might wish to observe, since we must apprehend the shepherd anyway —" Brausch broke off, shrugging. "It's a perfect opportunity, *nicht?*"

"For God's sake!" Brace began, and then looked at the lean, determined face and gray eyes of the Jäger. You fool, he thought. The worst thing you could have done was give the Jäger the idea you wanted to protect the shepherd.

"Sixty miles to see a buried animal!" the lieutenant from the medical detachment complained bitterly.

"Go to hell!" said Brace.

The lieutenant adjusted his sunglasses, jumped into his jeep, and ordered the driver to start away. Saul looked at Brace and hesitated as the Jäger and Polizeiwachtmeister Brausch began walking over the meadow toward the mountain; then he turned and hurried after the two figures plowing steadily through the wet grass.

Brace looked up the valley at the flock, and saw a glint of light. He strained to make out the shepherd, and saw another flash which came from the midst of the sheep, as if the sun were reflecting against a shining object. The sharp light cut into him and made him wince. It's the binoculars, he thought miserably. The old man's seen the three of them and he can see you also. Why in the name of God and in the first place could you not have allowed the fox the privilege of diagnosing his own ailments and being sick in peace?

The three Germans were striding briskly over the meadow, their heavy boots cutting parallel trails in the covering of dew. For a moment, Brace watched the rapidly diminishing figures, and then he started slowly up the valley; following their straight, purposeful swath, he found himself shivering in the first warmth of day.

The Wachtmeister had already begun to question the shepherd, but with Brace's arrival he turned his back on the old man and placed his hands on his hips in a gesture of triumph. "What d'you think?" he cried. "Our friend refuses to confirm or deny that he killed the fox!"

"Who can blame him?" Brace replied. "So would I in his position."

"But Herr Brace, it was you who told us of his intention in the first place."

Brace spoke to the shepherd. "Mathias, I told them you had said you would kill the fox, but not with the object of causing you any trouble."

"You've betrayed me," said the old man with contempt.

"Why bother with him?" said the policeman. "These poachers are all the same. They respect no one."

"What are you going to do now?" Brace asked wearily.

"What choice have I except to detain him? The killing of any wild animal without permission is forbidden by law. The Herr Jäger wishes to make a formal complaint."

"Suppose I had killed the fox — would you arrest me?"

"You don't understand, Herr Brace. The shepherd is of a type we don't want to have around. Therefore, we'll encourage him to move somewhere else."

"So it's a pretext!" Brace shouted, taking a step in the Jäger's direction. "The worst sort of pretext!"

The policeman interposed himself between them. "There's no point in blaming the Jäger," he said calmly. "The Herr Jäger is merely performing his duty."

"Yes, as Herr Zabern's flunky!" Brace replied. Now, seeing the insolent manner with which the Jäger was swinging the barrel of the shotgun cradled in the crook of his arm, he became enraged to the point of wishing that he had brought along his revolver. But Brausch, hands on hips, still stood squarely in front of him, watching him closely. It's your own goddam fault, Brace told himself bitterly. If you hadn't shot your mouth off at the tennis court last night . . . He turned again to the old man. "Listen, you've got to trust me, Mathias. I'll do my best to straighten things out with the Town Secretary."

The shepherd gave him a look of scorn. "You've betrayed me," he said. "Why should I trust you?"

Brace took him by the arm and pulled him aside. "Listen, they're probably going to take you down to the police station in the village," he whispered. "But whatever happens, don't admit you killed the fox."

"Judas!" the old man snarled, shaking him off. Now he advanced on the policeman. "Who'll take care of my sheep?" he demanded.

"That's no concern of mine," Brausch replied. "What do I care for your stinking sheep? You should have thought of them before you decided to make trouble around here."

"I'll take care of the sheep," Brace said. "Just remember what I told you."

The policeman smiled an impatient smile. "Come, come, Herr Brace, it's time to be off. The shepherd can get himself a lawyer later on. Besides, it's quite obvious that he doesn't want your help to begin with."

You sonofabitch, Brace thought, but he managed to keep himself in control. "At least allow the old man to put his animals inside the prisoner-of-war compound," he said.

"An excellent idea," Brausch replied with a laugh. "We certainly don't want them cluttering up the village."

Twenty minutes later, the sheep were swarming through the gate of the compound — a great clot of woolly rumps bobbing like soapsuds at the mouth of a drain. When the entire flock was inside the wire, the shepherd closed the gate and left his mongrels to guard it. Then he walked toward Brace, who had climbed out of his jeep, and the Wachtmeister and the Jäger, who were sitting astride their motorcycles.

"Here's your prisoner," Brace said contemptuously. "How are you going to take him in?"

The policeman shrugged. "If he wishes, the shepherd can ride in the Jäger's carrier, but since you'll be driving Herr Saul back to town, why not take him yourself?"

"Perhaps I could fingerprint him for you as well."

"You're taking things entirely too seriously," said Brausch with a laugh. "The charges against the old man are not that grave. They're merely designed to teach him a lesson."

And me also, Brace reflected morosely. The idea was like a bone in his throat. Whatever he did, he could only lose, which was the most galling thing of all. By acquiescing, he became the policeman's chastened pupil; by arguing, he damaged the shepherd's chances of a quick release. The only hope lies with Town Secretary Vogt, he thought.

He turned and looked inquiringly at Mathias.

"I am leaving the sheep under protest," said the old man, stiffly. "Who knows what may happen to them?"

"No one's going to bother your sheep," Brausch replied, pointing to the defaced sign on the barbed wire fence. "Can't you read, old man? It's *verboten* for anyone to come here." He glanced at Brace, and grinned.

"The Wachtmeister's right," Brace said to the shepherd. "Your animals are perfectly safe. This land belongs to —" He stopped in mid-sentence, struck by the realization of what he was about to say. "This land belongs to the United States Army," he said.

"Exactly," Brausch replied. "So the old fool has nothing to worry about."

"Nothing to worry about," Brace repeated with a smile. "You're absolutely right, my friend. You have no idea." He began to laugh.

"What're you trying to say, Herr Brace?"

Brace shook his head to stop laughing. "It's perfectly simple. The shepherd has decided to decline your invitation."

"Invitation . . . ?"

"To accompany you into town."

"Is this some kind of joke, Herr Brace? The old man is in custody. He hasn't the right to decide anything."

"You don't understand," Brace said. "Because he's on military property, he can't be taken into custody except with the consent of the proper military authorities."

The policeman flushed with a mixture of incredulity and anger. "Are you denying this consent?"

"Not at all. It's just that I haven't the right to give it. The training area is under the jurisdiction of the Sub-Area engineers. You'll have to apply to them, I'm afraid."

"This is a bluff, Herr Brace, a bluff of the most transparent kind!"

Brace grinned. "One pretext for another," he said. Hook, line, and sinker, he was thinking.

"The consequences for harboring a fugitive are very serious," Brausch replied. "In fact, now that you've had your little joke, I suggest —"

"But I'm not joking, Herr Wachtmeister. In fact, I intend to see to it that the Town Secretary is fully informed of what has happened."

Brausch started up the engine of his motorcycle. "You're going to regret this trick, Herr Brace."

"There's no sense blaming me," replied Brace with a mocking smile. "Like the game warden here, I'm merely performing my duty."

8

TOWN SECRETARY VOGT was profoundly disappointed; moreover, he was puzzled. The hunting party to which he had wished luck and waved farewell in the square, an hour before, had returned bearing not only the evidence of success — the carcass of the fox lay in a burlap sack on the stoop outside his office door — but also the weight of dissension. The Town Secretary peered out from beneath a pair of fleshy eyelids and studied the gloomy faces of the Jäger, the policeman, and the resident intelligence agent. Then he sank deeper into his chair, loosened several buttons of his vest, and began to nod his head.

Brausch was making a laborious summation. "You see, Herr Sekretär, the fox is dead but the affair has further complications. In the first place . . ."

The Secretary looked longingly at the volume of Tacitus's *Germania* lying open on his desk, and, feeling drowsy, fought the urge to doze. From experience, he knew that Brausch would have at least four points to make — possibly five.

"Secondly —" Brausch continued.

Secretary Vogt glanced at the Jäger, who did not conform to his scholarly and romantic notion that foresters were contemplative men. The Jäger's face mirrored the impassive scrutiny of a marksman. Looking at him, Vogt had the uncomfortable feeling of being aligned in the cross hairs of a rifle scope.

Still nodding, as if to reassure Brausch who was laying a third tier of charges, the Town Secretary examined Brace. There was a tinge of scorn at the corners of the young man's eyes; a certain amusement in the controlled inclination of his head; and a hard, stubborn line at the mouth.

"In the fourth place, Herr Sekretär, both the Herr Jäger and myself are fully convinced . . ."

In the trough of a deep and somber nod, Town Secretary Vogt sighed heavily. At least the end was in sight. Polizeiwachtmeister Brausch had never made more than five consecutive points before. A fact which doubtless explains why he converses arithmetically, the Secretary thought.

Flushed and angry, the policeman was approaching the climax of his summation, but Vogt was only half-listening. Within the soundlessly tolling head, the mediator in him was already plotting.

"And, finally," Brausch said — he had halted in mid-stride before the desk and was looking directly at Brace — "it is inadmissible, Herr Sekretär, that the shepherd who is under our civilian jurisdiction should be allowed to take refuge in a military installation!"

Now the inevitable pause had come. Nodding with the rhythm of a metronome set for adagio, the Town Secretary looked at Brace, who returned his glance levelly and in silence, and then at the Jäger, the man of forest shade, who leaned forward in his chair and gave an abrupt, inflexible nod of affirmation to what Brausch

had said, as if he were blinking in the glare of unaccus-
tomed sunlight.

Secretary Vogt raised a hand that admonished his
visitors. "Indeed the fox is dead," he said, smiling at
Brausch. "Now it must be determined whether he has
been infected with rabies. In the meantime, we must decide what precautions are to be taken for the common
welfare, for do we not agree, gentlemen, that it is the
public safety which most concerns us?" The Town Secretary waited an instant to affirm the incontestability of
his point; then he smiled again, leaned forward, and
picked up the receiver of the ancient nickel-plated telephone on his desk. The operator's voice was audible
throughout the room:

"*Bitte?*"

"*Kreisveterinärsamt,*" the Town Secretary said.

County Veterinarian Rees sat in a tiny office at the
rear of the administration building in Gerberstadt, and
dreamed of one day obtaining a post in the State Ministry for Agriculture and Forestry. The ministry was
located in Mainz, a scant thirty miles to the north, but to
Rees it might as well have been on some other planet. He
had been in Gerberstadt twelve years, and during all that
time there had been no openings in Mainz. Was it possible for a man to gain respect at Mainz by spaying cats
and examining ruptured oxen in a district that was behind the moon? For a long time, the county veterinarian
had not been able to pose this question to himself without a terrible feeling of hopelessness, but after talking
with Town Secretary Vogt, he suddenly dashed from
his office into the street, jumped into the Tempo tricycle

truck with which he made his daily rounds, and raced across the hills toward Weiersheim. At the outskirts of the village, he stopped the truck, shut off the engine, and deliberately waited to be overtaken by his old despair. Then, fully composed, he resumed his journey. When he entered the office of the Town Secretary, some minutes later, he was wearing his professional dignity and his surgeon's gray smock tightly buttoned.

Vogt addressed his latest visitor with studied formality. "Herr Veterinär Rees, the fox has been found dead and awaits your disposition in a sack outside the door. Naturally we are consumed with curiosity. We wonder if, perhaps, you could make a preliminary examination to determine whether he has been infected, as we suspect, with rabies . . ."

"Impossible, Herr Sekretär! At this point the fox is merely a lifeless animal — to me as well as to you. It must now be subjected to a most painstaking and scientific autopsy which can only be performed in a laboratory."

The Town Secretary smiled and resumed his meditative nodding. "Of course," he murmured. "You must pardon the ignorance of laymen in these matters, Herr Veterinär, but I'm sure we'll all be most grateful if you would indulge us with some explanation as to the nature of the disease." Vogt glanced at the serious, composed faces of his guests, and smiled. To abate passions, one must create a diversion that will separate the combatants, he thought.

The veterinarian folded his arms and considered his words carefully. "To begin with, the origins of the disease are quite mysterious," he said. "It is a virus invasion, of course, usually of massive proportions, with a special affinity for cells of the central nervous system, but whether it is always present in some form or whether it is somehow contracted by the various animals which are its vectors, we cannot be sure. For my own part, I am inclined to believe that the virus is indigenous to certain animals and that it may lie dormant for several generations before it becomes virile. But this is merely a theory. The one thing we can be sure of is that once the virus is activated, its victims will inevitably go mad and die."

Wachtmeister Brausch was drumming his fingers on the visor of his peaked cap which rested upon his knee. "This virus, Herr Veterinär — how is it transmitted?"

"Only by a bite contaminated with the saliva of the vector. It is a process of cause and effect, you see. The disease enrages its victims to furious assaults, new victims are created, and thus the virus endures."

"And once bitten by such a victim — is the disease inevitable?"

The veterinarian nodded solemnly. "It's almost a certainty," he said. "But the incubation period varies greatly. Progress of the virus from implantation to final establishment in the brain can take weeks or even months. Given certain conditions, it can be accomplished in a few days. If, for example, the bite is deep and close to the brain of the victim to begin with, and if the viral colony of the vector is large —" The veterinarian broke off and shrugged.

"And there is no possibility of recovery?" the policeman asked.

"None except inoculation with anti-rabies vaccine."

"Can all animals be so infected?"

"All, Herr Wachtmeister. Especially dogs, cats, and foxes."

"And what about sheep?" the policeman asked, with a glance at Brace.

"Sheep, too, if bitten."

The Town Secretary leaned forward quickly. "How long will your examination take, Herr Veterinär?"

Rees shook his head. "Impossible to know," he said. "I must open the brain of the fox and examine its tissue. If the viral colony is massive, I may be able to detect Negri bodies in the central motor neurons. I am not, however, a bacteriologist and I do not possess an electron microscope. It may be necessary, therefore, to take the tissue to Mainz for a more complete examination." The county veterinarian paused and looked reflectively at the ceiling. "Yes, in all probability I shall have to go to Mainz. There we can inoculate rats or mice with particles of the fox's brain. If, in a few days, the test animals show the usual symptoms . . ." The veterinarian smiled and shrugged again.

The Town Secretary nodded. "And in the meantime, Herr Veterinär?"

"I would suggest that all dogs be chained and kept under careful scrutiny," Rees replied. "Cats as well, if possible."

"And what about other animals that may have come in contact with the fox?" asked Brausch.

"Such as, Herr Wachtmeister?"

"Such as sheep," Brace said dryly.

"They should also be isolated and watched. In the case of dogs, the first symptoms are slight. The animal does not foam at the mouth as is commonly believed. He becomes uneasy and is often sexually aroused. He tends to snap and growl, even at his master. He is angered at the sight of other dogs. Gradually, as the virus invades his brain, he experiences several days of violent paroxysms. Then paralysis and coma set in, which is inevitably followed by death."

"And what of humans?" the Town Secretary asked.

Veterinarian Rees gave a rueful smile. "The symptoms are approximately the same, Herr Sekretär, but I am not a physician. My official interest is only that the animals which may have been infected are not allowed to roam freely. If any of the inhabitants of the village have been bitten, I suggest you contact the Ministry of Health immediately, for the anti-rabies vaccine must be administered without delay." The veterinarian got to his feet and shook hands with everyone in the room.

Secretary Vogt accompanied him to the door. "You will let us know as soon as possible the results of your examination?"

"At once, Herr Sekretär! I am almost certain, however, that the affair will be best concluded in Mainz." Rees picked up the sack containing the fox, and, holding it at arm's length, started down the steps to the square. "Yes, I will go to Mainz myself this afternoon."

Secretary Vogt returned to his desk and sat heavily in his high-backed chair. He was acutely aware that, having created diversion and stilled dissension, the burden of decision now lay with him. And now, as ever, the tolerance of the scholar was inextricably at war with the required authoritarianism of the leader. The Secretary felt diminished. Why, in his old age, had he chosen to divide himself? Why were there always so many con-

siderations? They swung before him like pendulums,
and, pondering them, he commenced to mark their slow
tempo. To antagonize the policeman, whose vested authority was second only to his own, was unthinkable;
to refute the Jäger was tantamount to degrading the
game preserve — that temple of autumn ritual and source
of communal drama and pride; and to alienate the American would sever an important link with the military
with which he had always maintained the most cordial
relations. For some moments, Secretary Vogt sat nodding above the volume of *Germania*, the first known
geographical and historical text of his country, which
had been set down by Cornelius Tacitus at the end of
the first century. The Roman had written of a wild
country under an inclement sky, and the description of
the cultured man writing about the land of barbarians
was a shaft that arched over the intervening centuries to
find its mark in the Secretary's breast. Now, pinioned
by the necessity of being absolutely impartial — scrupu-
lously fair — he smiled at the three men sitting before
his desk. As always, he had found comfort, if not solution, from his contemplation of the past.

"So, gentlemen, we have made progress!" Secretary
Vogt beamed at the impassive faces of his guests. "But
of course!" he continued briskly. "We have been en-
lightened. Now our path is clearer. I myself will post a
proclamation explaining the situation for the people and
requesting that dogs and other household pets be tied up
and penned. If you, Herr Wachtmeister, will be good
enough to supervise their compliance, the danger of
contagion from within will be largely controlled. And if
the Herr Jäger will kindly maintain his customary scru-

tiny of the forest animals, we can all await the Herr
Veterinär's findings with confidence."

"Not quite," Brausch said. "You have forgotten the
sheep and the shepherd's dogs, Herr Sekretär."

"Not for a moment. It is my decision that the animals
of the shepherd are to be in quarantine at the training
area until the veterinarian has made his report."

"And who will supervise *his* compliance?" asked
Brausch.

"I will," Brace said.

"It's indisputable that the sheep and mongrels have
been exposed to the fox," Brausch replied, addressing
Vogt. "Should they not be subject to restrictions equal-
ling those imposed upon the animals within the village?"

"They'll be enclosed in the wire compound," Brace
said shortly. He spoke to no one in particular, but when
he finished he looked directly at Brausch.

The policeman looked at the Secretary and shrugged.
"One wonders what motive lies behind this desire to
keep the shepherd in our midst."

"But if the sheep *have* contracted rabies, Herr Wachtmeister, would it be fair to send them on to some other
town?" There was a weary irony in the Town Secretary's voice, but it was masked by the almost palsied
shaking of his head.

"Such responsibility rests with you, Herr Sekretär.
For my part, I shall carry out your instructions." Polizeiwachtmeister Brausch had got to his feet and was standing very straight before his chair.

The Secretary came around the corner of the desk to
take Brausch's hand. "Herr Wachtmeister, the thorough-
ness with which you conduct your duties is a great aid

and reassurance to me." Vogt shook hands with Brausch and the Jäger, and accompanied them to the door. "Since the situation is potentially serious, gentlemen, I shall go with Herr Brace to inform the shepherd in person of my decision . . ."

Brausch allowed himself to be amused. "Perhaps, Herr Sekretär, the authority of your position will be sufficient to overcome the interdict of military protection now afforded to the old man." The policeman turned and extended his hand to Brace.

"*Auf Wiedersehen*, Herr Brace!"

"*Auf Wiedersehen*," Brace said.

The Town Secretary was squinting into the morning sun that hovered above the *Schlossberg*, illuminating the red letters of the slogan splashed upon its crumbling walls. "Today I must remember to have that removed," he said absently. "And when this business of the fox is settled, gentlemen, I should appreciate having a chat with you concerning your efforts to apprehend the culprit who is responsible for such desecrations."

Brausch scowled up at the ruins. "Don't worry, Herr Sekretär, sooner or later we'll catch up with him." He turned and smiled grimly at Brace. "Sooner or later," he said again, and started down the steps to the street.

The Town Secretary waited until the policeman and the Jäger had crossed the square; then, nodding with satisfaction, he glanced at Brace. "Well, Herr Brace, if it's convenient for you, perhaps we could take a little drive."

"Certainly," Brace replied. "The old man is waiting at the compound."

Secretary Vogt waved his hand indifferently. "There's

no need to bother the shepherd," he said. "I'm fully confident that you'll convey my wishes to him." The Secretary nodded toward the Ganders sitting on the watering trough. "Just a little ride for appearance's sake," he said, climbing heavily into Brace's jeep.

Brace grinned and looked at the Ganders who were taking the morning sun and staring back. The Secretary's a strategist, he thought. He got in behind the wheel and started up the hill out of town. "Where would you like to go?" he asked.

Secretary Vogt thought it over. "Would you mind taking me to the mountain? At my age it's too much to climb, and I haven't been up there for a long while."

Brace shifted the jeep into high when they reached the top of the hill and started through the forest toward Alpha Site. On the far side of the hunting preserve, he turned south on the same road he had followed the day before, when he had gone to find the shepherd, but now he drove across the bridge above his trout stream and climbed the opposite side of the valley, passing through rolling tiers of meadow and orchard which lay folded around the base of the mountain like cloth draped around the pedestal of a statue. The mountain was symmetrical and rounded, and rose above the gentler hills like a carbuncle. A cap of dense firs and hardwood trees fitted the top, ending like a hairline at the edge of the highest meadows. Here the macadam also ended, between rows of chestnut trees, at a village with a signpost that pronounced it the highest village in the Pfalz — the residual boast of an era before Autobahns, when it had enjoyed a certain distinction as a retreat for tuberculars and asthmatics. Beyond the village, a dirt road wound tortuously through the woods to the *Gasthaus* just below the top of the mountain. Brace and Secretary Vogt drove past the *Gasthaus* to the end of the road, left the jeep, and started up a footpath that led to the summit. The Secretary climbed slowly and with great effort, a hand grasping each thigh above the knee. When he reached the top, he sat down upon a large, grass-covered mound, and, panting heavily, looked out over the meadows in the valley and the forest covering the hills on the opposite side.

"Have you been up here before, Herr Brace?"

"In the winter," Brace answered. "To ski."

"And what did you like?"

Brace looked into the valley. He remembered the perfect brilliance of the mountain beneath the snow and the strange completion of his solitude when he had skied down through the trees and come across the tracks of his jeep.

"The isolation," he said simply.

The Secretary nodded. "It's the same with everyone, Herr Brace. On Sundays, the peasants and villagers of the district climb up here wearing their best black suits and dresses."

"I've heard them singing on their way back down," said Brace.

"But are they happy?" the Secretary murmured. "Below them they see the receptacle of their life's energy and their resting place after death. They have only built the *Gasthaus* to make it bearable. People climb mountains to look down upon themselves, Herr Brace. As a geographer and historian I see that except for a few short intervals we of this part of Germany have been under the rule of others for over a thousand years. We have been conquered by Rome, inundated by waves of barbarians, fought over by Merovingians, sacked by the Spaniards and the Swedes, burned by the French, annexed by Napoleon, and occupied following two great wars. We of the Pfalz—" Secretary Vogt trailed off into silence, and for some moments he stared into the valley, his face grave with the contemplation of centuries. When he spoke again, his voice was weary. "You must forgive me, Herr Brace. Age does not make for precision. I merely want to say"—here the Secretary looked up and smiled—"I merely want to tell you that I feel you were wrong to contravene the authority of Polizei-wachtmeister Brausch."

Brace looked at the Secretary's earnest face and flushed. "I apologize, Herr Sekretär. I felt certain at the time that the Wachtmeister would treat the shepherd unfairly."

"Did you think that I, too, might act unfairly?"

Brace sat down upon the mound. "No, Herr Sekretär, I wasn't thinking that far ahead. I acted on the moment and I'm sorry for it."

"Well, things will undoubtedly smooth out. At present it's merely a question of ruffled feelings." The Secretary paused. "This shepherd—is he a friend or an associate?"

"A friend," Brace answered. "There's nothing professional involved. Actually, I have no right to let him make a sheepfold of the training area. I've only done it because—" Brace suddenly found himself confronting an explanation that defied adequate translation. "Because he's alone," he said.

"I think I understand," the Secretary replied. "The

shepherd is a nomad and the nomadic life is always entrancing — especially to one who values solitude, and especially now in this age of technology. But this shepherd who is called Pucher, have I perhaps heard of him before?"

Brace smiled to himself. The Secretary is really a strategist, he thought. He wants me to say what Brausch undoubtedly told him I already knew. "According to the policeman, the shepherd was once suspected of snaring rabbits and of not having the proper grazing permits."

"Yes, yes! I remember now. It was long ago." The Secretary laughed with the recollection. "Sly Jacob," he said. "Sly, sly Jacob."

"Jacob . . . ?"

"The son of Isaac who tended the flock of his uncle Laban, and who became the first known breeder of sheep. Do you not remember the story of how Jacob tricked his uncle into a bargain whereby he would keep all the animals that were spotted and speckled?" The Town Secretary laughed again. "Shepherds have always lived by their wits," he went on. "They come by their reputation for poaching naturally. From my own childhood, I can remember many rhymes about shepherds, none of which were flattering." The Secretary shut his eyes and made a grimace of concentration. Then he placed a hand upon Brace's arm, and, with a sing-song intonation, continued:

> The miller from the peddler
> The shepherd from the thief
> They no more differ
> Than the radish from the beet!

Brace grinned. I'll have to tell that to the old man, he thought. "What's the reason for the great unpopularity of shepherds?" he asked.

" 'Abel was a keeper of sheep, but Cain was a tiller of the ground,' " the Secretary replied. "An elemental conflict, Herr Brace. As for the shepherd Pucher, I wonder if it isn't possible that his lineage from the Old Testament is even more direct than we might suspect."

Brace considered this remark in silence, remembering that the old man had counted boastfully in English and then in Polish and Yiddish. Was it possible that the shepherd was a Jew and that he had survived the holocaust? And was this what the Secretary was saying? Brace started to speak, but held back. If the shepherd is really a Jew, I could do him a disservice, he thought. For a while longer, he pondered this problem, troubled by the realization that by withholding his knowledge he was making an adverse judgment against the man sitting beside him. Then, tangled in the uncertainties of his thinking, he began to grope for words.

As if sensing his embarrassment, the Secretary interrupted him. "Of course, conjectures come all too easily," he said. "They're a form of indulgence. For example, Herr Brace, you'd be surprised to know the conjectures I've harbored concerning your own country." The Secretary paused and smiled. "I don't believe you've ever mentioned what part of it you come from."

Startled, Brace looked up. "I come from New England," he said. "From a place about halfway between New York and Boston." He realized that he had scarcely thought about home for months, even when he wrote his infrequent letters, and that he had no nostalgia for it.

But now, as he looked out over the valleys and forests of his district, he was reminded of certain rolling country in Connecticut. *His district.* An intangible possession at best. Was it anything more than a state of mind?

Secretary Vogt refrained from asking several questions about America and waved a hand toward the view with which Brace had become engrossed. "What I meant to say about the shepherd, Herr Brace, is that he is a man of no time or place, so we must endeavor to help him during the time he is in this place, *nicht?*" The Town Secretary gave several ponderously rhetorical nods to his own question. "That's to say whatever help we can give," he went on. "At my age one is constantly in doubt of his effectiveness — even of the effectiveness and wisdom of giving aid and advice. For many years, Herr Brace, I taught geography in the school at Gerberstadt. In the autumn, I used to bring my pupils to this very place. I showed them outcroppings of limestones accumulated from the billions of tiny shells of the sea life that lived and swam and died here in the great Mesozoic Age, when all of Europe lay beneath the Sea of Tethys. I showed them the hard rock of this mountain which was thrust up by some deep turbulence long after the Sea of Tethys had abated and diminished into the Mediterranean puddle. I told them that when the Romans came they called it Mons Jovis, the dwelling place of Jupiter." The Secretary laughed softly and patted the ground beside him. "And I also told them that long before the Romans sanctified it, the Celts had used the mountain as a military bastion and built a fort here to make a last stand against the tribes that eventually drove them to Ireland and to England. The mound on which we're sitting is what remains of the fort. Think of it!" The Secretary carefully placed his palm against the grass as if there might be some tremor of long forgotten life still to be felt; then he went on. "I taught my pupils, two generations of them, about the nature of the Pfalz, Herr Brace, hoping they would feel closer to the land for knowing it. But they were sent off to die in other topography — in the peneplains of Russia, in the deserts of Africa, and in the mountains of Italy — and those who came back were in no mood to hear their old professor's latest theories of erosion. The real erosion, you see, was not the timeless variety I had described for forty years in my classroom, but what had taken place in them. And so, during the war, I suddenly had reason to question the validity of my life's work. I decided for a time that geography was useless. I retired to write a history of the Pfalz. Now I am close to finishing it. But is there service even in that?"

Secretary Vogt got to his feet and started down the path toward the jeep, leaning on Brace's shoulder to steady himself. "It's one thing to know history objectively and quite another to live and be engaged in it," he said. "My service to the town, for example, is limited. I am old and out of touch. I am no longer certain that I understand the aspirations of the people. Because of my training, I can perhaps see a larger perspective than they, but do I understand their present condition? Do I realize their envy for the wealth of your soldiers? Can I fathom the anger and shame of our young men who watch the girls of their district strolling through villages with your Negroes? Do I sympathize properly with the feelings of our displaced citizens — the bitterness of the

[130]

innkeeper Weber who grows more and more dispossessed, or the restlessness of his wife?" Secretary Vogt shook his head sadly and lifted himself into the jeep.

Brace fastened the door, walked around to the other side, and climbed in behind the wheel. The Secretary certainly must have heard about you and Lisl, he was thinking. The whole town probably knows it. And Weber, too, which is something to remember even if you think he doesn't give a damn . . . Brace put the jeep in second gear, caught the engine on the roll, and started slowly down the mountainside.

Secretary Vogt remained silent for some time. "Do not think," he said finally, "that when I describe the suffering of my former pupils I am not mindful of the anguish they inflicted in other countries, and of the enormity of the crimes committed within my own. But there is always the dislocation between past and present, and what is history becomes inexorably more so. Man forgets his blame. Soon he strives again for plaudits."

"The war has almost been forgotten," Brace replied.

"Not really, Herr Brace, or I would not feel the necessity of making explanations."

They had reached the town at the edge of the woods, and as they drove through the street beneath the chestnut trees, Brace saw several of the villagers tip their caps to the Secretary. "In any case, your own plaudits are well deserved," he said.

The Secretary smiled. "Are you referring, perhaps, to the manner in which I became Secretary of Weiersheim? If so, I must tell you the real story. In addition to sheer topography, you see — to outcropping, upthrust, stratification, subsidence, scarp, and erosion — I taught my charges history. Not the kind of history which is mathematics and which consists of committing to memory the dates of battles and of the births and deaths of kings, but the kind that depends upon a present association with which my pupils, who were the children of peasants, could draw liaison with the past. Each year I gave lectures that explained the suffixes of the surrounding towns. I told them that the villages ending in *heim* were the earliest villages of all, having been founded by Alamannic and Frankish settlers in the ninth century, and that those ending in *hausen* and *dorf* were daughter settlements which had been built slightly later. I explained in detail the communal economy and field systems which characterized these villages, and how similar communal tendencies existed in the Pfalz of today. Then I told them that with the clearing of land in the centuries following new hamlets sprang up bearing such suffixes as *bach*, *berg*, *bronn*, and *thal* which, of course, denoted affinity to brooks, mountains, cliffs, and valleys; that towns ending in *pfaff* and *frauen* indicated allegiance to the Church; and that still others with suffixes meaning castle, rock, and corner furnished lasting proof of the preoccupation with defense that motivated the feudal lords of the later Middle Ages."

The Secretary lapsed into silence and stared out the window. They had recrossed the trout stream and were climbing up the other side of the valley toward the forest, where the shooters' lanes emerged from the gloom. Brace wondered if Vogt had forgotten the trail of his story in the recollection of his lectures, but a moment later the Secretary shifted in his seat and spoke again.

"One day — it was in the second year of the war and

shortly after I had delivered a talk on the communal economy of the early Frankish settlements — I was summoned before the Nazi *Kreisleiter* who demanded to know if I was a secret advocate of agrarian communism. I denied it vehemently, of course, but though nothing was proved I was thereafter required to submit a detailed curriculum for the approval of the party's county authorities. Perhaps you will laugh, Herr Brace, but I can assure you it was a terrible affront to me. I could not forget it. Three years later, on the occasion of my fortieth anniversary as a teacher, I was tended an honorary dinner in the *Rathaus*, at which time I made a speech that constituted a rebuke to the Pan-German geographical concepts and *Kulturraum* theories of Albrecht Penck, who had sat for many years in the chair of geography at the University of Berlin, and of his pupil and successor, Norbert Krebs. Krebs had written that Deutschland did not coincide with the changing area on the political map. He claimed it was an area that belonged to the German people on the basis of certain physical and cultural peculiarities. Both Penck and Krebs had defined this area of German *Kultur* as including not only the Swiss who accepted Haupt-Deutsch as their language, but also such peripheral peoples as the Dutch and the Flemish. Naturally they were looked upon with favor by party propagandists seeking to justify National Socialist expansion. In my speech I hinted that the geo-ethnic theories of Penck and Krebs were unsound and should be altered with a view to future serenity. It was the autumn of 1944, Herr Brace, and an unserene Germany, deluged with bombs, had seen the Westwall crumble. My heresy went unnoticed in the

Rathaus as, I suppose, I had really intended it should — probably because no one in my audience had heard of Penck or Krebs, and possibly because they were all fast asleep, but it was reprinted word for word the following week in the *Gerberstadter Volkszeitung*. A month or two later, it found its way into the information offices of the *Gauleiter* of the Pfalz, where it was spotted by an analyst whose assignment it was to read local newspapers for signs of civilian discontent. I was immediately arrested and interrogated, but my age, long service, and the fact that the Allied armies were already on the southern border saved me from jail. I was, however, dismissed from my post in disgrace."

"A recommendation," Brace observed.

The Secretary gave a harsh laugh. "Yes — so it turned out to be. After the surrender, my record of academic treason was unearthed by agents of the French First Army which occupied the Pfalz. Shortly thereafter, the citizens of Weiersheim were surprised, one morning, to discover in the market square a proclamation signed by the representative of the French Commander, General Koenig, appointing Herr Professor Vogt to the post of Town Secretary. Herr Vogt, for his part, was surprised to discover that he had been a valiant resistor of the National Socialist conspiracy, but in short order his surprise gave way to approval, and then, even to belief. He accepted his new post with pride and delight. Thus, you see, he received the plaudit he scarcely knew he was seeking."

They had reached the town and come once again under the scrutiny of the *Gänseriche* sitting on the trough at the end of the square. Brace stopped the jeep before the Secretary's office and tried to think of something to say. He wanted to say something encouraging, yet unpatronizing, but Secretary Vogt was pointing through the windshield toward the ruined *Schloss* that towered above the vineyards.

"And so, Herr Brace, my dignity was reaffirmed, and with it a certain confidence. But nothing was really quite the same again. For years I had been interested in the *Schloss* as a relic and a reflection of another age, but when my former pupils came home from the war, I realized that it was always people, not relics, that count. Still, it was too late for me to change my ways completely. I began to investigate again an old myth about some people who vanished from the castle during a siege. I think I may have told it to you before, and about my theory concerning the tunnel."

"I remember," Brace replied. "I promised I would speak to the colonel about the possibility of your making an excavation at the *Kaserne*."

"Just a modest one, Herr Brace. A small trench, perhaps, which could easily be filled in again."

Brace was touched by the eagerness in the Secretary's voice. "I'm sorry to say I forgot about it, but I'll mention it to the colonel the first chance I get."

"Thanks, Herr Brace!" The Town Secretary shook Brace's hand and climbed out of the jeep; then he reached across the seat and shook Brace's hand again. "And thank you for the ride."

"Don't mention it, Herr Sekretär. It was a great pleasure."

"*Auf Wiedersehen!*"

"I'll find out about the excavation today or tomorrow!" Brace called. He waved good-by and watched the Secretary disappear into his office. Then he drove through the square past the watering trough, where the *Gänseriche* were holding a council, and started back to the *Kaserne*.

When Town Secretary Vogt entered his office, he sat down at his desk and wrote in his journal:

"Able was a keeper of sheep, but Cain was a tiller of the ground." Is it possible that men such as the Jäger, the Wachtmeister, and myself, who are rooted to the land and the institutions of town and farm, must always be in opposition to the nomads in our midst? And is this opposition not, on the grander scale, the whole story of anti-Semitism? Have I seen today the recurring pattern derived directly from original history? Have I sought to protect Jacob's heir — sly Jacob who stole his brother Esau's birthright, and who, at his uncle Laban's expense, became the first known breeder of sheep?

For some minutes after he had set down these words — the trip and the climb had tired him — Town Secretary Vogt closed his eyes and pressed his fingers against the folds of his hooded lids in an effort to clear a vision that had begun to swim in the opaque advent of sleep. He was struck by the backward leap his mind had made. Was it vision, then, or simply fatigue? One did not, after all, span the millenniums since Genesis with total facility — even one whose life's work had been the survey of ageless upheaval and disintegration. The Secretary found his breathing suddenly labored. But after a few minutes more, he returned to his journal:

If I am correct, if today there is a migratory Israelite wandering through these ancient valleys of my beloved Palatinate, and if it is Jacob who has somehow survived the terror — then I am on the brink of a profound discovery, for if I can now determine the secret of his survival, the instincts that have caused him to endure, I shall have latched on to a fragment of the secret of life itself. Have I for fifty years wasted my time studying the upheaval of mountains and the erosion of hills only to learn that it is the study of man, not that of the crust, which will eventually reveal the eternal secrets? Yes, I was wrong to speak of human erosion to the American. Only man endures. Only he does not erode.

Town Secretary Vogt read over what he had written; then he rested his head on the back of his chair and looked up at the ceiling. Was it justice to quarantine the shepherd's sheep? he wondered. Could I have done anything else? Have I counteracted my edict with sufficient forbearance?

After the Secretary had asked himself these questions, sleep came quickly. But just before he shut his eyes, he thought again:

Fifty years studying the crust . . .

And then:

"Abel was a keeper of sheep, but Cain . . ."

And now, as always, the ages — Permian, Triassic, Jurassic — swirled through his brain, bringing the timeless torpor. Ah, what was it Faust had said?

"Fly. Up, and seek the broad, free land!"

How? the Secretary wondered. How? How . . . ?

He slept.

9

GRETA WAS ALREADY at the tennis club. Brace parked his jeep beside her pale blue Volkswagen, and watched her batting balls against the wire fence on the far side of the courts. She was standing close to the fence, with her back to him, idly scooping the balls at ankle level, and hitting them at such angles that the rebounds alternated between her backhand and forehand. She was wearing shorts today, and in the shorts she seemed much younger — a grave child at play, totally absorbed by her own grace and rhythm.

Brace climbed out of the jeep, pushed through the gate in the fence, and started across the courts. The gate catch clanked shut behind him, and Greta turned. "I hope you haven't been waiting long," he said.

"No, just a few minutes to practice." She smiled and extended her hand. "Good afternoon, Herr Brace."

"Good afternoon," Brace replied.

Greta was retrieving her balls, picking them up by wedging them against the side of her foot with the tip of her racket. "And how are you?" she asked.

"I'm fine, thank you," Brace said. The formality of his words was disconcerting. It erased his sense of their previous intimacy. Suddenly he felt shy and awkward.

[138]

His eye roved over the courts which had been freshly raked and broomed. Everything between them now seemed as unmarked and untrammeled as the newly manicured clay. Brace bounced one of his own balls, watching it rise and recede with studied concentration; then he looked at the jumbled pattern of footprints made by her tiny sneakers before the fence. Had there really been any intimacy? he wondered. Or had he simply imagined it?

"Shall we start?" Greta said. Already she was walking into the nearest back court.

Brace went around the net to the baseline on the other side and hit a ball to her, softly, from his hand. They engaged in several listless exchanges. He found it difficult to concentrate. He kept glancing at the table where they had sat and talked the day before.

"Shall we play?" Greta took a few tentative steps toward the net.

He nodded in reply, and lobbed the balls in his hand to her. Perhaps she was bored. The thought depressed him. "You start serving," he said.

"Oh no," she protested, "rough or smooth."

"Smooth," Brace said, and spun his racket. Like her greeting, Greta's adherence to the formality of rules seemed to increase the distance between them. It was surely deliberate, he thought. "Smooth," he called out, bending over the racket.

"Your service!" she cried with a bright smile.

Brace waited for her to send him the balls she was holding; then he walked back to the service line. He was certain now that she was deliberately seeking an equality between them. He tried several practice serves, all of which went into the net. His timing was off, and he knew that he was throwing the ball too high and too directly above him to obtain the best leverage. He walked to the net to retrieve the balls and saw Greta setting herself just behind the baseline.

"I'm ready," he said.

Once the game got under way, Brace immersed himself in the competition, but instead of trying to win points, he became preoccupied with keeping the ball in play. Though he had never been a capable volleyer, he found himself hitting soft shots into Greta's forecourt — shots that enticed her to the net, where they came face to face, a few racket lengths apart, to dance an agile, always equidistant dance. Greta played effortlessly and with complete concentration, unaware that he was studying her. Brace won his service, lost to hers, and then lost his own. She had passed him three times in a row with hard backhand volleys, and then she had lobbed over him, driving him back in a vain attempt to retrieve. His momentum carried him into the wire mesh fence, against which he shielded himself by throwing up an arm. As he stooped to pick up the ball, he was breathing heavily. Trickles of sweat ran over his forehead and stung his eyes. In spite of himself, he was annoyed.

Greta was smiling at him from the net. "Are you all right?" she asked.

Brace grinned and nodded, and waited grimly at the baseline for her service. When it came, he lashed it down the line and took the point. But when he tried the same thing again, Greta returned his shot with a slow, arching ball that landed deep and almost at his feet. For several exchanges, he continued to swing with all his strength, but though his shots were hard, they were too much down the center of the court to throw Greta off balance. Her slow, studied returns enabled her to get into position for his, and, in addition, Brace found that his new strategy was tiring him considerably. He soon realized that he could not overpower her. Her game was too pliable — she was countering him tactic for tactic; now, having forced him into a series of errors, she won the fourth game with a deftly sliced drop shot that found him hopelessly deep and out of position.

"*Ein-drei*," he called with a rueful smile. Standing at the service line, he watched Greta bend forward, her supple legs shifting with nervous anticipation, her grave face peering at him above her racket. He was amused but also chagrined — he had scarcely made her run! Suddenly he was beset by the idea that she might become disinterested if he allowed her to win too easily. He had begun by indulging himself with the sight of her; then he had sought to demonstrate his superiority through sheer strength. Now he determined to be cunning.

With her first return of service, he started driving deep to Greta's backhand, and when he had forced her toward the sideline, he began to mix his shots, alternating them from corner to corner, and then varying the pattern to keep her guessing. During several long rallies, he resisted the urge to try winning shots; instead, he worked patiently at his placements, and watched Greta run. She ran gracefully — back and forth along the baseline — and she continued to stroke the ball smoothly, but the running took its toll. Between points, Brace saw her plucking at a wisp of damp hair which tickled her neck. Her shots were shallower now. He won the game at love.

"*Prima!*" Greta cried.

He broke her service for the first time in the next game, and thus evened the set. As Greta came forward to send him a ball that was lying in her forecourt, he could see a faint but diffuse flush upon her face, and some tiny beads of perspiration on her upper lip. He ran quickly around the net and retrieved the ball himself; then he watched her trudge slowly back to her baseline, and returned to his own court to serve. He continued to play safely, chancing only to the extent of aiming his shots for corners. In this way, he kept her constantly on the move. Her own shots began to lose speed and precision, and at the end of the eighth game, she was running noticeably slower. Brace began toying with her — back and forth, back and . . . back again. Once, she looked at him almost pitifully and shook her head, but he pretended not to see. At set point, he served softly to her, and then slammed her return as hard as he could toward the opposite corner. Greta started for the ball, and stopped. Lowering her racket, she spread her arms, arched backward, and lifted her head.

"*Ja, ja,*" she murmured, looking up at the sky as if at him.

They met at the net and exchanged compliments. The hand she offered was small and damp — a polite token; then, paralleling each other, they walked toward the sidelines. At the post, Greta turned and held out her racket.

"I promise to do better now," she said.

"Aren't you tired?" he protested. "Shouldn't we rest?"

"Oh no!" smiled Greta, with a kind of fierce joy. "Two sets, and then we'll rest."

Brace placed the balls he was carrying on the strings of her racket, and laughed. "You'll wear me out."

"No," she said gravely, looking him in the face. "I don't think so."

Considering this remark, he ran happily into the back-court to await her service. His exuberance sustained him and he took the set easily, allowing her only a single game. When it was over, and they had sat down at one of the tables on the sidelines, he was appalled at his lack of generosity. But he consoled himself with the thought that things might have dragged on too long. He clapped his hands for the caretaker, and looked at her.

"Apple juice or lemonade?"

She smiled and refused the cigarette he offered. "Orange soda," she said.

"Two orange sodas," Brace told the caretaker. He lit his cigarette and watched Greta arrange her hair in the mirror of a compact. "I've been thinking about your carp," he told her. "What do you feed them?"

For an instant, Greta regarded him coldly, as if he had made a demand. "Bread," she answered finally, with a tiny shrug. "And sometimes scraps."

Brace puffed reflectively on his cigarette. "Herr Saul feeds the trout in his stream bits of liver. In the winter, he chops holes in the ice so the liver will sink to the bottom. Perhaps if your gardener were to do the same with the carp pool . . ."

Greta laughed. "But you forget that the ice freezes to the bottom and the fish are locked inside it."

Brace was delighted at the disappearance of her reserve, but the satisfaction he derived from directing the conversation also contained an edge of doubt. Would he, by probing, uncover more than the loneliness he had sensed in her yesterday? He knew almost nothing about her — a fact that filled him with regret — nothing except some skeletal information contained in an old report: "*Zabern, Greta (nee Müller); Date of birth 1927; Place of birth Ludwigshafen; wife of Zabern, Konrad, owner of the Pfälzische Hartsteinfabrik.*" Now he remembered the sense of guilt with which he had looked her up in his files. "I've thought about the ice," he said. "Perhaps a hose that would blow air bubbles into the water, or some smudge pots such as they use in the tobacco fields —"

"Perhaps one should not tamper with destiny," Greta replied. "That of fish or of people."

A reproach? Or a genuine sense of fatality? Brace was intrigued by the possibility of the latter. In men it was a commitment to life; in women, a promise of license. Immersed in these considerations, he was not prepared for her question.

"What is it that you do for the military?"

He looked at her quickly, and then avoided her eyes, detesting the shade of evasion he knew must be reflected in his own. "I gather information," he said with a shrug.

"Do you like this?"

"Yes, very much." He wanted to tell her why, but he realized that it would necessitate explaining too much. How could he explain the freedom he had usurped, the enchantment of his domain, and the contentment with which, each morning, he studied the map on the wall of his office? "My work enables me to meet many people," he said, smiling at her.

"Such as Herr Saul, who feeds liver to trout."

"Ah, but that's a business relationship." The caretaker had brought the sodas and two glasses, and now Brace poured each glass half full, and lifted his own toward Greta in a silent toast. "Herr Saul leases me the right to fish in his stream," he said.

"You're free then," she murmured. "You're not confined to the *Kaserne* like other soldiers."

He nodded happily, relishing the luxury of sitting at the tennis court with her, but a moment later he found himself studying the mesh fence that encircled them, and thinking about the chain link barriers that surrounded the *Kaserne* and Alpha Site, and the barbed wire that enclosed the shepherd's flock.

Greta was sipping her soda, and scrutinizing him over the rim of her glass. He sensed another question. "I enjoyed playing tennis with you," he said. "Perhaps we could play again."

"If you like," she replied. "But I'm afraid I'm not enough competition. I had seen you play before, of course, but I hadn't realized you were . . . so clever."

Once again she had inextricably shifted their relationship; now he no longer felt masterful or clever, but filled with the necessity to retrieve himself, to overcome the subtlety with which she had altered their course. He plunged on: "Shall we play tomorrow?"

He knew he had made a mistake the moment the words were out.

"I'm sorry," said Greta, frowning. "Next week, perhaps."

He nodded and looked away. "I really shouldn't play myself," he said. "I've too much work." It was not true; he had said it out of quick pride, and now, aware of its transparency, he was impelled to continue. "I have a new responsibility these days," he told her. "The shepherd I spoke of last night — he's keeping his flock at the training area near the preserve."

She listened politely as he went on about the fox and the events of the morning.

"It's too bad there has been so much trouble," she said, when he had finished.

"The Jäger is sure he's a poacher," Brace replied lightly. "He's probably afraid the old man will set snares for some of your husband's rabbits."

"And will he?" asked Greta.

Brace laughed. "I've warned him not to, but he's a very independent old man. Still, what if he did? There must be lots of rabbits."

"Shouldn't he buy them, however?"

"He doesn't have any money. He lives off the land. He catches trout by tickling them with his fingers."

"Then I should think he'd have an easy time with rabbits," said Greta, solemnly.

"I'll see that he doesn't deplete the supply too much," Brace replied with a smile. He leaned back in his chair and lit another cigarette. My God, he thought. I've already implicated her in a plot against Zabern himself.

"When I was a little girl, we used to visit friends in the country near Speyer," Greta said. "There was a ferry over the river there, and one day I saw some shepherds bringing across their flocks. The bargemen

[146]

were annoyed with the sheep because they were afraid of the river and cried so."

"You may even have seen my shepherd," Brace said. He looked again at the wire mesh fence. My shepherd, my district, he thought, and smiled to himself. I'm getting pretty possessive . . .

"What's he like, your shepherd?"

"He's a regular patriarch," Brace replied. "He's straight out of the Bible. He looks as old as Methuselah, but he tells me he's only seventy-three."

"And with how many sheep?"

"Nearly fifty," Brace said. "When I first met him, he was looking for a barn to keep them in during the winter. I told him he could fix up the training area and keep the sheep inside the prisoner-of-war compound. No one ever uses it."

"And the shepherd — will he be happy there?"

Brace gave a quick shrug and shook his head. She has a facility for asking precise questions, he thought. "I don't know," he said soberly. "The old man doesn't like the idea of the barbed wire, but I think he's probably tired of wandering around and glad to have found a place to stay."

Greta had got to her feet. "I must be off now," she said abruptly, as if it were a duty she was embarrassed to have forgotten.

Surprised, he jumped up and watched her gathering her things. He could barely restrain himself from asking her to stay. Stupid, stupid, he thought. Why did you wait so long?

"I also enjoyed our match," said Greta, holding out her hand. "Perhaps we shall play again next week."

He mumbled a reply and followed her through the gate and across the yard to her car. As he was holding open the door of the Volkswagen, the bus from Alzey passed through the street beside them, bound for the center of town. It was a great green ark of a bus with a superstructure that hung out over the frame of its chassis. He had often seen it wallowing over the treeless hills of the countryside like some ponderous excursion boat on the open sea. Now it passed slowly in the narrow street like a ship through the lock of a canal, and, glancing at it, he saw Lisl Weber's impassive face staring back at him — staring back and turning around to watch him even as the bus passed out of sight.

He watched Greta climb into the tiny car, and suddenly, for no reason, he remembered a fragment of a conversation he had overheard about her, months before. "She married him because he was a war hero," someone had said from across the courts. A hero, Brace thought. That much was true — Zabern had won the Iron Cross with one of Kesselring's mountain divisions in Italy, and had spent the last year of the war recovering from a chest wound. But had she chosen him because of that, and was she looking for some new hero now with the cool green eyes of her quiet, grave child's face? The possibility stunned him.

"The shepherd," he began lamely — it came out like a gasp.

Greta had her hand on the ignition key; she looked up at him.

"You must come out and see us." He looked blindly over the car and heard his own words drowning in the desperation that had suffused him. "I think the old man

[148]

would like it," he said, recovering himself. "And I, too," he added huskily, touching his hand gently on the roof.

"Perhaps," Greta said. She had withdrawn into the car, out of sight, and her voice seemed distant.

"Why don't you come tomorrow afternoon?"

"Perhaps," she repeated.

"Does the daylight bother you?" he asked, amazed at his boldness. "Or is it the Jäger?"

He could barely hear her.

"What things?" he asked.

"The way we are talking."

Now she looked directly, coolly, at him.

Reflexively, he removed his hand from the roof, and straightened.

"Come anyway," he said.

"Good-by."

The engine coughed and started.

Smiling, he bent down close to the window. "Don't come from the village," he said. "Come by the cart path that cuts in from the road through the forest. It's more prudent."

The car shot forward — a faint, familiar echo strangled by the engine's growl.

Was it laughter? he wondered. Her grave laughter?

He stood in the courtyard of the tennis club, trying to decide, until the car passed out of sight and he could no longer hear it sputtering in the stone-lined street.

10

THE SUN WAS LEAVING the market square of Weiersheim. A wall of shadow cast by buildings on one side had advanced halfway to the circular watering trough on the other, and the trough itself, as if by a gnomon's mark, had been bisected in the slanting light by the shadow of a chimney on the *Gasthof* roof. Like clock hands, the village elders moved around the dial of the trough, maintaining their position in the sun as if to acknowledge both the waning of the day and of themselves. For a moment, Brace watched them with an acute awareness of his own youth and vitality; then he walked toward the doorway of the inn, where he was intercepted by Weber.

"I was wondering when you'd come!" Weber exclaimed. "I've been expecting you." The innkeeper poked his head outside the door, and then recoiled into the dark hallway.

"I've been playing tennis," Brace said dryly. "I stopped by to have a beer."

"Too bad you didn't come earlier. You've missed everything!"

The innkeeper stepped away from the door so that Brace could enter, but Brace chose to remain outside on the steps. Now he glanced slowly and deliberately around the square. He was, as always, annoyed by Weber's conspiratorial familiarity.

"Just look at the *Gänseriche*, Herr Brace! They're sitting on the edge of their seats. They're the ones to sniff trouble, I can tell you."

"They look the same as ever to me," Brace replied.

"Do you really think so?" For a moment, Weber pretended to consider the possibility seriously; then he laughed. "You should have seen them when the Wachtmeister went up to old Huy's house and shot his dog!"

"Why did he do that?" Brace asked, scowling at the smile on the innkeeper's face.

"It's a long story, Herr Brace. I might have known something was up when the *Gänseriche* returned to the trough after lunch without Huy." Weber ventured out into the sunlight, and lowered his voice. "How long d'you think it's been since those old birds congregated without Huy?"

Brace shrugged. This sonofabitch wants to be plied, he thought. "How long?" he said.

"Not since I came here, Herr Brace. Three years! Even the *Gänseriche* thought it was unusual. I can hear their cackling all day long, you know."

Yes, I'll bet you can, Brace thought. I'll bet you can even translate the ones who haven't any teeth.

"The *Gänseriche* decided Huy must have eaten something that made him sick," Weber continued. "They were going to send an emissary to make inquiries at his house, but when the Town Secretary posted his proclamation about rabies, they forgot about it. Naturally, everyone began to speculate about the proclamation and about whether it was a result of the big meeting at the Secretary's office this morning."

"Naturally," Brace said. Nobody misses a trick around here, he thought.

"The next thing I knew, there was a woman screaming in the square. Herr Brace, I can tell you I haven't heard screaming like that since the war. I ran to the door, of course, and whom do you suppose I saw?"

"Huy," Brace answered, intending it as a joke.

"Exactly!" Weber cried. "Huy himself being dragged through the streets by his own daughter-in-law. And by the *ear*, mind you! Oh, it was wonderful to see. It did my heart good. The whole village came out of doors. Never have I heard anything like her screaming. Old Huy was bellowing like an ox in a burning barn. What a grip she had on him! Why, the blood was running down his face and neck! She's such a thin, sickly thing —who would have thought she had such strength?" The innkeeper paused to shake his head. "First she dragged him to the Secretary's office," he went on, "but the Secretary had gone out, so then she pulled him back into the middle of the square where there was a large crowd gathering, including the Wachtmeister who had hurried down from the station. By this time she had stopped screaming, but she still had poor Huy by the ear, and she was yanking his head from side to side as if he were a dog on a leash. Well, that was only the beginning."

Brace lit a cigarette and smiled. Keep talking, he thought. Keep talking, Weber, old boy. "Go on," he said.

"Well, it turns out the Huys dined on chicken last

night," the innkeeper said, rubbing his hands together as if to savor the event. "A nice fat bird deposited in their yard the night before by a thief who was attacked and driven off by the dog. Huy's daughter-in-law says the chicken wasn't one of theirs, so it must have been Saul's, since Saul claims his coop was robbed that same night. In any event, when the daughter-in-law went out to the yard yesterday morning, she noticed the dog had got himself a nasty bite high up on the neck beneath the jaw. Yesterday evening, of course, the bird appeared on the dining table, and this afternoon, when the daughter-in-law came down to the square to do her marketing, she read the proclamation concerning the possibility of rabies and the new restraints imposed on the village dogs." Weber chortled gleefully. "One doesn't have to be very bright to put two and two together, hey, Herr Brace?"

For some moments, the innkeeper waited for Brace to comment, but when the latter merely continued to puff on his cigarette, Weber went on with his story. "The minute she read the proclamation she dropped everything and ran back to the house," he said. "She was screaming like a cat out of hell. She has two children, you know, and the brats had evidently swallowed plenty of chicken. Old Huy had taken a short nap after lunch and was just pulling on his coat to rejoin his cronies on the trough. Well, he rejoined them, all right. Oh, you should have been here to see it, Herr Brace. What a reunion!"

"I'll bet it was," said Brace, laughing.

"Just think of the humiliation! Held by the ear in front of the whole town and branded as a chicken thief and a potential murderer of children. It was some performance, I can tell you. And all the family linen to boot! It turns out the old buzzard has made life miserable for them up there. He has a married daughter living in Göllheim, you know, and he's forever threatening to leave the property to her if he's not pleased at home. If you ask me, he might just as well croak tonight. You should have seen him slink away when she finally let go of him. People were laughing, but you couldn't help feeling sorry for the poor devil."

"Who decided to shoot the dog?" Brace asked.

"The Wachtmeister, but that came later. First the woman had to be calmed. She was hysterical about the children. Brausch told her it was impossible to swallow rabies but she wouldn't believe him. No one could make any sense with her so Brausch sent a boy to fetch Secretary Vogt. You can imagine what he was doing." Weber pointed to the ruined castle above the vineyards, where Brace could just make out the black-frocked figure of the Town Secretary, who was standing between and below two other figures perched on ladders that had been placed against the crumbling walls. "By the time the Secretary got down here, the woman was wailing out of all control. He also told her it wasn't possible to swallow rabies, but she wouldn't believe him either. So he sent her and the children to the hospital in Alzey. It was then that Wachtmeister Brausch suggested shooting the dog. The Town Secretary agreed and also ordered Brausch to see to it that all the other dogs and cats were secured immediately, whereupon everyone rushed home to prepare for the policeman's inspection.

People are plenty worried, I can tell you. Everybody's trying to remember what he ate the past week."

"But the Wachtmeister and the Secretary are right," Brace said. "You can't contract rabies by eating."

The innkeeper was smiling and shaking his head. "I know, Herr Brace, I know. But they're convinced of it, so what can you do? These peasants are full of superstition. What evolution have they achieved here in the Pfalz? It's a shame, Herr Brace. Germany without Prussia is like a body without its spine. Oh, they're smart enough in the Rhineland and the Ruhr, but the Bavarians and the Schwabs are hopelessly provincial, and your Pfalzers are incredibly stupid. That leaves the Hessians and the Holsteiners, but it's not enough, Herr Brace, it's not enough. Germany will never be the same until it is reunited."

The old refrain, Brace thought. "I suppose you're right," he said soothingly. "The villagers have good reason to be worried, however. Rabies is nothing to joke about. When the shepherd first told me that, I didn't take him too seriously, but after listening to the county veterinarian this morning, I realize he was right."

"Ah, the shepherd! Perhaps you'd be interested to know what they're saying about him!"

Brace flipped the butt of his cigarette into the square. "Yes, I'd be interested," he said, keeping his voice casual.

"After Secretary Vogt went back to the *Schloss*, Herr Zabern and the Jäger arrived on the scene. When he heard what had happened, Herr Zabern told the people who stayed in the square that the shepherd was a poacher and that his flock had been exposed to rabies. He said it was intolerable that the sheep be allowed to remain so close to the village, and that something would have to be done about it."

"Like what?" Brace asked.

"He didn't say, but the *Gänseriche* are saying the shepherd should be driven away."

Brace looked at the old men sitting on the trough, and smiled. That's a bad sign, he thought. Like all retainers, the *Gänseriche* are echoing their patron. "The *Gänseriche* had better worry about their daughters-in-law," he said.

"Exactly!" Weber cried. "That's exactly what I said myself! Besides, whose business is it if you want to put the old fellow up? Perhaps you've enlisted him in the army, hey?"

"Perhaps," Brace said. "And who cares about the *Gänseriche*, anyway?"

"Ha! ha! You and I think alike, Herr Brace. Come inside for some *Schnaps*."

The innkeeper is in corking good spirits, Brace thought as he entered the *Gasthof*. It's too bad there isn't a catastrophe every day . . .

"Come into the kitchen!" said Weber, crossing the dining room. "Look at these hares my wife brought back from Alzey! Aren't they the beauties? But d'you think anybody'll want to eat 'em now that the rabies scare is on?"

As Weber reached into a cabinet for some glasses, Brace fingered the soft fur and malleable bones of three hares hanging upside down from a peg on the kitchen wall. There was a strange note in something the innkeeper had said, but he could not place it. Then Weber poured the glasses to the brim with *Steinhäger*, and, taking the bottle with him, led the way back into the dining room.

"Königsberg!" he said.

Brace nodded and lifted his glass. Königsberg, he thought. A city as fictitious as Shangri-La . . .

"How my wife and I would like to go back!"

"Perhaps you will," Brace replied absently. He had just remembered that, until a moment ago, he had never heard Weber refer to Lisl as his wife. It was as if the man had tacitly renounced any proprietary rights. But now, suddenly, the innkeeper had asserted himself, as if his sense of cuckoldry had diminished with Huy's public disgrace. Brace studied him with a new interest.

"We've had our troubles, of course," Weber was saying, "but who doesn't, hey?"

Brace nodded and held out his glass as the innkeeper refilled it.

"One can always start over again, isn't that so?"

"Yes," Brace replied. "At least one can try."

"That's the whole secret, Herr Brace! One must try." The innkeeper downed his second glass with a gulp and then sat back in his chair, beaming. A moment later, he had launched into one of his political diatribes.

Brace listened impassively, but he was aware that the impassivity on his face was a deception. The events of the day had suddenly conspired to engulf and pull him from his vantage point. As long as he considered them singly, he could remain intact and uninvolved, but when, as now, he found himself confronted with a welter of rural mysteries, his fatality gave way to frustration, and he was seized with a longing for anarchistic expression that was almost unbearable. As always, in these moods, he was filled with desire. It was an admission that, once made, calmed him.

"One can always start over," Weber had said. Brace wondered if the innkeeper had intended it as both a hope and a warning. Yes, beyond a doubt, he thought. So don't kid yourself about it. Or about the fact that it means he's made some kind of decision . . .

"Perhaps an enclave will provide the ultimate solution," Weber was saying. "A free city such as Danzig used to be."

Brace heard the sound of the words without any other focus. For a moment, he reveled in the luxury of his new objectivity about Weber, but this too was merely another form of domination, and even now his gaze traveled toward the familiar grate in the ceiling. Then he was inside the enclave of Lisl's bedroom, giving rein to wild and improbable dreams that were heightened by the inaccessibility with which she had been cloaked by Weber's new resolve. He thought about the first time he had made love to her. He had come to the inn for lunch in the middle of the afternoon, when Weber was away, and Lisl, wearing a bathrobe, had come down from her room to serve him. Afterwards, on some vague pretense, she invited him upstairs, where for a time they sat on her bed, smoking cigarettes. Both of them were filled with nervous excitement that soon became a torment of lust. Lisl kept glancing through the window at the square below, professing to watch for the arrival of customers, but really with the intention of goading him about the possibility of Weber returning early; and Brace kept reaching inside her robe for the breast she exposed each time she bent toward the ashtray between them. Finally, she seemed to grow tired of the game, and of fending him off, and stood up with her back to him. Seizing the opportunity, he came up behind her, and, lifting her robe, which he bunched in the small of her back with one hand, gave her a generous and accurate caress with the other. Annoyance and desire mounted within Lisl at once. Then, as if thankful that she did not, at least, have to watch him, she had placed her elbows on the window seat, leaned forward, and pressed her face against the curtains. In the next few minutes, her breath had clouded over the pane completely.

For some moments, Brace was wholly absorbed in this memory, but then he progressed to another level from which he saw himself drawn time and again to the inn — impelled not so much by the prospect of losing Lisl as by the desire to retain everything. He knew that if he were to see her now, he would lie to reassure her. But perhaps she had seen nothing at the tennis court. Or perhaps she didn't care . . .

Weber had stopped talking and was smiling at him. "You're worried about the shepherd, Herr Brace?"

"No, no," Brace said quickly. "I was daydreaming." He smiled back at the innkeeper, but he knew that he was flushing.

Weber drew apart the curtains of a window that looked out on the watering trough where the *Gänseriche* sat. "Imagine them wanting to drive the old fellow off!" he muttered. "It makes my blood boil, I can tell you. Ex-beet-diggers, Herr Brace, that's all they are. Ex-collectors of their own excrement! But we'll fix 'em, you and I, hey?" The innkeeper glared up at the windows of the opposite houses as if he expected to see curtains twitching in reply.

"Don't let them bother you," Brace said.

"Don't worry, I know what it is to go against the current." Weber released the curtain and leaned forward, resting his arms on the table top. "D'you think I don't know what they say about me?"

Brace shrugged in reply. My God, he thought, is he playing a game with me or doesn't he know, after all?

"No matter, hey? But the Wachtmeister and Herr Zabern — when I heard the way the wind was blowing with them, I telephoned you, Herr Brace."

"I haven't been in my office all afternoon."

"I know," Weber replied. "They couldn't tell me where you'd gone, so I took matters into my own hands. Under the circumstances—" The innkeeper broke off and poured himself another touch of *Steinhäger* — "I went up to see your shepherd."

For a moment, Brace was silent — stunned by an anger he recognized as the purest jealousy. Then, seeing the irony of it, he nearly laughed out loud. "What did you tell him?" he asked.

"Why, I told him what they were saying, Herr Brace."

"And what did he say to that?" Brace looked impatiently at Weber, who was smiling. His amusement had given way to a sudden fear that the old man might leave the sheepfold. He even imagined himself arriving there to find it empty.

As if sensing this apprehension, Weber smiled even more broadly. "He didn't say anything, Herr Brace. He just listened. I think he distrusts people. It took him a while to warm up."

I'll bet it did, Brace thought. "The old man has lived alone most of his life," he said.

"*Ja*, with only the sheep for company. Just between us, Herr Brace, I don't think there's a chance his animals have rabies. They look healthy enough to me."

Just between us, Brace thought, I find your palship wearing awfully thin, Weber, old boy.

"It must be a lonely life," the innkeeper said. "There must be times when a nice fat ewe looks pretty tempting, hey?"

"I'll bet you didn't say that to the shepherd," Brace replied sharply. He regretted the words as soon as he had spoken them. "The old man's a friend of mine," he explained.

"And of mine, too!" the innkeeper exclaimed in an offended tone. "Surely you don't think I would insult him, Herr Brace. I was merely repeating what one often hears about shepherds."

"Sure," Brace said. "I'm sure the old man appreciated your coming up."

"Yes indeed, Herr Brace. He was very polite. I brought him a few supplies, you know. Just some things I thought he might be able to use."

"Very nice of you," Brace said, and drained his glass. He had a sudden urge to relegate the innkeeper back to the role of informant. He got to his feet and extended his hand. "Get in touch with me if you hear anything else," he said. The words were the same as always, but in spite of his resolve, Brace found himself nodding meaningfully toward the window and the trough beyond, and he had the feeling that as they shook hands they were somehow sealing a bargain as equals.

"The very moment," Weber replied. He followed Brace to the door and watched him descend the steps to the square.

"Thanks for the drink," Brace called.

"It was my pleasure, Herr Brace. Tell the Herr Schä-fer that if I can be of any assistance—" The innkeeper shrugged a self-effacing shrug and smiled.

Brace nodded in reply and walked to his jeep. He was wondering if he should pretend to return to the *Kaserne*, or take the road that led directly up the hill to the sheepfold, and he was full of doubt about the meaning of Zabern's sudden intervention. Before he got into the jeep, he turned and waved to Weber, who was still standing in the doorway. "The hell with you, Weber," he said softly, but the words sounded hollow to him, and as he started up the hill, he found himself shaking his head as if to clear it.

11

THE OLD MAN SAT with his back against a wall of the shed, and looked out past the compound to the beet fields where some peasant women were laboring with long-handled hoes. Beyond the fields, the escarpment and its crown of ruins seemed to rise directly from the green leaves of the sugar beets, giving no hint of the hollow that lay between, cupping the stone and cobblestone conglomerate of the village. The afternoon was wearing on, and though the guard towers blazed in the last, flat trajectory light of the sun, they were no longer stark reminders of the compound's original purpose, but muted now, as if appendaged into less grim context by the calm union of the flock feeding on the grass beneath. The old man knew that when the sun dropped behind the mountain, the shadow of the forest would breach the wire and climb the sides of the towers; then the sheep would crowd together for warmth, and the compound would become grim again, lacking only the gaunt, despairing faces that had stared from the camps in Bavaria. The shepherd hated what the shadow did to the compound, and he was thinking of the prisoners as Brace's jeep appeared at the edge of the plateau and came toward him over the dusty track through the beet fields.

His serious expression moved Brace to be jocular. "Hullo, Mathias!" he called. "What're you dreaming about?"

"Hello," the old man replied. "What are you doing in your underwear?"

"Haven't you ever seen a tennis player before?"

"Certainly I've seen them. Have you never heard a joke?"

Brace laughed and climbed out of the jeep.

"I saw tennis before you were born," said the old man, gruffly. "Once I saw a nobleman play at Baden."

"Was that von Cramm?"

"I didn't know his name. He was playing with a Frenchman."

"What were you doing at Baden?"

"I was bringing my sheep north from the Swabian Alps."

"No kidding," said Brace.

"Yes, I tell you," the old man replied testily. "In my time, I've seen all the spa towns."

"Sure," Brace said. "I'll bet you're known in the best watering holes."

"Listen, don't joke when you don't know anything yourself. I've been to all of these — Bad Kreuznach, Bad Münster, Bad Nauheim, Bad Kissingen, Bad Vilbel, Bad Homburg, Bad Ems, Bad Dürkheim, and Wiesbaden." The shepherd ticked off the towns on his fingers, and when he finished he was still trying to think of others.

"You must be a famous tourist," Brace said. "I've only been to two or three."

"Listen, I've been to so many I can't remember them."

"You should write a travel book."

"You don't understand anything. Why should I write a book about what I already know? Only academicians write such books. They write them because they don't know anything and they want to fool themselves."

"What academicians have you read?" inquired Brace.

"A great many, my friend. The newspapers and the government are full of them. During the war, the government gave us pamphlets telling us how to take care of our sheep. Those were written by academicians, I can assure you, because none of them made any sense."

"First you should write about all the famous watering holes you've visited, and then you can start a definitive work on sheep herding."

"What a waste of time! Why write on something I know all about?"

"Having made a great success with your first two books, you can engineer a literary triumph by writing a handbook for poachers."

"I know all about that, too."

"What don't you know?"

"A great many things. I don't know anything about the ocean or ships."

"Then you should write a book about sailing."

"Then I would really be an academician!" the old man shouted in triumph. "You are a lamb!"

"I'm a lamb, am I?" Brace replied testily. "How about this morning?"

"Not this morning," the old man admitted. "With the policeman and the Jäger, you were a fox."

"Things went very well for us in the village," Brace said. "We have a friend down there — the Town Secretary, who is a very wise and just man. He has decided to put your sheep in quarantine until the county veterinarian examines the fox for rabies. Thus he has legalized your refuge here at the training area."

"What has the fox to do with my sheep?"

"It has to do with all animals," Brace explained. "The Sekretär has also quarantined the village dogs. It's just a precaution."

"You're a lamb!" the old man shouted. "They've tricked you!"

"Listen to me," Brace said patiently. "Two nights ago, the fox is believed to have bitten a dog in the village, and today the policeman had to shoot it. So naturally the Town Secretary has restricted any animals that might also have been infected."

"It's a trick! None of my animals have been infected."

"I know that, but the Secretary has to be certain. He's got to treat everyone the same way."

The old man shook his head incredulously. "Did you tell him my animals were infected?"

"Of course not!" Brace replied. "Get some sense in that hard, stubborn head of yours. The Town Secretary is our friend, and the quarantine is only temporary — a matter of a day or two."

"You talk like an idiot! D'you think the hunger of my sheep is something temporary? By tomorrow this patch will be bare of every blade of grass."

"Tell me how much fodder you'll need. I can bring it in the jeep." Brace looked toward the compound where the sheep were crowding both sides of the barbed wire fence, eating the last tufts of grass. There was not a head in the entire flock that was not lowered and nothing to be seen but fat woolly rumps. He considered his new responsibilities with a surge of contentment. No longer would he come out here just to "wet a line."

"Listen," the old man said. "We should have an understanding. After the middle of November, I must depend on your vehicle for everything."

"Count on it," Brace replied. "And for the next few days as well."

"But you have other work."

"Don't worry about that. You can count on me to bring everything you need."

The shepherd sat down again. "I don't like the idea of this isolation," he said.

Brace shrugged. "It's only temporary."

"Just until the veterinarian examines the fox, *nicht?*"

"That's right."

"But you've been tricked! The fox has rabies for certain! Haven't I seen him myself?"

Brace shook his head wearily, without reply.

"Listen, I'll be here forever! Like a piece of cheese under glass!"

"Aging cheese," Brace said with a grin.

"Listen with your jokes! I know these administrators. When they say it is temporary, they mean it is forever!"

"You can leave any time you want," Brace said, "but remember that once you do you won't be able to come back. The policeman and the Jäger will see to that."

"Look at me!" the old man demanded. "Am I afraid? Not of them or of your friend, the administrator, either."

"Harder and harder," Brace said. "You've made a cult of it, old man."

"I am nobody's tenant. Let the beet farmers be tenants."

"I'll remember that," Brace said.

"Yes, and tell it to your friend, the administrator."

"Perhaps I should bring him up here so you can tell him yourself."

"Certainly. He won't fool me. I know these administrators."

"This one is different."

"You're a lamb," the old man said. "And they are all the same — like policemen."

"This one was arrested by the National Socialists."

"Listen, I know all about that, too. It's a rot. It's the same kind of worms that poison my sheep in the autumn, when the pastures are filled with snails. The worms live in the snails who vomit them so the sheep can eat them with the grass. Only the sheep can't vomit them because the worms infect their livers until they die."

"Isn't there anything you can do for it?"

"Nothing for the National Socialists and very little for the sheep. Sometimes I make a powder from juniper berries and feed it to the animals with oats and salt, but the best medicine is not to let them eat grass that is infested with snails in the first place."

"Did you have trouble with the National Socialists, too?"

"No," said the old man. "I stayed away from them."

"Easier for you than for others, perhaps. Shepherds aren't supposed to be political, are they?"

"Who told you that?"

"The Wachtmeister."

"Listen, you are young and easily influenced. The National Socialists were everywhere — just like the worms in snails — and they got into shepherds the same way they got into other people."

"I take it all back about what you should write," Brace said. "You should write political history."

"Listen, I know something about it. In the old days, I belonged to the Guild, as did all shepherds. There were always festivals in the small towns at dipping and shearing time, and at Saint Bartholomewtide, all the shepherds gathered for a whole week at Markgröningen, in Württemberg. A king and queen were chosen, and the young men ran footraces in black lederhosen and white shirts. There were violins and pipes and piccolos, and the winners of the races could choose the best girls for dancing. There was the cockcrow dance and the beer-mug dance and the butcher's dance — listen, there were so many dances I can't remember their names, but I could still do them if I wanted to. There were the most beautiful girls in Germany there, and when I was young I could have any of them. They would stay in the fields with me all night. But after the National Socialists came, they took the young men for the army and made the older shepherds take larger flocks. It was never the same, and after twenty years ago I never went back."

"But you can still remember the girls," said Brace.

"Listen, when you are as old as I am, you will remember everything. You will forget most of what you said or heard, but never what you took or touched."

"So all your memories are pleasant."

"No, but they become that way. The war does not seem pleasant, but I have almost forgotten it. What I remember is a woman I stayed with in Lindau, when all the men were away. She was the wife of a soldier."

"So you poached women as well as rabbits and trout."

"Yes," said the shepherd, proudly. "Even though I was already old. But the war ruined it."

"Too bad," Brace said.

"Yes," the old man grinned. "The men came back."

"Then it's not true that shepherds go with their ewes."

The old man looked at Brace without expression. "You are not only young and easily influenced," he said, "but also foolish."

"No offense, Mathias."

"Don't call me Mathias until you become mature."

"Look, I apologize for having said it. It's a story I heard somewhere, and not something that I believe myself."

"I'm glad to hear it," the old man said, "but your foolishness is in having mentioned it to begin with. If you had mentioned it to me ten years ago, I would have cracked your skull."

"Then it's a good thing I've met you in your old age."

"Good for you, perhaps, but not for me. What you mentioned is another kind of rot which, like the National Socialism, afflicts some people but not others."

"Okay," Brace said. "Accept my apologies."

"Certainly," the shepherd replied. "You may call me Mathias again if you wish."

"Thank you, Mathias. Will it be all right if I bring someone to visit you tomorrow?"

"Your friend, the administrator?"

"No, a lady friend."

"Some girl from the village . . . ?"

"No, a woman," said Brace, smiling. "In fact, the wife of the man who leases the preserve for hunting."

"So you're poaching women yourself!"

Brace grinned. "The lady is coming to see your sheep," he said.

"Certainly," the old man replied with a grave face. "I shall be very busy tomorrow and won't disturb you."

"What do you need in the way of fodder?"

"Hay," the old man said. "As much as your vehicle can carry."

"In bundles or loose?"

"However you find it. And also a sack of oats and one of rye or some other grain."

"I'll get it in Gerberstadt or Alzey, but perhaps you had better come with me."

"No," the old man said. "Under the circumstances I don't want to leave the sheep."

Brace nodded. "I'll also bring tools, nails, and lumber. What else will you need?"

"A sack of salt," the shepherd said, "and some chemicals. For rot and cachexia, I'll need a kilogram of mixed sulphur and aniline, but if this seems too expensive I can always use juniper powder and salt. It's very important to have arsenic and green vitriol, however, for with these

I can make a bath which will cure the sheep of scab, itch, ticks, and ailments of the hooves. I will need two kilograms of arsenic and twenty of the green vitriol. In addition, I will need other chemicals such as camphor alcohol and ammonia, but these we can obtain later."

"I can probably get everything except the arsenic," Brace said. "That's an awful lot of arsenic."

"There are always laws and details about the arsenic," the old man replied, "but if the apothecary won't sell it to us, we can get a permission from the *Veterinär*."

"What will you mix the bath in?"

"I've been thinking about that," the shepherd said. "If there's no tub, we can use a large cloth. Can you find one that holds liquid?"

"I'll steal some tarpaulins from the Motor Pool."

"Steal some buckets and gloves and old clothes as well. Afterwards, we must burn everything for the arsenic is dangerous."

"I'll steal some kerosene," Brace said. You had better be careful, he thought, or you may steal your way into the stockade at Crailsheim. "Will you need anything else for the sheds?" he asked.

The old man frowned. "A shovel," he said. "I've already scraped away the soil from the interior. Now I must replace it with sand and gravel."

"And where do you propose to steal that?"

"From piles beside the roadway."

"I'll have to attach a trailer to the jeep," Brace said. Sly Jacob, he thought. Sly, sly Jacob . . .

"What is a trailer?"

"An addition to the vehicle," Brace answered with a smile. He was thinking that the piles of sand and gravel

[172]

had been placed beside the roadway so the battalion trucks could get out to the storage area during the winter. It was gravel that had been crushed in the quarry of Konrad Zabern and sold at a great profit to the Americans. Now it would be stolen away, and he himself would be an accomplice in the conspiracy.

"I hope all this won't trouble you too much," the old man said.

"No trouble, Mathias. You're my good luck charm. We're part of a boondock epic, you and I — a Teutonic western."

"What are you talking about?"

"Nothing," Brace replied. "Just to hear myself."

"Be careful," the old man warned. "It's a bad sign. I have to guard against it myself."

Brace got to his feet, laughing.

"By the way, what was it the innkeeper came to see you about?"

"Business," the old man replied shortly.

"Okay," Brace said, "but watch out for him. He's a clever one."

"D'you think I am blind?"

Brace grinned. "No, you're a clever one, too, but watch out for him in any case. And don't worry about any rumors he may have brought with him."

"It's you who worries, young fellow."

"A bad habit," Brace said. "What did the innkeeper bring you, anyway?"

"Some paint."

"Paint . . . ?"

"Yes, and some bread and beer," the old man growled. "I'm going to put the paint on the sheds and the bread and beer into my stomach. Do you have any more questions?"

Brace shook his head and started for the jeep. "So long, Mathias," he said. "See you tomorrow."

"Certainly," the old man replied. "Don't worry so much. Look at me. I'm not worried. I know I can depend on you."

After he had climbed into the jeep, Brace held the door open and leaned out. "The innkeeper had three nice rabbits hanging in his kitchen today!" he shouted.

"Did he?"

"I've been wondering where he got them."

"You should have asked him!" said the shepherd.

"He told me his wife bought them in Alzey."

The old man shook his head. "A waste of money, *nicht?*"

"Try to remember what I told you about taking rabbits here!"

"Yes, but remember also that I am no one's tenant!"

"You'll be a tenant of the county jail if the Jäger finds you poaching."

"You're too young to worry so much," the old man said.

"Stay inside the compound until I come tomorrow!"

"Yes, yes. Don't worry so much."

Brace lifted his hand in a salute. "Good luck!" he called.

"Certainly, Harry, but I won't need it," the old man replied.

PART IV

All Manner of Venery

12

BRACE ALWAYS THOUGHT of Alpha Site as sitting on the crest of a very high hill. It was, in fact, not on a hill but in a turbulent part of the forest where steep ravines and gullies gave it an illusion of height such as the trough creates for the crest of a wave. There were many higher points of elevation in the vicinity, and these appeared clearly marked on Brace's maps, but his mind's distortion of the topography was not so much a question of overlooked contour lines, or of the illusion created by ravines, as it was an extension of his professional preoccupation with Alpha Site and with its implications. Once inside the double chain link fences, however, all perspectives contracted — all visions shrank into the earth. Here beneath a vault of trees, subterranean igloos wrinkled the forest floor into elongated mounds of turf and needle, sprouting ventilators that looked like the spores of some gargantuan burial grove. Built as an arsenal for the *Wehrmacht*, updated and renovated by American ordnance engineers, and camouflaged with subtlety and nonchalance by landscape gardeners and by nature, Alpha Site was a truly hidden citadel. Was it the city of a future that was now too close at hand to be comfortably imagined, and that already seemed so impermanent? Would it survive, as had the Celtic rubble, with sufficient evidence of its secrets for distant historians to explain, or would the excavators be forced, as with Stonehenge, to speculate on unknown treasures, obscure gods?

Brace considered these questions as he drove past the last funereal bunkers to the Operations Building which, like an iceberg, was only one-quarter visible. He rarely thought about the mechanisms themselves — the warheads planted deep beneath him — not even to the extent of trying to imagine what they were like. He had never seen one, of course, for he had "no need to know" — the criteria upon which all operations at Alpha Site were based. In spite of this, he felt no real apprehension — a matter of familiarity, of having been there too many times. There existed among the officers and soldiers at the site a certain quiet camaraderie in which serious discussion was avoided and fear masked by endless variations of old jokes concerning the protection afforded by nonexistent lead suits, and the magical healing powers of Unguentine. But unlike the other installations Brace had visited, there was a special clarity to this one that always engraved itself upon him, and now, as he sank with the elevator into the bowels of the Operations Building, he carried with him the last vivid patch of sky, the detail of firs etched against it, and the stiff movements of some soldiers going out on patrol over the umbilical ribbon of macadam which ran through the trees beyond the control gate, and on which, every once in a while, a truck would appear, unbelievably, amazing everyone.

The elevator stopped with a hydraulic sigh and

opened into a concrete corridor that echoed with footsteps and the scrape of a carbine butt as a seated guard
shifted his weapon to examine Brace's pass. When his
pass had been checked and he had signed the logbook,
Brace walked to the end of the corridor, and entered a
conference room where the battalion adjutant, a captain
in dress pinks and greens, was distributing copies of a
mimeographed report before chairs arranged around a
large table.

"Good morning," Brace said.

"You couldn't prove it by me," the captain answered
with a rueful smile. "I got out here before daybreak and
haven't been above ground since."

"The colonel around?"

"He'll be down shortly."

"Any idea what he wants?"

The adjutant licked his fingertips to separate the pages
he was distributing. "Not with you," he said. "But with
us he wants to have a big powwow."

"Well I'm surely not invited to that," Brace laughed.

The adjutant shrugged. "I think it's about the I.G. inspection we stood yesterday, and the maneuver we've got
to go on next week."

"How did you do with the Inspector General's boys?"

The adjutant shook his head wearily. "The usual gigs,"
he said. "Oil in the Motor Pool bays and mildew in some
of the bivouac stuff."

"How about document control and perimeter security?"

"Okay on all of that."

"Then I must be in good with the colonel," Brace replied.

"I wouldn't know," the adjutant said primly. "He was trying to get hold of you yesterday afternoon."

"No kidding," Brace said, knowing as he said it that his nonchalance would irk the adjutant. "Funny there was no message."

"I believe the colonel wanted to see you in person," said the adjutant stiffly.

"Well, better late than never," Brace replied. Male secretaries are easily miffed, he thought. They resent the lack of their own bondage in others. "I guess the colonel wants everybody to shape up," he said soothingly.

"You should try it," the adjutant replied, waving one of the mimeographs. "Why don't you go out to the field with us the beginning of next week?"

Brace picked up one of the reports and grinned. "I've got an aversion to camping," he said. When the adjutant made no reply, he walked across the room to a table where a percolator sat rattling on a hot plate, and poured himself a cup of coffee. The percolators were a fixture in nearly all the offices at Alpha Site, where great quantities of coffee were consumed. They were never washed before the end of day, but merely dumped and refilled. Thus the brew grew progressively stronger until, by nightfall, it rose black in the cup after the first quarter inch. Since milk was rarely provided, sugar remained the sole ameliorative, and the coffee became potable to the degree that it became syrup. In the morning, however, the situation was not so serious. Brace put in two teaspoonfuls of sugar, and took a sip; then he added another teaspoonful, sat down, and scanned the report. It was a scenario of the maneuver entitled *Operation Windfall,* and described its subject as *a simulated nuclear exercise of containment and counterattack that will dem-onstrate the resiliency and retaliatory power of a modern army composed of pentomic divisions.* For some moments, Brace read on in silence; then he looked up at the adjutant.

"How d'you like the levels of political and ethnic symbolism here?" he asked. " *'Operation Windfall* will be contested in Bavaria by two opposing forces of nearly equal strength and capability, called *Natonia* and *Slavia.'* " With a harsh laugh, he tossed the scenario on the table. "What's your preference, captain, cops or robbers?"

"No sweat," the adjutant replied. "We're going to be *Natonians.* All we have to do is send a dummy convoy out to the Rhine."

Brace leaned back in his chair. "Dummy convoy," he mused. "You know, I've developed a theory about Alpha Site. I figure it can't be on the level, but if it's not on the level, it's a fake, right? Everybody's going through the motions as if it were real, but that's just to fool people while they stash the real stuff someplace else. So here we sit, pulling guard on a dummy nuclear storage site, and next week you're going out with a dummy nuclear convoy to take part in a dummy nuclear war. How about that?"

"Very funny," the captain said. "You intelligence people are real cards. If one of us talked that way, you'd probably write him up for subversion."

"No, no — disaffection. But why waste time writing up a whole battalion?"

"I'll bet you wouldn't tell that to the old man," the adjutant said.

[181]

"I'll bet you're right," Brace replied lightly. You'll tell him for me, he thought.

While the adjutant finished distributing the scenarios around the table, Brace stood before a huge map of the surrounding area that covered one whole wall of the room. For a few moments, the effect was kaleidoscopic: the wall became his district and the room encompassed both as if it were a lofty point of the universe from which he, a privileged conspirator, could look into a crevice of the earth, unmindful of the unreality of crushing land so flat that trout streams, village walls, forest roads, and sculptured hills appeared only in symbols of blue, brown, black, and green, and rose in relief and sank in depth only in contour lines, hash marks, and mathematical notations. But, slowly, a twinge of envy pierced Brace's absorption — a nagging twinge of the type that afflicts a man who knows that a photograph of his mistress is being carried in the wallet of a rival. A moment later, he shook it off. Technicians, he told himself, thinking contemptuously of the colonel and his staff. Technicians who substitute terrain for life, tactic for adventure, eventuality for mystery . . . Now he found himself studying the sheepfold and the adjacent preserve. In relation to the other tracts of forest, the preserve was larger than he remembered. He noted that the shooters' lanes traversing it were not indicated, nor were the sheds and the POW compound of the training area. Off the map, he thought happily. Out of sight behind the moon . . . Behind him, he heard the door open, and, turning, he saw the adjutant straighten at the table as Colonel MacIntyre entered the room.

Brace did not come to attention or salute the colonel

because he was considered to have civilian status, and to be in no way a subordinate of the military commander. He was, as always, careful to be correct, however, for the colonel ruled his command with all the patriarchal jurisdiction and prerogative of his rank, and was accustomed to treat the resident intelligence agent with the formality and reserve a patriarch accords an outsider who holds a position of autonomy within the tribe. As he advanced across the room, Brace saw the colonel apply the flame of a match to the end of a cigar, and regard him through a billow of blue smoke. The colonel always seemed surer of himself at Alpha Site. Nervous and suspicious at the *Kaserne*, he was full of composure here beneath the level of the ground. The new breed of man, Brace thought.

"Good morning, sir," he said. "I understand you were trying to reach me yesterday."

"Yes," the colonel replied. "The I.G. people brought up some questions I hoped you'd be able to answer. In the first place, they seemed interested in the fact that we illuminate the perimeter fence at night. They didn't say they disapproved, you understand, but they were definitely interested, which is generally the same thing." Colonel MacIntyre smiled mirthlessly and blew a mammoth, unconcerned cloud of smoke into the room. "I thought that you, being a security expert, might be able to shed some light of your own concerning the latest theories of what to do and not to do with floodlamps."

"I've never made any official recommendations about them," Brace said, choosing his words with care. "My own opinion, however, is that they should not be turned on automatically at nightfall, but should be used as the

[183]

occasion might warrant to augment the guards stationed between the fences, and the patrols that cover the forest outside the perimeter."

"Interesting . . . But since you're my adviser on security matters, why is it you've never given me the benefit of this particular bit of wisdom?"

"Because I didn't feel it was sufficiently urgent, sir. If the political situation should change, and if we were suddenly subject to open harassment —"

Colonel MacIntyre shook his head abruptly. "We always used lights at Sandia," he said. "I don't see why in hell we shouldn't here!"

Brace nodded politely but made no reply. The colonel is piqued, he thought. Surely he must know there was not the same danger of pinpointing a target at Sandia.

"Lights are the best device I know of to scare people off!" the colonel said.

Again, Brace nodded. But that's not it, he was thinking. The lights calm the colonel's nerves. He's the kind of man who, at the slightest noise, turns on all the lamps in his house . . .

"Nobody coming through those woods is going to try any monkey business when he sees the place lit up like daylight!"

No, Brace thought. He's going to think we're playing night baseball, or testing for burned-out bulbs.

"Okay," the colonel said. "So if the I.G. says I have to black out, I'll do it. But if they refer the matter first to you, I trust you'll tell 'em about what you told me."

"Yessir," Brace said, and grinned. The colonel is a master at preparing concealed positions, he thought.

"Now the second thing is this business of the bus that brings the electronics specialists out here from the *Kaserne*."

"I *have* made recommendations about that," Brace said.

"I remember," the colonel answered. "And my memory was refreshed by the I.G. boys yesterday."

"I recommended that the specialists come out in three or four vehicles, each by a different route, which would be switched around every once in a while."

"Uh, huh. It impressed the I.G. no end."

Brace chuckled. "I hope it doesn't inconvenience you too much, sir," he said.

Colonel MacIntyre put his hands on his hips. "If you want to know, it's one hell of a bother! Extra vehicles, extra drivers, paperwork about the routes — we've got enough to do here as it is!"

Brace had a sudden urge to turn around and look at the adjutant. I'll bet the captain's enjoying this, he thought.

"By the way," the colonel went on, "we got excellent marks on document control and I appreciate your help on that."

"I'm glad to hear it," Brace said. Watch out, he thought. The old boy has just paid you a compliment, which means there's something else on his mind.

The colonel peered up at Brace and shifted the cigar orally from one side of his mouth to the other. "The third reason I wanted to see you yesterday is something else again. A German cop appeared at the gate out here, right in the middle of the I.G. inspection, to deliver a letter from the County Administrator in Gerberstadt. I shouldn't have said letter, I should've said protest — a formal protest about some shepherd you've seen fit to house up at the engineer's training area. The letter claims there's a rabies scare because of that damn fox, and that the shepherd's flock poses a health danger to the entire community. Now I've got too goddam much on my mind to start worrying about German–American relations these days, so what about it?"

"I'll be glad to handle it for you, sir."

"You will, hanh? Well, I've been wondering if maybe I shouldn't forward the letter along to Group."

"That's up to you, sir," Brace said coolly. "Since the training area is in my jurisdiction, however, I'll repeat the offer."

"Okay," the colonel replied. "But I don't want any more trouble on that score. It took a sergeant and two clerks the whole of yesterday morning to make up that dog report for Group."

Brace smiled. "I guarantee you won't have to bother yourself about sheep," he said.

The colonel was not amused. "I'd better not," he replied. "Next week, half this battalion has to go into the field, and I've not only got to show up well out there, I've got to run the *Kaserne* and this installation as usual. Now where the hell would I be if I was already bound to follow that damnfool suggestion of yours about shipping specialists out here in four vehicles? Up the creek, Brace, that's where! Hell, I haven't got enough vehicles to begin with. And I don't want to hear any crap about the dangers of surprise guerrilla attack, either. You intelligence people like to think there are guerrillas under the leaves for Chrissakes! Maybe someday they'll get around to indoctrinating you to the fact that this is the nuclear age."

Brace nodded and kept on smiling. Yessir, Colonel Technician, he thought. The Nuclear Age is here and simulated. Someday soon you and I will get indoctrinated in how to fight guerrillas with the atom bomb and scare crows out of cornfields with flame throwers . . . While the colonel was talking, he had been thinking that the shepherd had probably not heard of the mysteries of modern physics, did not know the secrets man had wrested from nature, which she, in turn, now threatened to retrieve with an apocalyptic tyranny. Perhaps the old man had heard of the bombs, but could he imagine they lay buried in the soil like seeds wafted into unsuspecting gardens? Could he know that another mysterious gestation — no less immutable than the one that would soon swell the bellies of his sheep — was now taking place in the earth, having been fertilized by the mad sperm of man's mind, and that the resulting mutation would dwarf in horror any two-headed lamb he might once have plucked from the womb of a ewe?

"I can appreciate your problems, sir," he heard himself saying to Colonel MacIntyre. "Will that be all?"

"That'll be all, Brace. Thanks for coming out. By the way" — the colonel had plucked the cigar from his mouth and was aiming it at Brace like a dart — "why have you got this shepherd up there, anyway?"

"He's an informant," Brace answered quickly. "I'm trying to crack a case."

A few moments later, alone in the elevator that was ascending to daylight, he laughed aloud. It's official now, he thought. Officially approved and stamped . . .

The doors opened, and he beamed at a major who was waiting before them.

13

HALF AN HOUR LATER, Brace was rapping on the door of the Gendarmerie Station in Weiersheim. When there was no answer, he tried the door, found it locked, and started down the steps to the street. Then he heard a shot. The shot came from the outskirts of the village, and there was no mistaking it. Brace stood beside his jeep, listening for another, and heard instead the sputter of a motorcycle descending toward the square, followed by a roar as the machine accelerated on the hill leading up to the station. In a few moments, Polizeiwachtmeister Brausch came into view, steering close to the walled houses on the opposite side of the street until he drew abreast of Brace, at which point, using his left leg as a pivot, he wheeled the machine around with a flourish, and brought it to a stop behind the jeep.

"Good morning," Brace said.

"*Morgen*, Herr Brace!" The Wachtmeister raced and idled his motor several times; then he shut it off, sat back in the saddle with the heels of his boots touching the cobblestones, and extended his hand.

Brace took the hand warily, remembering the occasion of their first meeting, seven months before, when Brausch had made him wince. Now he set himself to counteract the policeman's grip, and a stalemate of carefully controlled pressure ensued.

"Have you been waiting long?" Brausch said.

"I arrived a few minutes ago," Brace replied. "Just before the sound of a backfire."

Brausch smiled and patted the holster on his hip. "That was no backfire, Herr Brace."

"Trouble?"

"Not exactly."

"I thought you might have apprehended our sign painter."

"No such luck," said the policeman, who dismounted, rummaged through the carrier bag of his machine, and pulled out a plastic sack that was smeared with blood.

Brace leaned forward to examine the sack and saw that it contained the severed head of a small dog. "What was the offense?" he asked.

"The dog got loose last night, Herr Brace. This morning the owner called to tell me that it had returned with a laceration on one of its legs. Naturally, under the circumstances . . ."

"You're going to mount it, of course."

The Wachtmeister shook his head. "This affair's no longer a joking matter, Herr Brace. In fact, there's been a disturbing new development." Brausch climbed the steps, unlocked the door of the station, and led the way into his office, where he handed Brace a typewritten letter. "Here's the preliminary report from Kreisveterinär Rees," he said. "As you can see, he states that he found the brain tissues of the fox riddled with rabies virus."

Brace took his time reading the letter. From the corner

of his eye he could see Brausch tapping his foot and switching the rim of his peaked cap against the side of his knee. "But isn't this what we expected?" he asked finally.

"One might say it confirms our worst suspicions," Brausch replied. "It also clarifies the necessity for strong precautionary measures. But there's a new mystery, Herr Brace."

"A new mystery," Brace echoed, wondering if the conversation was about to slip into the trading game he and the policeman often played — a game in which one tried to interest the other in a piece of insignificant news, hoping to use it as a lever to acquire more important information. "And what is that?" he asked.

"Three different henyards were robbed during the night. In each instance, the yards were well fenced and the gates were latched. Also, in each instance, the chickens were found nearby in badly mangled condition."

"Could the dog have done it?"

"I think not, Herr Brace. The dog was the pet of a household with chickens to begin with, and it had no history of chasing them. In addition, there was no blood on its muzzle when I shot it."

"So the list of victims grows."

"Yes, regrettably, in proportion with the danger."

"Perhaps the culprit is some kind of hawk."

The policeman shook his head. "The Jäger informs me that a hawk would not have released its prey," he said. "He is certain it must be a fox."

"Would a fox release its prey?"

"Who knows, Herr Brace? Perhaps we are dealing with another renegade. Perhaps the disease has spread. In any case, we must assume the worst. The developments of last night have finally aroused everyone. The owner of the dog I shot *insisted* that it be exterminated. Several other animals that have behaved strangely are under close surveillance. If, by nightfall —" the policeman broke off, and shrugged.

"You're convinced, then, that it's another fox."

"I'm convinced of nothing," Brausch replied. "In your profession and mine, one must plan for all eventualities. This includes the possibility, of course, that the predator may not be an animal to begin with."

Brace lit a cigarette and looked carefully at the policeman. "Suppose it's a man," he said. "Will he be surveyed and exterminated, too?"

The Wachtmeister flushed with anger. "You're talking nonsense, Herr Brace! But if it *is* a man, he must be dealt with, *nicht?*"

Brace smiled and nodded. "And whom would you tend to suspect?"

"Why the shepherd, of course!" Brausch laughed. Now he motioned Brace to a chair, and sat down himself at his desk. "Let's forget these remote possibilities," he said. "Since I know you're a reasonable man, Herr Brace, I will also suggest that we forget the events of yesterday which have tended to come between us. In view of the new danger, it has been decided today that we must institute sterner measures. After all, what are dogs or sheep compared to the public safety?" For some moments, the policeman waited for Brace to respond; then he continued, "Naturally, such measures must be comprehensive, for it would hardly be fair to the people of the village if they were not administered with the utmost impartiality. I've been instructed, therefore, to step up the program of eliminating, removing, and chaining any animals that may have been exposed to the contagion which the *Veterinär* has now verified, and I have also been instructed to carry this out methodically and without favor to anyone."

"What are your instructions regarding the shepherd?" Brace asked.

"Merely to prevail upon you to see the necessity of removing him and his animals from their present location. Frankly, Herr Brace, we're for giving the old fellow the boot. Let him go make trouble elsewhere."

"But you covered the bet yesterday, when you delivered Administrator Kemp's letter to the military commander."

"Yes, that was perhaps a mistake," Brausch admitted. "But that was yesterday. Today we appeal directly to you."

"Who is 'we,' Herr Wachtmeister?"

"The County Administrator and myself."

"And Herr Zabern."

"As lessee of the forest, it's only natural for him to be concerned also."

"Only natural," Brace murmured. "What about Secretary Vogt?"

The policeman shook his head. "The Herr Sekretär is full of good intentions, Herr Brace, but he is really quite obsolete. He cannot forget the past and he does not understand the realities of the present."

Poor old Vogt, Brace thought. He's become a figurehead, and in addition you forgot to ask the colonel's permission for him to dig up the *Kaserne* and find his precious tunnel. "The realities you mentioned, Herr Wachtmeister, what are they?" he asked.

"But they're apparent, *nicht?* First of all is the fact that to carry out our program efficiently, the shepherd's flock must be removed from the vicinity of the village. Secondly, Herr Brace, one must consider the importance of the hunting preserve both to the community and to Herr Zabern, who has invested heavily in it. When Administrator Kemp conferred with him yesterday, Herr Zabern expressed deep concern over the present situation. And, finally, is there not a question of good relations? Considering the importance of the neighboring military installation, you surely wish to avoid unfavorable publicity that might arouse the local populace and attract the attention of hostile elements."

Brace forced a smile. Concisely put, he thought, especially the last part. This Brausch has a talent for planting the barb. "I can guarantee that the shepherd's animals will continue to remain in quarantine at the compound until the matter is settled," he said.

"But how can you guarantee such a thing unless you are prepared to stay up there yourself?"

Touché the second barb, Brace thought. This Brausch has become a regular banderillero. "Because the old man understands the gravity of the situation and will agree to any restrictions," he said.

Brausch smiled and shook his head. "And how can this be explained to the townspeople who are being called upon to sacrifice their pets?"

"That's your problem," Brace answered. "My only contribution is to see that the old man stays put."

"Then we cannot count on your cooperation."

"I have no authority over the shepherd unless he remains in the compound."

"And as long as he remains in the compound, your assumption is that we have no authority over him either."

Brace shrugged without reply. Whatever's fair, Herr Polizeiwachtmeister, he thought. Whatever's fair . . .

Brausch had got to his feet. "Your assumption is in error, Herr Brace. Under the statutes of the sovereignty agreement, no German civilian who is guilty of a crime can take refuge in a military installation."

"What's the crime?" Brace asked dryly.

"What's the crime," the Wachtmeister repeated. "Yesterday afternoon, Herr Brace, the innkeeper was seen going up to the training area. He went with one package and came back with another. This morning, when I went to the *Gasthof* to see him, I noticed several hares hanging in the pantry. Herr Weber told me his wife had bought them yesterday in Alzey, but when I asked my confrère in that town to check on this, I learned that while Frau Weber did some marketing in Alzey yesterday, she did not purchase any hares."

Brace smiled. "So the shepherd is a poacher. I'm surprised at you, Herr Wachtmeister. Circumstantial evidence of that sort wouldn't hold up anywhere."

"Perhaps not, Herr Brace, but perhaps you will remember that on Monday I promised to investigate your shepherd. Well, I have done so. This morning I also called the gendarmerie in Grumbach which is listed on the old man's identity card as his place of birth. A preliminary check reveals that the Mathias Pucher born there in 1884 died in Bavaria in 1944."

"There are often errors in records," Brace replied. "Especially in wartime."

"A further check is being made," the policeman said. "I am expecting to hear about it this afternoon."

"Let me know when you do," said Brace, getting to his feet. "Maybe the old man will turn out to be a ghost. Maybe we've just imagined him."

"You do not amuse me, Herr Brace."

"When you have preferred formal charges against the shepherd, I'll have to acquiesce to the statute," Brace replied. "Until then, I warn you not to violate a military area. That's also in the statutes."

"I'm well aware of it," Brausch said stiffly. He crossed the room, opened the door, and held out his hand. "*Auf Wiedersehen*, Herr Brace."

"*Auf Wiedersehen*," Brace said.

Once again, the pressure of one grip canceled out that of the other.

When Brace returned to the *Kaserne*, he found his chief, Mr. Moran, waiting for him in the downstairs corridor of the Headquarters Building. Like Brace, Moran wore mufti, but it was mufti of an unmistakably American variety — the ensemble consisting of a blue double-breasted suit, white socks, and gray gabardine topcoat — which he had purchased with his clothing allowance at the post exchange in Kaiserslautern. He was a tall, heavy man in his middle forties, with weighted jowls that caused his face to sag into what would have been an expression of worry had the smile playing constantly at the corners of his mouth not changed this to a look of perpetual self-effacement. An uncertain salesman, Brace thought each time he saw him. Now he led Moran upstairs to his office, hung the topcoat on a hook beside the door, and sat in the swivel chair behind his desk.

"I called to tell you I was coming," Moran said apologetically, "but you were out."

"Just as well," Brace replied. He gestured vaguely at some dead flies on the window sill. "I might have been tempted to clean the place."

"How's everything?"

"Fine," Brace said. "The way it always is." The colonel must have sent Kemp's letter to Group, anyway, he thought.

"I phoned you several times yesterday. I thought maybe you were sick or something."

"I've been getting ready for hibernation," Brace replied with a smile. "Winter's coming." Remember to phone in, he told himself, it keeps everybody happy.

"Another month or two and the roads will get bad. You sure you want to stay up here?"

"Yes," Brace said quickly. "Very sure."

Moran fingered the creases of his trousers. "Look, it's not exactly my business, Harry, but I'd like to know why."

"It suits me," Brace replied, shrugging. "I like it here."

Moran frowned, and then grinned in fatherly fashion. "A woman?"

"No," Brace said, thinking briefly of Greta. "No, this is hardly the spot for that."

"You're telling me," Moran said, and glanced out a window. "Nothing but farm villages. I haven't been through here for months. I'd forgotten how bleak it was."

Brace was suddenly struck with the thought that

[197]

Moran, who lived with his wife and three children in one of the huge apartment developments the army had erected for dependents at Vogelweh, probably considered he was lonely. The idea touched and amused him. He looked out the window at the series of cuestas that diminished eastward toward the Rhine; far away, a train bound for Worms emerged from a wrinkle in the ridges, crawled like an insect the width of a pane, and disappeared behind another fold. Could he tell Moran how inexpressibly happy these bleak vistas made him?

"It's not so bad," he said. "I'm used to it." He saw Moran's shy smile of embarrassment, and felt the guilt of a man who, through sheer cupidity, has concealed a "good thing" from a friend.

"A batch of replacements has just come into Stuttgart," Moran went on. "I could get you transferred to one of the cities — Mannheim or Karlsruhe maybe."

"Thanks," Brace said. "I'd prefer to stay here."

"That's final?"

"Final," Brace said with a smile. "I get out next April, you know." The words sent a pang through him. During his first year of service, he had thought only about "getting out," even to the point of imagining it with the same heady and disoriented euphoria that prevails when one leaves an afternoon cinema and goes into a sunlit street. Yes, he had always felt he would leave the army as he would walk out of a bad movie; then they had sent him to the Pfalz — the most remote theater of all — and now his discharge loomed before him like an unavoidable reproach. He wondered why. Was he afraid to emerge from behind the moon and go back into the world?

Moran relaxed in his chair and folded his hands awkwardly across his lap. "I had Coolidge check out the
rumors about that shepherd. Just as you thought —
nothing to them."

Brace nodded. "The shepherd's become quite a friend
of mine," he said. "I helped him . . . get located for the
winter." For a moment, he was tempted to describe the
rhythm of his new regimen, but he did not. Was it because he feared Moran would disapprove? Or not understand? Or was it because he did not understand himself?

"Well, the old boy's clean as a whistle," Moran replied.

Brace had to laugh in spite of himself, but it was also, in
part, a laugh of relief. So Moran suspected nothing,
after all! You're still in the clear, Brace thought. Business
as usual . . . When Moran leaves, you'll be off to pilfer
the Motor Pool, and this afternoon the Wachtmeister
will hear from the gendarmerie in Grumbach . . .

As if sensing the younger man's reflective mood,
Moran began to reminisce about a tour of duty he had
spent at Regensburg, during the time of the Berlin block-
ade. "It was a lot different then," he said. "We controlled
the works — government, business, press, police. When
you control everything, you can be anonymous. Today —" Martin broke off and glanced out the window
again at the rolling, treeless hills — "everything is abstract."

Today we no longer control, Brace thought. The Occupation is finished, Moran, old boy. Today we're guests.
No, less than that. Janitors of forts and sheepfolds . . .

For some time, the two men continued their discussion, swapping gossip about headquarters, and talking in

reassuring generalities about the coming maneuvers and the latest Bundestag elections, but behind the façade of conversation, Brace had an uneasy awareness of Moran's malaise. "Everything is abstract," Moran had said. It was true. Here they sat in their bastion behind the Rhine, but was it really a bastion, or were these the same vague assurances the French had felt behind the Meuse in 1940?

Standing at the window, a half hour later, he watched Moran's sedan pass through the gate and disappear into the soft gold and brown folds of the countryside. Some soldiers were strolling across the courtyard, bound for the mess hall and lunch. At Alpha Site, they would be coming up out of the bunkers. We're like the fox, Brace thought. Nothing really matters. The disease creates a total listlessness, masking the hint of madness . . .

For a moment longer, he continued to stand by the window, looking down at the sill covered with the dead and dying flies of the season's changing. Then he pulled on his jacket and started for the Motor Pool that he knew would be deserted now, at noonday.

14

WHEN BRACE ARRIVED at the sheepfold, he found the shepherd standing at the entrance of one of the vehicle bays that divided the shed. The old man was leaning against a makeshift railing of saplings with which he had blocked off the bay, and did not look around, even when the mongrels ran up to bark at the jeep. Brace switched off the engine, and swung open the canvas door at his side.

"Hullo!" he shouted.

The old man did not move.

I wonder if it's his deafness, Brace thought. Maybe I should buy him a hearing aid for Christmas. The idea filled him with exuberance. "Hullo, Mathias!" he shouted again.

Without turning, the shepherd gave a short, irritable wave with his hand.

Brace climbed out of the jeep and walked to his side. "What's going on?" he asked.

"Be quiet," the old man muttered. "You'll distract the ram."

"Distract him from what?" Brace said, and looked at the animal — a deep, thick-bodied stud with well-sprung ribs, wide loins, and immense testicles.

"His ideas," the old man replied. "He's begun to have ideas about the ewes."

The ram was standing in the center of the bay, watching the two men with bright, unafraid eyes. Now the shepherd climbed between the rails and moved slowly toward him. "*Tag*, Herr Wachtmeister," he said softly, and then reached out to tweak the animal's ears. The ram butted him vigorously, and pushed him back against the rails. The old man retaliated by crowding the animal to the other side of the bay, but the ram feinted, caught him from the side, and drove him against the wall. Grinning, the old man bent down and thrust his shoulder into the ram's brisket; then he reached around, grasped the animal's forelegs, and threw him to the ground. A moment later, the ram regained his feet and caught his antagonist on the side of the ribs with his horn. The old man gasped for breath and climbed back through the rails, and the ram trotted around his pen, tossing his head.

"Look at him!" said the shepherd. "There is half my flock. Even the mongrels are afraid of him."

"What's the point of the combat?" Brace asked.

"It's for exercise, and to keep him interested. I don't dare let him run free any longer. This morning, even with the linen tied around him, he was after the ewes. He knows it's getting to be the time for it."

"But if he's interested to begin with —"

"Yes, but now that I've penned him, he's like a goat. If he knows I want him to do something, he may do the opposite. So I must keep him stirred."

"Poor ram," Brace said.

"Don't feel anything for him. He knows he has the

best job of all. Sometimes I've had to rub their bellies and even smear their noses with stuff from the ewes, but not this one."

"Where's your other ram?"

The old man turned and pointed toward the flock inside the compound. "The other one's a yearling," he said. "He doesn't seem to know anything, so perhaps I'll have to pen him up and teach him. Did you bring some lumber?"

"As much as I could find," Brace said. "I also brought the tools and tarpaulins and some oats. I'll have to get the grain and the chemicals tomorrow."

"Don't forget the chemicals, especially the arsenic."

"I'll get them tomorrow," Brace promised. "I would have got them today but some business came up."

"And what if business comes tomorrow?"

"Don't worry about that. There are going to be some war games soon, but they won't interfere with the work we do together."

"Will the soldiers come here?"

Brace shook his head. "The games will take place in Bavaria."

"With shooting?"

"No, but there'll be the noise of it. Everything will seem real except for the lack of real shells or bullets."

"So no one will die," the old man said.

"No dying," Brace replied.

"Still, it's strange to call them games. War is never a game."

"Perhaps it would be better to call them practices."

"That's no good either. One practices for what is going to happen."

"Maybe it won't happen. The bomb makes it impossible."

"Nothing is impossible," the old man said, "but we can hope it is. Speaking of games, our friend the Jäger has begun to play his own. When I got up this morning, I found him sitting in his big chair."

Brace looked at the hunter's *Hochsitz* that blended perfectly with the tree trunks at the edge of the forest. "How long did he stay?"

The old man shrugged. "Until he became bored — an hour or two."

Frowning, Brace walked to his jeep and unhooked the tarpaulin that covered the trailer. Then he began to unload the supplies he had stolen from the Motor Pool. The shepherd helped him carry the booty into the shed, and for several minutes the two men worked in silence. When they had finished, the old man said, "Don't worry about the Jäger. It's only a question of nerves."

Brace nodded and looked again at the *Hochsitz*. He was thinking of the possibility that Greta might be seen. For a moment, he considered telephoning her, but he rejected the idea at once. If Zabern himself should answer, or if one of the girls at the Gerberstadt switchboard recognized his voice, or — which was the most likely — if Greta had decided not to come . . . The vulnerability of his position suddenly intruded upon Brace, leaving him frustrated and filling him with annoyance at the old man's quiet confidence. "You're going to be in quarantine a while longer," he said. "The veterinarian found that the fox had rabies."

"It's what I expected," the shepherd replied calmly.

Brace remembered that he had told Brausch the same

thing. "The Wachtmeister knows about the rabbits you sold to Weber. The innkeeper lied about them."

"Don't worry about the innkeeper. He'll continue to lie."

Brace grinned in spite of himself, but he could not overcome the urge to undermine the old man's assurance. "The Wachtmeister's been asking questions about you in Grumbach," he said.

"He'll find out nothing. I haven't been there for years."

"He already knows that Mathias Pucher died in Bavaria, in 1944."

"Then let him prove it." The old man shook his head and smiled. "The policeman has tried to worry you, and succeeded," he said.

"If he *does* prove it, there'll be no more protection for you here."

"You worry too much about things that won't happen."

"Listen," Brace said harshly, "I don't give a damn what your name is, but the policeman will use it against you if it's false."

"Not even if he should live as long as I have."

"Then the name is really yours."

"No, the policeman is right about that. Pucher died in the mountains in 1944. I buried him myself and I have even forgotten where. After the war, I went to Grumbach and told his sister what had happened to him. She was then very old and ill, but perhaps she told her children and they, in turn, have told the police. In any case, there's no need for worry. None of the children had ever seen Pucher, and I never had to identify myself in Grumbach, except to the Americans for whom I made some translations."

Brace had a renewal of faith in the old man that was attended by a certain feeling of relief and shame. "Well, if worst comes to worst, the hell with them!" he exclaimed. "Tell 'em who you are and the hell with them!"

"Why should I volunteer anything?" the shepherd said. "I know who I am, and where I have been. That's enough for any man."

Brace wanted to clap him on the back, but the mongrels had suddenly growled, and the old man had raised his binoculars and was peering across the field to the forest, where Greta's Volkswagen came bouncing over the logging road, gleaming in the occasional patches of sunlight that pierced the trees. "It's Frau Zabern," Brace said, with amazement.

The old man chuckled softly. "Yes," he replied. "The lady who is coming to see my sheep."

Brace was already hurrying toward the shed, and beckoning the vehicle toward him with wide sweeps of his arm. "I'm going to have her put the car inside!" he shouted.

"You're going to die young," the shepherd replied. "Of worrying."

The exhaust of the Volkswagen stirred up a cloud of dust within the shed which was already filled with the odor of urine and wool oil. Brace smiled at Greta, but when he opened the door to help her out of the car, he saw that her fingers were still gripping the wheel. He began to loosen them, one by one. "Come on," he said, a trifle gruffly. "The coast is clear."

"You know, I am ashamed."

"No," he replied. "You're afraid."

"Yes." She looked at him defiantly. "Also afraid."

[206]

For a moment, he found himself returning her angry stare. Then, looking past her, he saw a picnic basket on the seat — a modern wicker affair with woven cylinders for wine bottles — and felt a surge of joy that he could not contain, but only mask.

"Come on," he said, taking her by the arm. "The old man is waiting for us."

The shepherd was all joviality and exaggerated gestures. "Well," he cried, "you are very welcome, my lady!"

Greta smiled and gave him her hand. There was a silence. Then she said, "Do you have any lambs?"

"Three," the old man replied. "The ram fooled me one day in April and got in with the ewes."

They began walking toward the compound.

"When are the lambs usually born?" Greta asked.

"In the spring, my lady."

"I should like to see it."

"Then you must come back."

"Is it true that you can use a dead lamb's skin to induce its ewe to nurse the orphan of another?"

The old man smiled. "I've seen that done," he replied, "but it's not necessary. The grief of a ewe is the grief of any mother, and the desire to nurse and fondle a lamb need not be brought about by any deception. Sometimes, however, a very old ewe will refuse to nurse her lamb. In that case, I will put her and the lamb into a pen, and send in one of my dogs to bark at them. The dog makes a true mother of the ewe for she will always face him to protect the helpless lamb. Then, when I have called the dog away, she will allow the lamb to suckle."

"You must have many worries with the ewes."

"I have more with the rams, my lady. They become jealous of one another. The younger ones prefer the younger females, which causes them to forget their proper duty, and if one ram should see another with a ewe he wants himself —" The old man threw his hands into the air. "Ah, those rams!" he said. "They have a pleasant task, yet they are always making trouble, especially the younger ones, when the ewes make them lose all good sense."

"But I think it's nice that the rams prefer certain females."

"But the females must not have their feelings injured," the shepherd replied. "They are very affectionate, my ewes. After they have been taken by the ram, they like to crowd around him and nuzzle him, so I must let them stay with him for a day or two."

"Then there is love among sheep," Greta said.

"Certainly. Come back next week and you will see it."

"I will try."

"Don't let my cautious friend influence you."

"One must be a little cautious," Greta replied with a smile. "Especially in daylight."

"Don't worry, I'll keep watch with my binoculars."

The shepherd raised the glasses, adjusted the lenses to his eyes, and looked up at the sky. "I can see a hawk," he announced, "even though it is at least a kilometer away." He pulled the glasses from his neck and handed them to Brace. "Are mine not as good as those of the military?"

"Better," Brace said, and focused on the hawk that

was wheeling above the beet fields east of the training area.

"If I were a soldier," the old man said, "I would ask for the job of watching for the enemy."

"Today this is done with a machine called radar."

"Today everything is done with machines," the old man replied.

"The radar detects airplanes at great distances — even beyond the horizon."

"Does it hear them?"

"No," Brace said. "It senses."

"Like the animals."

"Yes, something like that."

"I prefer the radar in animals," the old man said. "Wait until you see my ram detect the ewes that are in heat. There is radar!"

"Be careful, or you will embarrass Frau Zabern."

"I'm not embarrassed," Greta said.

The old man grinned. "Neither are the rams."

"I've brought lunch," Greta said. "Will you join us?"

"Thank you, my lady. I never eat in the middle of day. Besides, it's time to exercise the sheep." The shepherd opened the gate of the compound and signaled his dogs to begin rounding up the flock. Then, when Greta had started back to the shed for the picnic basket, he turned to Brace. "The world changes and I don't always understand the new machines," he said.

"Neither do the rest of us," Brace replied.

"Still, some things never change."

Brace nodded in silence.

"I'm talking of the woman," the old man said. "She's even more beautiful than the woman I knew in Lindau."

Brace smiled.

The old man placed a hand on his shoulder. "Listen!" he whispered — there was a ring of astounding violence in his voice — "she has risked everything to come here. Don't be a lamb!"

Brace felt the immense strength of the shepherd's hand. Wrinkled, veined, scarred — like the eroded land itself — it held him in a tenacious grip. Turning, he shook it off with a force that surprised them both, and started toward Greta, who had come out of the stable.

The grove they entered was a dark tentacle of the forest which projected into the yellowed fields of the hill country like a tongue of water lapping on a beach. Because it lay close to the village, it had long ago been combed for kindling by kerchiefed old women who pulled wooden carts through the gloom, and whose fingers, gnarled as the litter they gathered, had plucked even the tiniest twigs from the soft wash of needles that surrounded the trunks of the pines with hardly a ripple. Light filtered into this pillared interior as a pale reflection, after innumerable bendings; the merest puff of a cloud brought darkness. Looking up at the vault of branches overhead, Brace could understand how beholden to the gothic forests were the cathedrals that studded the flatlands beside the Rhine.

When they had spread the blanket, Greta dropped to her knees and began to unload the wicker basket.

Brace watched her, fascinated.

I'm forgotten here, he thought. She's setting table in the forest. For a moment, his heart was filled with a private, greedy joy; his mind spun with images of ancient rites — wood nymphs and processions of priest-esses. He sat beside her on the blanket.

"You know," he said, looking at her grave child's face, "you civilize these woods."

She brushed aside the hair that had fallen over her brow, and regarded him with cool green eyes.

He watched her bite deeply into her sandwich. After-wards, holding the bread with both hands, she examined with evident satisfaction the marks her teeth had made. Was this also the absorption of a lonely child? he won-dered. But she was not a child, and now he remembered that she was even older than he — at thirty-one, a woman, with the grave face of a child. He thought again about the card in his files — a meaningless card filled with meaningless, skeletal information. Abruptly, he put it from his mind. What value had statistics here in this immaculate grove not quite removed from the world that glimmered beyond the trees?

"Are you thinking of me?" she asked suddenly.

He was startled. A child's ego? Or the uncertainty of a woman alone in the forest? But again, her eyes denied the precocity of her words.

"I was thinking of how you played tennis yesterday," he said. It was a lie. He had been thinking of the old man's hand on his shoulder, and the fierce possibility of his exhortation.

Greta nibbled at her sandwich. "Did I play well?"

"Yes, and gracefully."

"And did I civilize the tennis court?"

"To the enjoyment of everyone present."

"What nice compliments you pay!"

He opened the bottle of wine and filled two small

glasses she produced from the basket — tiny, fragile glasses so dwarfed in the forest as to seem doll-house accouterments. "How long have you lived in Gerber-stadt?" he asked, filled with the stunned wonder evoked by the sight of wildflowers in harsh and treeless alti-tudes.

"Since the last winter of the war. Why do you ask?"

"Because . . ." He faltered a moment. "You don't be-long here."

"What a strange thing to say. You don't like the Pfalz."

"Oh, I like it very much," he protested. "I don't even want to leave."

He looked away, aware of the sudden desperation he had detected in his voice. Could he tell her what had happened to him since he had come to the Pfalz? Could he explain that he wanted to remain behind in-definitely, suspended in these bleak features of ter-rain?

He studied her a moment. Her gray wool skirt, fash-ionably short, stretched tight and smooth across her thighs; his eyes lingered at the point where her blond hair lay against her suede jacket. "Your clothes," he said with a smile. "They weren't bought in Alzey. They're not even German."

She laughed with pleasure, and touched the hem of the skirt. "No, they're French! The jacket was a gift from Paris. The skirt I made from a pattern — also French."

"I had thought perhaps you shopped in Frankfurt."

"No, I've only been there once. And never to Paris. My husband doesn't like to travel."

A silence followed. Finally, Greta said, "There were many French here during the Occupation."

"And then we came."

"Yes, with all your rooting in the forest."

"Like boars."

She laughed.

"Were the French popular?" he asked.

She made a tiny grimace. "We had an officer billeted in our house. A very polite officer. Gallant, even. I loved his little round kepi."

"I suppose he was stationed at the *Kaserne*."

"For a while. Then his detachment was moved to Alzey. But he continued to stay with us."

"Was he from Paris?"

Greta fingered an edge of the suede jacket, and smiled. "From Paris," she said.

Brace refilled the tiny glasses, pouring with a studied concentration.

"Of course," Greta went on, "the French weren't popular with everyone. The peasants say they cut down too much wood."

"The traditional enemy," Brace murmured.

"Yes." She made a small wave of her hand. "Always a question of nationalities."

He watched the hand held still at the end of its gesture. A dismissal of politics? Or of an old lover? He felt his eyes become veiled with curiosity — a skim congealing like the first ice over a pond.

"The first Americans who came were friendly," Greta said. "An engineer battalion for building roads and fortresses. Some of the officers played tennis, and the soldiers had many girl friends in the villages. We used to see them Sundays, walking. Then, one day, they went away."

"This was their training area," Brace said. "Where the old man keeps his sheep."

"Where are they now?"

"In Kaiserslautern."

"Ah," said Greta, with a little face. "An ugly town filled with soldiers. Ugly since Barbarossa. I'm sorry for the engineers, but perhaps they'll come back."

Brace shook his head. "No, the battalion that's here now will be replaced by a similar one from the States."

"They're not so friendly, these soldiers — very correct, but not friendly."

"They're —" Brace broke off, searching for the word. "They're technicians," he said harshly. "Not the usual kind of soldier."

"Too much preoccupied, perhaps, with their fortress in the woods."

He smiled. "You know what's there, of course."

"Everyone does," she replied with a shrug. "More or less."

Already a fact of life, he thought. How incredible — even in these warlike forests where, centuries ago, Teuton tribesmen hurled themselves against the fringes of an empire.

"I should like to return your nice compliments," said Greta, laughing. "But I'm afraid your technicians don't civilize these woods."

"No," he admitted, "but let's not think about them." Once again, his vision of her became opaque. He recognized the fact that his vague desire to probe, to question, was also to possess. Ah, the limitations of fences,

he thought, glancing at the vault of branches overhead. Abruptly, whistling, he started off on a short tour.

When he returned, he was pulling a wooden cart that
he had found nearby, beneath a bush. The sides were
stove, the handle partly splintered, and the wheels
wobbly on their wooden axles. Still, it was serviceable.
Strange to find a cart abandoned in a part of the world
where people made use of everything. Perhaps one of
the old faggot gatherers had reached the end of her
endurance. But the cart was empty. Had its precious
cargo been pre-empted by other scavengers? Or was it
empty to begin with, hidden by some peasant girl en
route to a rendezvous — a girl ashamed, perhaps, to drag
a cart into the presence of her lover? A perishable relic,
Brace thought, hearing it creak behind him — a casualty
of death or love. Here in this damp climate, it would
surely rot to pieces long before it gathered significance for the next man who should poke among these
trees.

He saw Greta sitting on the blanket, smiling gravely
at him, and he was filled with exuberance and a sudden,
wild desire to surprise her. "Come on," he said, extending his hand. "I'll take you for a ride."

She protested only feebly, crouching in the bottom
of the cart and clutching its rickety sides, as he darted
around the tree trunks, trailing her behind him as a child
pulls his boat, ludicrously, across a lawn — knowing,
even before they reached the edge of the ravine that
sloped away to the meadow (and despite her wild laughter) that their motion had exceeded their capacity for it,
like the cartwheels themselves, whose revolutions, im-
peded by rust and the swelling of rotten wood, could

[215]

not keep pace, but only scrape up great mounds of needles and gouge a fierce, weird track. Still he kept on, until, at the top of the ravine, he halted, climbed in behind her, and, reaching over her shoulder to grasp the handle, pushed off. The cart jolted a few yards toward the meadow gleaming below; then it struck a soft gully beneath the needles, tilted as it lost a wheel, and spilled both of them to the ground.

He was grateful for her laughter but acutely embarrassed as he helped her up and brushed the needles from her skirt. Then, unaccountably, he retrieved the wheel and refixed it to the axle of the wagon. Stupid, he thought. Stupid, stupid . . .

Trailing the cart behind him and grasping her by the arm, he helped her over the slippery needles to the top of the ravine. Afterward, they walked back to the blanket.

She was amused and touched. "A vehicle of antiquity," she said. "Not the one for us."

"No," Brace said, and dropped the handle of the cart, and, clumsily, tenderly, holding her awkwardly at the elbows, brought her face to his.

When, minutes later, on the blanket, he drew away, he found her eyes shut tight, and sat up, breathing deeply. Somehow, she had removed her shoes, and for a while he studied them, lying askew beside her naked feet — a profound permission. Without further prelude, he touched the soft underside of her knee, and then, continuing, knowing even without looking, from the slight pressure of her hand upon his wrist, that her eyes must still be closed, he lifted the skirt above her waist. Her hips were dissected by a band of tinted lace — a pair of incredibly licentious panties, as if from the pages of a men's magazine. Brace gasped with stupefaction. Had this mere gesture of a garment been worn for him? Ah, but they were, like the suede jacket, so agonizingly French. Again he looked at her eyes, still closed, her naked trembling feet, and the single soft flesh fold at the tuck of her waist, which stirred with measured breathing. He imagined her pulling on the panties — this woman with the grave face of a child, who attended him now with eyes tightly shut, face in repose, fingers exerting a slight, yet excruciating pressure on his wrist. Then he drew his hand away, inserted his thumbs beneath the elastic, and unsheathed her thighs, her hard, shaped calves, the tiny, lusting feet.

Once, as he undressed, he found himself looking wildly along avenues that suddenly opened between the tree trunks, lanes offering incredible vistas, lanes through which hunters surely traveled. Zabern's forest . . . And, gasping in the empty hush, he realized that he had been holding his breath. Stupid, he thought again. But a moment later, he was suffocating with an unbearably sweet torment, an aching moment of lust and terror, when nothing seemed so possible as discovery — when, in the first soft settling thrust, he listened, all awareness, to the murmur of the trees, his elbows conduits of the faintest rustle like one of those South Sea tribesmen in whose culture the culminative ecstasy consists of fear and triumph; who, having crept into a forbidden hut and glided between the woman's just awakened thighs, listens to his own heartbeat, and the measured breathing of the husband sleeping at her side.

When he awoke, he saw the hawk still circling, slipping at regular intervals across an opening in the treetops. He lay on his back, very still, not even blinking, and counted off the seconds until the bird, varying the periphery of its orbit, returned to view — a shadow flickering above the light-filled branches. Then he lifted his head. Beside him, Greta slept, and for a time he marveled at her face. There was a profound beauty about her when she slept. Her arm stretched beyond the edge of the blanket, and on a careless hand were needles fallen from the trees. Never would he see anything more alive, but nearer death, than this hand already being covered in the forest. Brace lay back again. Something had happened — something barely audible that neither the bird circling above nor the woman sleeping at his side had heard — the clicking of a final, precious bolt, a door locked securely behind him. He closed his eyes and thought about the bleak vistas beyond the trees, this space the hawk surveyed, where he, looking at himself as in a tepid pool, had disappeared from view.

When the sun left the treetops, he wakened her, but reluctantly, as if her sleep were superstition. She reached for him even before opening her eyes, and he touched her lips and pointed to the sky where, breathlessly, the hawk slid by.

Greta burrowed against him with a shiver. "Does it see us?" she whispered.

He shook his head.

"No wonder the peasants fear God," she said. "Out there everything is bare."

He lay back overcome with a feeling of total surveillance; how naked joy had made him!

Suddenly, Greta was all insistence. Kneeling beside him, she rained a shower of kisses, bites, and breathings. For a brief time, he tried to match her ardor; then, over-matched by eyes no longer shut but searching, and by a mouth that knew exactly what it wished to find, he gave in, as to a summer shower. Like some Lilliputian giant, staked out luxuriously on the surface of the earth, the last peg driven, he reveled in captivity, with only his eyes open. Now he understood why the barbarians had always entered the mystic groves in fetters, and why Woden hung of his own free will on the sacred tree as he tried to penetrate the mysteries of the universe. Beyond Greta's shoulders and the halo of her blond hair — too close to be in focus — he saw the forest at that hour of approaching dusk, when, for a single moment, the smoke of twilight is dissolved, and everything becomes distinct and pale. Then the shadows deepened and the trees lifted mock trunks, suddenly soft, as if made of papier-mâché.

"To here," Greta whispered, and touched her belly.

All at once, the forest drained of light.

"To here," she moaned, tracing a finger upwards. "Ah," she said hoarsely, "to here," and, leaning over him, shook her head, feeding him tiny wisps of hair that fell like blinders beside his eyes.

15

FOR BRACE, who was on his way home, there had as yet
been no collision — no telephone's ring, no awareness
of the ceiling overhead again. Action was still a com-
placent reflex — a eurythmic sense of timing; vision
was linear within the trajectory of headlights; the mind
had been anesthetized in the profound torpor of night.
Only faint support came from the chassis mounted on
wheels that, like a boat keel upon a bar, barely grated in
the tracks of the roadway through the beet fields. Now,
ahead of him, a man stepped aside to let the vehicle
pass, but it was not until Brace had gone beyond,
slowed to a stop, and reached across the empty seat to
open the door — only then, in that act of accommodation,
did he come awake, was he conscious of breathing again,
of time no longer flowing toward him on the mist, but
suddenly still, deep, past . . .

The face that appeared in the doorway was Weber's.

"Get in," Brace said.

The innkeeper hesitated and then laughed — an excited laugh, but tenuous as the hand fingering the flap of
the canvas door.

"Get in," Brace said.

"Certainly, Herr Brace! For a moment, you've surprised me, but we're here for the same reason, *nicht?*" Weber climbed into the jeep, and rolled his head back with significant exaggeration. "The old boy's quite a drawing card, hey?"

Brace lit a cigarette and blew out a cloud of smoke that rebounded from the roof and fell in an opaque curtain before Weber's face. One hoodwinks falcons with smoke, he was thinking, but not this bird.

"Why do we come here, Herr Brace? Have you thought about that? What does he offer us?"

Don't talk, Brace thought. Let him run on. Let him tell you . . . But he looked at Weber, and shrugged, in spite of himself.

"Strength, that's what! It's all there in that weathered physiognomy — continuing epidermal erosion, scorn in the mouth, character in the eyes, plus a good dose of craft, hey? Yes, Herr Brace, we are seeking from the shepherd something we lack for ourselves."

"Rabbits, perhaps."

"Jokes to the side, my friend. Jokes to the side. Confidence, aloofness — the confidence to remain aloof — that's what drives 'em crazy, you know. The idea of him sitting up here alone — they can't stand it. Mystery is prestige. What a mistake I made in the old days with the BHE! Posters, exhortations — that's not the way. If I'd just dropped a few hints, and then clammed up and kept 'em guessing . . ."

Brace thought of Lisl and smiled. Poor Weber — to think he might keep people guessing politically when the biggest parlor game in town is to guess who has been pollinating his wife . . .

"Take Herr Zabern!" the innkeeper cried. "You don't see him lowering himself."

"What brings Zabern to mind?" Brace asked. You're wrong about Weber, he thought suddenly. You're about to become a practice dummy for his new thesis of leadership.

"But he's the perfect example, Herr Brace. Half a dozen public appearances a year — once for the wine tasting, and the other times for his hunts. Otherwise, he keeps a nice distance. No unnecessary hobnobbing for him."

Brace put the jeep into gear and started slowly through the beet fields; then he stopped again. "I should've asked whether you were on your way to or from the sheepfold," he said.

"It doesn't really matter, Herr Brace. I had something to tell the old man, but when I drew close and saw your vehicle I decided not to intrude."

"You're very discreet."

"Not really. It's just that one hates to barge in."

He's seen Greta, Brace thought. Anyway, you've got to assume that he has. "What is it you wanted to tell the shepherd?"

But even as he spoke, the innkeeper cocked his head and held up a hand for silence. Now, from far off, came a series of shots — soft plops swallowed quickly by the mist.

"Another dog," Brace said.

Weber shook his head. "Not tonight, my friend. This morning it was dogs. Tonight it's cats. There are plenty of strays around, you know. They hang out near the farmhouses. The Wachtmeister's convinced they're a menace, so he's persuaded everybody to go out and eradicate 'em. Goes to show how scared people are, hey?"

"You've heard about the new fox, I take it."

"More than that, Herr Brace, I've seen the victims! Heads torn right off, you know. Makes you wonder."

"What kind of animal decapitates chickens?"

"That's it exactly! Nobody's stopped to think. Nobody's in the streets for that matter. When I walked up here, it was like going through no man's land."

"You want to watch out," Brace said. "Somebody might take a shot at you."

"Not anyone in that platoon of Brausch's. You should've seen them when they lined up for inspection at the trough. Blunderbusses and breechloaders, Herr Brace. It was ludicrous." The innkeeper opened the door as a new volley reverberated in the distance. "Imagine them going after the cats," he chuckled. "Fast as you knock 'em off, there's a new batch coming in, hey? I mean where'll it end?"

"Probably with some awfully gun-shy kittens," Brace replied.

"I wouldn't be too sure, my friend. You notice how they've expanded operations? First it was strays in the street, now they're beating the bushes on the outskirts. Pretty soon . . . well, a sheep makes a tempting target, you know."

"So would the man who shot one," Brace said. "You might just pass that on, if you get a chance."

"Oh, I'll have plenty of chance, Herr Brace. There's been plenty of talk."

Brace had put the jeep into gear again, and now they were bouncing over a deeply rutted stretch, where the

[223]

road provided a sluiceway for rainwater running off the plateau. As they approached the village limits, a large hare dashed out from beneath the beet plants and skittered ahead of them, dodging from one tire track to the other. Suddenly it turned broadside, and, pierced into immobility by the headlights which ignited its eyes, crouched in the sparse strip of grass that divided the road. Brace grunted and swerved the jeep sharply to the left, but the hare leaped toward them and disappeared beneath the hood with a thump. Brace steered back into the tracks, and stepped on the brakes; then he threw the jeep into reverse and swung it back and off the road so that the rear wheels climbed a shallow bank at one side, and the headlights tilted down at the rabbit which was flopping helplessly on the other side.

"He's cooked," Weber said calmly. "His back is broken."

With a grimace, Brace yanked at the hand brake; then he jumped out of the jeep and ran a few steps along the roadway. When he returned, he was carrying a large, flat rock. The hare had managed to writhe out of the headlights' glare and was now quivering feebly in the shadows. Using both hands, Brace raised the rock above his head and threw it down with tremendous force. The shadow of his arms stretched across the body of the hare and disappeared in a grotesquely rippled extenuation over the leaves of the sugar beets, and just at the moment of release, the animal lifted its head toward him, and screamed. Brace wheeled around and saw Weber's pale, impassive face staring at him through the windshield. He hurried back to the jeep. He could hardly breathe.

"Did you say something?" he asked.

"My God, no!" said Weber, softly. "That was the rabbit, Herr Brace."

He's scared, Brace thought joyously. Scared as you are. For some moments, they drove on in silence.

"The rabbit," Brace observed finally. "You could take him as a perfect example, too. Night after night, he must have popped out into the road and escaped being squashed. But tonight, or tomorrow night . . ."

"Your meaning is not entirely clear."

Brace shrugged. "Why does a rabbit appear suddenly in the middle of a roadway? There are several possibilities. Perhaps we shouldn't read too much into this little fable, but we can certainly start out by saying that he's committed a grave error of judgment. Do you agree?"

"Yes, Herr Brace, that's obvious. But what are the possibilities?"

"The first is that the rabbit knew, or thought he knew, precisely what he was about. Saw the awesome headlights night after night. Wondered about them, what they were, until driven to find out their secret. Overconfidence to the point of foolishness, hey? Sheer bravado! The rabbit deliberately placing himself in situations he could not understand or control. Value of the experience was hardly worth the slim chance of survival. Our rabbit should have profited better from what must have been a series of narrow escapes." Brace fished in his shirt pocket for a cigarette, and glanced inquiringly in the innkeeper's direction.

"Go on to the next possibility," Weber said.

"There's only one other," Brace replied with a laugh. "We've got Aesop beat to hell as it is."

Weber smiled.

[225]

"The other possibility tends to vindicate the rabbit. Perhaps he was being chased by a predator, or thought he was endangered by the guns of Brausch's vigilantes, and jumped into the road as a calculated risk. The wisdom of his decision turns out to have been doubtful, but we can't fault the rabbit on that score since we're undoubtedly ignorant of what it must be like to fear continual pursuit."

"I like the second possibility, Herr Brace. The first seems too contrived."

"I agree," Brace replied. "In the end, there's nothing brave about a rabbit. But it doesn't really matter, does it? Either way he's dead."

They had reached the square, and were parked before the *Gasthof*. Above them, on the second floor, a crack of light showed through the blinds of Lisl's bedroom; across the way, a lamp glowed on the desk of the Town Secretary. For a time, the two men sat in silence; then the innkeeper stirred as if to leave.

"Parables are not uninteresting, Herr Brace, but they're too easily applied. For each possibility, a parable, but no one parable for all the possibilities that must be taken into account."

"One has to draw the separate lessons and apply them in a composite, perhaps."

"But the composite would be a mass of contradictions."

"Which is probably what Aesop would not admit, and why they threw him off the cliff."

"Still, there's always appeal in simplification, Herr Brace, if each man will interpret in his own way. It happens I've recently come across a parable myself, or at least the makings of one. If you have a moment . . ."

"Go ahead," Brace said. The innkeeper's recovered himself, he thought.

"Since we've been talking of animals, you may find it pertinent — it's about the old man's flock. Has he told you how he keeps track of the ewes that are bred?"

"No," Brace said.

"The ewes come into heat every sixteen days until they are inpregnated by the ram. To keep track of the ram's performance, his brisket is painted so that the various ewes will be marked as served. The color of paint has to be changed every sixteen days in order to know which ewes are rebred, and if all are rebred, to know that the ram has failed. For example, red the first sixteen days, yellow for the next sixteen, and after that, blue, perhaps. D'you follow me, Herr Brace?"

"Sure," said Brace. "If the ewe comes out looking like a rainbow, the ram is something less than a ram."

"Exactly! It's quite an ingenious method, isn't it? Suppose it could somehow be applied to people."

"There'd be a lot of trouble."

"Yes — a lot of trouble." The innkeeper nodded solemnly, and then grinned as another ragged volley resounded from the heights above them. "Must be quite a bag, hey?"

"Maybe they're just shooting in the dark," Brace said. "To keep up their spirits."

Weber laughed and climbed out of the jeep. "Unfair to the cats, Herr Brace. Nothing should die by chance."

For some moments after Weber had gone, Brace sat in the jeep, debating whether or not to call upon Secretary Vogt. In the end, he decided against it, and reached for the ignition switch. There was a sharp cramp in his hand,

and he realized that for a long time he had been clutching the steering wheel.

"Relax," he told himself aloud. "It was only a rabbit." But when he had reached the top of the hill, and started down the other side, toward the *Kaserne*, he suddenly had a picture of himself standing above the fox, his arms raised, his whole spirit poised to bring the rock crashing down upon its skull.

Too late. Tendrils of mist were curling over the meadows that surrounded the walls of the *Kaserne*. Even as the headlights played across them, Brace could see the tendrils spreading, merging, and filling in gaps behind them. Autumn had finally come. Soon, he knew, a blanket of fog would obscure the land.

PART V
Fog Behind the Moon

16

DURING THE NIGHT, Brace dreamed he was standing on the old Celtic ruins at the summit of the mountain. Below him, the terrain was shrunken into a unity that allowed of trees, declivity, and open fields, while denying distance. From his vantage point, he could see the sheepfold, the game preserve, the grove in which he and Greta had lain, and Alpha Site, and this strange juxtaposition was compounded by a blanket of snow, enormous in depth, which covered everything. Light rebounded from the snow, which sparkled in sunshine, but the snow was trackless and without a sign of life. There were, however, noises; from the stable, covered to the peak of its corrugated roof, came a low wail, and from the hunting preserve a soft, crunching sound as if men were tromping through the shooters' lanes. Brace looked for footprints between the shed, where the old man slept, and the stable that housed his sheep, but all around lay snow, unbroken. It occurred to him that his eyes were affected by the glare of the sun, and so, making a visor of his hand, he stooped down and scrutinized the land again. Nothing. Not a trace or track of stirring. Now he straightened and continued his vigil, scarcely breathing, his serenity troubled only by the noises that threatened to shatter the perfection of the snow. Distantly, a voice he recognized as the colonel's echoed from the ravines of the storage site. The colonel was shouting orders, as if to a troop of men, and there were voices in reply. "Poles" — Brace heard the word distinctly. They're prodding for spores, he thought, for the spores that may still be breathing beneath the snow. Suddenly, he was aware that he was not alone on his perch; Greta stood beside him, and she, too, was surveying the land below, her attention directed toward the grove, where, immaculate and untouched, the snow fit tight against every ragged edge. Brace scanned his world again, and then shook his head, calmly, but with fear rising within him, for now there was a tumult of shouting from the preserve — the excited shouting of hunters closing in on game — and, mingled with this, a frantic, hopeless calling from Alpha Site, and a new and terrible clamor from the buried stable. Beside him, Greta stood, her gaze still fixed upon the grove. Brace shook his head a second time and lifted his arms in a vast, pacific gesture to calm the untouched brilliance of his solitude . . .

There was a knock at the door and he awoke without believing it. Another knock, more insistent; then the door opened. A crack of light penetrated from the corridor, and in it, faceless in shadow, appeared the head of the duty corporal.

"Morning, sir."

"Good morning!" Brace said jovially, sitting up in his bed and fairly shouting with sudden false awareness out of sleep.

The duty corporal was embarrassed. "Call for you at

the CQ desk, Mr. Brace. German fellow. Asked me to rout you out."

"Fine! Thanks!"

The door closed. Brace swung himself out of bed. His feet touched the cold floor, and, as if by a circuit completed, he came awake.

The courtyard was clotted with fog and drained of sound — the silence of water at the bottom of a well. A trace of daylight edged the tops of the walls, which gleamed slippery green and gave off the musty smell of stones that have been long submerged; one sensed a vast expanse beyond them, as if, at a low level adjacent to the sea, the water table had been imperceptibly sucked away by an ebbing tide. It's like waiting for the turn, Brace thought, or the forest to grow back. His mind was filled with a familiar sense of well-being. Snatches of his dream returned, but without apprehension now. A few wet leaves lay plastered against the cobblestones, stuck there like postage stamps by the wheels of some truck back from the storage site. Nothing could touch him within these walls; from here to the Rhine and beyond — throughout all of central Europe — nothing moved except by crawling.

The corporal in the Charge-of-Quarters Room had gone back to sleep, having pulled the blanket over his head in dozy protest. A pair of shiny, misshapen combat boots protruded from the bottom of the blanket and hung in awkward repose over the edge of the cot. On the far side of the room, a short-wave receiving set gave out a faint hum. The last link, Brace thought. He was suddenly filled with a tender and protective concern for this soldier who had buried his head in sleep. Now, looking out the window, he saw the floodlamps' blunted glow, and felt the breathless joy of a schoolboy waiting to be reprieved by the radio's announcement of a blizzard. But the short-wave set merely hummed, and the phone, removed from its cradle, sat on the CQ's desk. Brace picked it up, sure that the lines must be cut.

"Hello?" he said.

"*Ja!*" an excited voice replied. "Here is Secretary Vogt. I regret to awaken you, Herr Brace, but something has happened."

Brace sat on the edge of the desk and shifted the receiver to his other ear. Above the crackle of the *Deutsche Bundespost* telephone line, he could hear the Secretary breathing heavily; from the corner of his eye he saw the corporal stirring beneath his blanket.

"The whole square has been smeared with slogans!" Vogt went on. "Every wall! Like a rainbow. When the fog clears . . ."

"I'll be over," Brace said, and hung up the phone.

But as he hurried back across the courtyard, his sense of urgency disappeared, and suddenly he found himself standing in the center of the *Kaserne*, feeling slightly ridiculous, like a man who has run a few steps into the street after a bus that has closed its doors and moved along. Even now, the fog was spilling over the walls — a sluggish pall diffusing light, muffling everything. What's the hurry? Brace thought abruptly, and started off toward the mess. "Like a rainbow," Vogt had said. The phrase stuck in his mind — a curiously inappropriate expression. The fog wouldn't lift for hours.

The mess was empty except for a few cooks and the doctor, who, unaccountably, was sitting by a window at the far end of the hall. The doctor's profile, inclined toward a cup of coffee held between his hands, was barely distinguishable in the metallic light that glimmered on the table tops and on the freshly washed tile floor. Brace felt strangely buoyed as he crossed the room. The doctor's eternally disconsolate pronouncements were as much of a prospect as the Pfalz itself; he found himself anticipating them with the same distaste and relief with which one takes a purge. Now he sat down opposite him, nodded a silent greeting, and stirred some sugar into his coffee. One waits for oracles to speak, he thought.

"Croup," the doctor said with a grimace. "Croup and bronchitis. Every brat on post is wheezing. It's this goddamn fog."

"You'll go home famous," Brace replied. "You'll have the reputation of a wilderness medic. Like Grenfell."

"Grenfell didn't have a telephone. They couldn't get at him except by dog sled, you know, and then it was always something dramatic, like appendicitis."

"What's the cure for croup?"

"Time," the doctor said.

"How do you prescribe it?"

"You don't — at least not to officers' wives. You give 'em camphor oil, tell 'em how to make a steam tent, and wind up doing it yourself."

"I bet you inspire reverence."

"None of that," the doctor said. "Leads to adultery. Gets you into Leavenworth."

"Still, it must be a satisfaction to ease the suffering of children."

"I'll tell the world. Every brat saved is an increment

of life insurance. This army's breeding like rabbits. Pretty soon there won't be any need to ship over replacements. The army will send down roots and perpetuate itself. Of course, there'll eventually be mutations, but by that time . . ."

"You're a fraud," Brace said. "You're not as lackadaisical as you pretend. You caused me a lot of trouble this week."

"Yeah . . . ?" The doctor grinned briefly.

"With the colonel," Brace said. "That business about the fox — it got back to him from Area Command. He had to make out a master canine list."

"You don't say. How'd it go, anyway?"

"Did what go?"

"That business about the fox."

Brace got up to leave. "It's not over with," he said.

"That why you're up so early?"

"No, there's some trouble up in 'Sleepy Hollow,' " replied Brace.

"Croup?" said the doctor with a smile.

Smoke was curling from a stovepipe on top of the gate sentry's hut, and the soldier who came outside to wave Brace on through was wearing a belted overcoat. Beneath the helmet liner, his face wore the assumption of his duty, but the unavailing gesture — almost an afterthought as he turned to go inside — was a flip of the hand, a futile salute to the fog which had deprived him of authority. A sentinel for the middle of nowhere, Brace thought.

Now he was abroad, like a boat loose from its mooring, his sense of drift paced by the slow, metronomic

sweep of the windshield's wipers. Alone — with useless
headlights, a raincoat sleeve to rub away the condensa-
tion of his breathing — I'm alone, he thought. Here, on
the road, the fog was clinical and soothing — a wet com-
press. At the top of the hill, patches of macadam suddenly appeared, only to plunge away like mats of kelp
beneath a bow. There was a moment of gauzy light, but
as he descended between the first rows of houses, Brace
felt as if he had entered the stifling confinement of a
sick ward. The cobblestones and the scaling walls gave
off the sweet stench of wounds suffocating beneath
bandages soaked in antiseptic; street lamps glowed
through the murk with the diminished wattage of night
lights. Then, at the entrance to the square, a front wheel
slipped into the trough of an open gutter, and, for a
second, the jeep teetered out of balance. With the shudder of a man who has lurched against an invalid's bed,
Brace jammed on his brakes, jumped out into the street,
and ran around to the front, only to find that he was
perfectly parked before the bakery shop.

The door of the Town Secretary's office was locked.
Brace knocked hesitantly, and turned away, almost re-
lieved that no one answered. From the far reaches of the
shrouded square, he heard the engine of a car; then a
door slammed shut and there was a murmur of voices,
followed by a shuffling of feet, which was muffled by
the fog. He took a few steps in that direction, but found
himself strangely abstracted, overcome by a strong desire to withdraw. He started back toward his jeep,
stopped, headed once again toward the Secretary's office,
and ran headlong into the Jäger and Polizeiwachtmeister
Brausch.

The Jäger sidestepped quickly and plunged on, but Brausch shouted a bluff greeting and held out his hand.

"*Nacht und Nebel!*" he cried. "Have you seen the art gallery?"

"Gallery?" Brace repeated dully.

"Some technique! Our friend has blossomed — a real flair for color and composition."

"I've been trying to find Herr Vogt," Brace said. He was suddenly oppressed by the fog. He looked about him, shaking his head as if to clear it.

The policeman grinned and pointed through the murk. "The old boy's gone up to make sure of his castle. Everybody's running around the suburbs these days, Herr Brace."

The gibe annoyed Brace, but he was careful not to let it show. "What's the Jäger up to?" he asked.

"He's assembling the *Gänseriche*. Herr Zabern's called a hunt."

"A hunt! In this weather?"

"Probably practice," Brausch said, shrugging. "It's the bird season, you know."

"They'll need radar in this stuff."

"Don't worry, Herr Brace, the fog will clear. These early ones always lift by mid-morning."

"Sure," said Brace. "Let's go look at the gallery."

"But we're in it! One could hope for better lighting, perhaps, but since we're amateur critics . . ." Brausch walked to the nearest building and began a circuit of the square. "Undoubtedly the artist's later period," he went on, tracing a gloved finger across a blue and yellow smear. "By this time, his canvas was thoroughly wet."

"At what point did he start?" Brace asked.

"No one's sure," Brausch replied with a grin. "There really hasn't been time to sort out the exhibit."

Brace laughed. The Wachtmeister's missed his calling, he thought. He should have been an usher.

"Here's a more deliberate composition. 'Ka-Pay-Day' — in red, of course." Brausch was standing before the familiar set of letters that one saw on the sides of bridges and underpasses, and, more recently, on the walls of the ruined *Schloss*.

Now they cut across the square near the watering trough, where a group of men was standing in loose formation. A muster of feudatory retainers, Brace thought. He was surprised to see Saul there. The lessor of his trout stream was wearing a pair of old-fashioned knickers and carrying an ancient double-barreled hammer lock shotgun. He had taken off his glasses and was studiously wiping the lenses on a dry tuft of undershirt which he had plucked from within the buttoned front of his coat. For a moment, Brace was tempted to call out their customary greeting — the invocation to the patron saint of fishing — but Brausch was setting a fast pace, and the mist had closed in again.

"Now comes the interesting part, Herr Brace!" (The policeman had assumed a stance of mock appraisal before the wall of the apothecary's shop, to which had been affixed, in red and yellow, the initials of the Chancellor's Christian Democratic Union.) "From this point on, our friend has experimented with the entire political spectrum. A nice sense of proportion, *nicht?* His chef-d'oeuvre is truly representative. Over here . . ."

Spectrum, Brace thought. Rainbow . . . Sudden knowledge brought him up like a noise at night; he whirled around, half expecting to find someone standing behind him, but there was only fog. The policeman had disappeared; ahead of him, Brace could hear his faint, mocking drone. He hurried along the wall.

". . . but notice the uneven letters, the blurred lines. Perhaps our master was in a hurry. In any case, he's too modest."

"Wait a minute," Brace said. "You haven't any idea who he is?"

The Wachtmeister shrugged eloquently. "I'm not even certain he exists! By obscuring vision and muffling sound, the fog insures that all the evidence remains circumstantial."

"Is the *Gasthof* open?"

"Doubtful," said Brausch, glancing at his watch. "It's still quite early, you know."

"Then you haven't seen Weber."

"The innkeeper? One assumes he's in bed. If it's coffee you want —"

"I want to see Weber. Come along if you wish."

"Thanks, Herr Brace, but I think I'll finish my little tour. Who knows? I may turn up a clue. Perhaps I'll find they're forgeries."

Brace gave a curt nod and started off toward the inn. What a pleasure to see the Wachtmeister's mug when he learns that the evidence, though circumstantial, is no longer obscure, he thought. As he cut back across the square, he nearly stumbled over the mist-soaked corpse of a cat that had succumbed to the policeman's nocturnal efforts in behalf of the public health.

Moments later, he was standing in the *Gasthof* hall-way, pushing a night buzzer hopefully installed for the convenience of late-arriving guests. From somewhere on the floor above, he heard the sound of it seeking egress with the insistent, swollen humming of an autumn fly. He peered through a glass pane of the door to the dining room, which was locked. A faint gray light laced with strange, tangled shadows had filtered into the room and fallen across the waxed floor. For some time, Brace pressed his nose against the pane; then he remembered the chandelier of stag antlers that hung from the ceiling. He stepped away from the door, and glanced at a pair of roebuck prongs nailed to the top of the frame. Horns everywhere, he thought. In this place, there was no end of mocking gestures.

At the top of the stairs, he paused, uncertain as a prowler; then, testing the floor with his toe, he groped along a corridor, opening doors on empty, cold, gray rooms — monochrome interiors in which porcelain bedside pitchers gave off the only luminous hue. Abruptly, he turned back, and walked toward the front of the inn. Here there were two doors, side by side, opposite a staircase leading to the third floor. One of them, he knew, was Lisl's. Turning the handle, he pushed against the first, which seemed locked; then he pulled hard, and, half falling, lurched backward into the bannister, startled by a pack of sheets and pillowcases that jumped out at him from the shelves of a linen closet. He struck a match, holding it until his hand steadied, by which time the flame had singed his fingertips. "Stupid," he muttered, and took several deep breaths. Then he opened the second door.

His eyes still suffered from the flare of the match, and the room swam into sight by stages. It was a room like

Lisl herself. Austere as the dark tavern below, female in the disarray of clothes pasted to the backs of chairs, and with a touch of femininity in the gauzy curtains hanging before slatted shutters, it was filled with the heavy smell of sleep. Now the bed came sailing up, piled high like a ship awash, and festooned, as if with rigging, by cords that stretched from the posts of the headboard and disappeared into a canopy of puffs and covers. From the stern of this decorous barge, as if in some ludicrous reversal of nautical design, protruded a pair of flanks supported on kneeling knees and held in place by ankles splayed wide apart and bound to the legs of the bed. When Brace reached to fling away the covers, his hand touched warm flesh — Lisl's buttocks, draped over a footrest thrust beneath her belly, and marked with identical daubs of paint. Without uncovering her further, he fumbled to undo the knots that fettered her ankles; then he untied the cords at the head posts. Afterwards, he sat heavily in a chair by the window, sick with a wave of relief and nausea, yet fascinated to the point of desire as he watched her untangling herself from her harness and the robe that had been peeled up over her torso and bunched around her head.

She came up breathing heavily, her face blowzy, her hair matted with ringlets drenched in perspiration.

"Take it easy," he said. "There's no one here but me."

Lisl, leaning on the footrest, began to laugh.

"How long since he left?"

Lisl was still laughing.

"You're afraid."

"Lisl, listen —"

"Or d'you think I've been clock watching?"

He saw now that her wrists were bound, but when he got up to free them, she pulled away.

He sat down again.

"Did he . . . ?"

"No, you fool!"

She was kneeling on the coverlets, flicking her wrists so that the rope ends which he had loosened from the head posts fell upon the floor and slithered toward him in tiny, mocking ripples. Her laughter was immoderate, flaunting . . .

He got up and closed the window.

"My God, you *are* afraid. I can see it in your face."

He shook his head, but only with resignation.

Lisl pulled at the flesh of a thigh, and turned her head to examine the mark on her buttock. "Look at that!" she said.

"Don't worry, it'll come off with turpentine."

"Idiot, it *tickles!* Look how it's cracked already. Like an old painting . . ."

"Lisl, tell me where he's gone."

She gave the briefest shrug to taunt him.

"Listen, after what he's done —"

"My God, I only wish he had," she whispered. "Or could have. Who'd have guessed he was that strong!"

"Crazy, you mean."

"No, strong, my dear."

With one of those transformations that had always intrigued him, Lisl's face broke into a smirk — a dreamy smirk that seemed to engage him in some intimate conspiracy, while excluding him from its final secrets.

Brace leaned toward her. "D'you know why he marked you — d'you know?"

But when she made no reply, he faltered in his resolve to tell her. "Because you are stronger," she had once said. He nearly winced at the memory. Now he went to the window again, opened it, and pushed out the shutters. The fog was steaming up along the walls as if some brew were cooling in the square below. The Ganders, tugging at their sleeves and caps, had drawn themselves into ragged formation by the watering trough. Off to one side, talking with the Jäger and Brausch, stood Konrad Zabern, with legs apart, and the folds of his loden cape open to show the swank hunting habit beneath. Brace turned his back on them, and sat on the sill, facing Lisl.

"The whole square is painted with slogans. When the Wachtmeister finds out he's disappeared . . ."

She was making fillips with the rope again. "He left hours ago," she said. "They'll never find him. He's gone back."

"Gone back!" Brace exclaimed. "To Königsberg?"

Her reply was a peal of laughter that caused him to glance over his shoulder and lift a finger to his lips.

"But he doesn't even have a car!"

"Does he not?" Eyes wide open, Lisl mocked him with feigned surprise.

"We can still intercept him at the border."

"We can . . . but why? Why? Why?" Convulsed with laughter, she bent forward and touched her forehead against the footrest.

Brace stood and slammed the window shut. Then he walked to the bed and tugged savagely at the knots on her wrists which she held out for him in a derisive gesture of penance.

At the door, he turned. He felt absurdly stiff. "Lisl —"

"Oh, my dear," she said softly. "In the future, stick to tennis."

Brausch was waiting for him in the entranceway downstairs. "You've seen Madame?"

Brace lifted his eyes toward the ceiling. "She's in her room. Weber's your man, but he's disappeared."

"So I've discovered," Brausch replied. "Herr Zabern just told me he had a visit from Weber last night. He said the innkeeper claimed a cousin of his was dying in Giessen. He asked Herr Zabern for the loan of a car and" — here the Wachtmeister shook his head — "incredibly enough, Herr Brace, Herr Zabern gave him one."

"Oh my God," Brace murmured.

"To think we never suspected him!"

"Who?" said Brace, absently. (He was thinking that Weber had surely told Zabern about him and Greta, and this realization, together with the fact that Zabern was outside in the square, had a numbing effect.)

"Who?" the policeman exclaimed. "Why Weber, of course! Who else?" He pushed past Brace and started up the stairs.

For some moments, Brace stood alone in the hallway, peering out at the fog that swirled through the square. Then he glanced at his watch; it was nearly seven o'clock. Weber must be in the Fulda Gap by now, he thought. Poor Weber. Like the rabbit — first bravado, and then a calculated risk, a leap into the middle of the road. But could he know what awaited him in the East?

When Brace finally summoned up the courage to leave

the hallway, he went quickly. The fog made him feel
less vulnerable. There was a soft degeneration in the fog.
Cloying, persistent, it touched him like a balm as he hurried, on the brink of running, toward the Town Secretary's office.

17

⥃⥃⥃⥃⥃⥃

"THERE COMES A POINT after which one is sometimes outraged but never again surprised," said Secretary Vogt so
slowly that when he paused, there was a long and uncertain silence. In spite of this, Brace found himself curiously at ease, as if he had chanced upon neutral ground.
A chalky light slipped through the windowpanes, film-
ing the office with a still glaze — the ageless sadness of
one of those municipal rooms in which people are com-
pelled to whisper. There was something profoundly
calming and judicial in the clutter of documents, regis-
ters, and volumes of history that lay scattered on the
Secretary's desk, and in the annually bound and labeled
ledgers stuffed into bookshelves against the walls; it was
an office that seemed suited for nothing so much as sono-
rous summations, solemn oaths, and binding adjurations,
a place where only reason should prevail, where, like the
sanctuary afforded by medieval churches, nothing could
touch him until he chose to venture forth. On the wall
beside him hung an ancient map of the county on which
bridges, cuts, viaducts, chapels, cemeteries, towers, chim-
neys, water mills, terraces, footpaths, quarries, vineyards
and orchards had been duly marked until the sum of
their delineation — a maze of inscribed detail — covered

the paper like the fine print of a Bible page. A truly civil map, Brace thought absently. The colonel and his technicians should see this map. Everybody should see it. They should see what happens to terrain after generations of people have lived in it . . .

"And yet," the Town Secretary continued, "one is often puzzled by oneself for not having drawn the most obvious conclusions."

"For that matter, I should have suspected him myself," said Brace. "He was an informant of mine, you know."

"A good one?"

Brace shrugged. "Like all the rest, he furnished an occasional piece of information."

"You paid him for this, of course."

"No, that wasn't necessary. Informants are motivated by one of three things — money, patriotism, or political hatred — and Weber fitted nicely into the last category."

"But I don't understand, Herr Brace. In this tiny village, what could an innkeeper possibly have to offer?"

"Nothing but gossip," Brace replied candidly. "Like any innkeeper, he was bound to overhear the conversations of his patrons, and since the *Post* is not far from the storage site . . ."

"Of course," said the Town Secretary. "I had forgotten that even spies drink beer."

Brace felt himself flushing with embarrassment. "No, nothing so dramatic," he said. "It's just that Weber was well located to give some indication as to how much information about the site was leaking out to the general populace."

"Not a very big job," the Secretary observed, peering out from beneath his hooded lids.

"I'd also asked him to keep his ears open for any news about the slogan painter," Brace replied with a wan smile.

"So he was not a very reliable informant — at least in that respect."

"You might say he was a double agent," Brace laughed. The Town Secretary opened his eyes. "I'm not familiar with the expression."

"It means a man who works for both sides."

"You think Weber was a Communist, perhaps?"

"No, in his case the other side was obviously himself."

"Then the last category needs no qualifying adjective," the Secretary murmured.

"Last category . . . ?"

"Of motivation," the Secretary replied. "Can't it be simply hatred?"

Brace nodded dumbly. The conversation seemed at the same time labyrinthine and inconsequential, yet he thought he had detected a strange note of censure in the interrogative quality of the Secretary's pronouncements. I must be tired, he decided, or perhaps the Secretary is disturbed about my use of citizen Weber as an informant. Now he glanced through an intricately latticed window at the square — still shrouded by fog — and relaxed in his chair. As long as the fog holds, I've got no worries about Zabern, he told himself. But how can I broach him as a topic to Vogt? And what about Greta? What's happened to her? For a moment, Brace tried repetitiously and vainly to concentrate upon her — Greta, Greta, *Greta!*

"Hatred," the Town Secretary repeated — he had

folded his hands over the front of his vest, and commenced, as always, to nod — "it's a motive that bears a certain scrutiny. For example, against whom was it directed? By painting his slogans on the walls, whom did the innkeeper seek to inconvenience?"

"The whole town," Brace said, "and certainly Wachtmeister Brausch."

"Yes, certainly Brausch, and myself, for that matter, but wouldn't any slogan have sufficed? Why was it, until last night, that Weber only painted Communist slogans, especially when, as we all know, he was an ardent member of the Refugee Party?"

Brace shook his head without reply. He was thinking that Secretary Vogt had developed a tendency toward complications.

The Secretary was still nodding, as if the motion were a residuum of his unanswered question. "Perhaps we should not rule out, after all, the possibility that Weber was a Communist — a double agent as you've put it."

"On the contrary, I think we can definitely rule it out, Herr Sekretär. No agent, even one with the simple mission of harassment, would have behaved as Weber did."

"Then the motive was definitely not political, and if not political . . ."

"Personal," Brace said briskly. "But that's an obvious deduction."

"We've been fooled by overlooking the obvious all along," said Secretary Vogt, with a chuckle. "Let's not continue our mistake."

"All right, then, we've narrowed the category of the innkeeper's hatred. What now?"

"What now," the Secretary said — it was a repetition

that imparted a certain impetus to their dialogue, even as it gave indication of his own perplexity.

"Well, there's this business of the fox . . ."

"Yes," agreed the Secretary, "there's the fox."

"I'm willing to bet there was no second fox," Brace went on, "and that those chickens killed the other night — the ones with their heads torn off — were more of Weber's work. The way he described them — why it was with *relish!*" Brace caught himself leaning forward in his chair as he said this, and realized that he had raised his voice. Now, with a great effort, he sat back. Take it easy, he thought. You're not here to prosecute the innkeeper.

"Yes," the Secretary said quietly, "it seems reasonable to assume that Weber may have wished to capitalize on the fear created by the fox."

"By allying himself with the fox, he probably hoped to further upset the townspeople. For all we know, he may even have killed the first chicken — the one Huy fed his family by mistake. Remember, that was the same night he painted the walls of the *Schloss*."

"But remember also that Huy's dog was bitten, and that the fox finally proved to be rabid."

For some moments, Brace was silent; then he leaned forward again. "Both of them were mad," he said. "Both Weber and the fox. Doesn't that explain everything?"

The trace of a smile appeared on the Secretary's face. "It explains a great deal, Herr Brace, but not everything. Irrationality on the part of the innkeeper might help us to understand the sudden promiscuity in his choice of slogans last night, but does it account for his previous actions? And, indeed, were these entirely irrational?"

"They seem damn well crazy enough to me!" Brace exclaimed.

"In appearance, perhaps, but if Weber was really seeking to avenge himself against the town, as you've indicated, then his actions could be construed to be rational insofar as they had a definite purpose. Do you follow me?"

"Yes, I follow you," Brace said wearily. This Vogt has not only developed a feeling for the complexities, he was thinking, they've become an obsession with him.

"So now we come to the inevitable question," said the Town Secretary, nodding almost imperceptibly now, as if his momentum were being slowed by contact with some kind of bedrock. "Why did the innkeeper detest the town?"

Brace could barely conceal his exasperation. "Because he felt he'd been wronged, of course! To begin with, he was disappointed at having been deprived of his rightful property by the Soviets. Then he became dissatisfied with his fellow citizens who turned out to be disinterested in his predicament. On top of that, he found himself discriminated against because of his refugee status, dishonored by —"

"By everybody, Herr Brace? Discriminated against and dishonored by everybody?"

"No, but he *felt* he was. That's the paranoiac for you. Gradually, he begins to think everybody's against him."

"Ah, gradually! But to begin with — whom did he feel was against him to begin with? If we could ascertain only that much."

"The Ganders," Brace replied promptly. "He used to hear them cackling away at the trough, you know. Just

the other day, he told me they were always making fun
of him."

"Did he tell you why?"

"No, he simply mentioned it in passing."

"Well, we couldn't very well rely on the assessments of
a paranoiac, anyway." The Town Secretary looked directly at Brace, and smiled.

A nice point, Brace thought.

"Exactly," he said.

"Still, it would be interesting to know why the *Gänseriche* had it in for poor Weber. It might even lead us to
the conclusion we've overlooked."

"There are three reasons," Brace replied. "First, as tribal chauvinists, they hated him for being an outsider.
Secondly, being staunch Christian Democrats, they disapproved of his agitation for the Refugee Party. And,
thirdly, proud of their waning masculinity —" Breaking
off, Brace reached into his shirt pocket for a cigarette,
and glanced once more at the square, where the fog —
that comforting pall — continued to obscure everything.

The Town Secretary waited until the cigarette had
been lit; then, with a gentle inclination of his head, as if
to encourage a student who has faltered in the middle of
a recitation, he said, "Yes, and thirdly?"

"They scorned him as the town's most notorious cuck-
old," Brace answered coolly, and exhaled a cloud of
smoke.

"Very good, Herr Brace. Now we're getting somewhere! Tribal chauvinists — yes, I'll make a note of
that." The Secretary took up a pen, and, bending over
his desk, wrote on a pad of paper. When he finished, he
nodded vigorously at the words and looked up again.

"You've heard of the comitatus . . . No? It was an important cultural development during the main phase of the Great Migrations. The *Völkerwanderung* had their prologue in the wars of the Cimbri and Teutones, and the attempt of Ariovistus to found a Germanic kingdom in ancient Gaul. The Cimbri and the Teutones were defeated at the end of the second century by a consul general named Marius, and Ariovistus and his Swabian allies were pushed back across the Rhine some thirty years later by none other than Julius Caesar. Thus ended the first major confrontations between the tribes and the power of Rome, but in the centuries that followed . . ."

Brace was only half listening, yet even as he stole another glance out the window, the sound of the Secretary's voice came to him as a soothing monologue, reassuring as the fog itself.

". . . pressed from the East by Visigoths, Huns, and others, and meeting the resistance of the Roman confederacy in the West, it was only natural that the peoples caught in between should unite, and that this should contribute to the breakup of the tribe as a basic political unit. Time after time, there is mention of the comitatus, especially in the Nibelungen and Beowulf sagas. It was a body of men from many tribes, who transcended blood loyalties by voluntarily joining the personal followings of various great chieftains. Originally, these followings were elite organizations for raids and wars, and, for better or worse, the concept they embodied has remained an integral part of German life. In fact, it has provided the one outstanding ideal among the German people."

"Discipline," said Brace, with a grim laugh.

"Perhaps, but there's a more precise word."

"Obedience."

"No, Herr Brace — fidelity!"

Brace tilted his head back, and studied the Town Secretary through half-closed eyes. Was this the chance statement of digression, or a gentle snare? No matter. Vogt had provided him with a perfect opportunity.

"If I'm not mistaken, you're implying that the Ganders are some kind of holdover," he said. "It's a theory I'm inclined to agree with — not the least of my reasons being that they call Zabern '*Chef.*' "

"An excellent point, Herr Brace!" Secretary Vogt made a scrawl in the margin of his note pad, and smiled happily. "My own intention was merely to amplify your description of them as 'tribal chauvinists,' but I think we've hit upon something really significant!"

Brace had got to his feet, and walked to the window. Now, peering out at the fog, with his back to the Secretary, he felt a sudden surge of confidence. "Let's not lose the thread of our little discussion," he said harshly. "Whatever we call the Ganders, we should remember that they hated the innkeeper for being an outsider!"

"Yes, yes — that's certainly possible."

"More than possible," Brace replied, turning around. "Your comitatus, Herr Sekretär — this embodiment of unswerving loyalty — isn't it always aligned against outsiders? How about the S.A. of Roehm, the S.S. of Heydrich and Himmler, and even before that, the private armies of the Bavarian aristocrats after the First World War?"

"Yes, there's no disputing —"

"Hatred of Jews, Communists, and all foreign elements."

"Yes," the Secretary murmured.

"And now for the Ganders, though you could hardly call them elite."

"No, certainly not."

"But full of hatred for outsiders like the innkeeper, and certainly loyal to their *Chef*, eh?" Brace turned to the window again. "Has it occurred to you that this is a strange day for hunting, Herr Sekretär? After all, what can they hit in the fog — rabbits? partridge? Yet the comitatus is gathered in the square, and the comitatus, as you've said, is an organization for raids and war."

"*Was*, Herr Brace, a thousand years ago! And, anyway, the innkeeper has fled."

"But the shepherd is still on the hill!" Brace answered, wheeling around again. It's not going to work, he thought helplessly as he saw the Secretary's uncomprehending look. He returned to his chair, and sat down in it, heavily. It's not going to work unless you tell him about Greta, everything . . .

But a moment later, the Secretary surprised him by saying, "The shepherd — yes, we should certainly keep him in mind, Herr Brace, but if you approve, let's finish what we've begun before we come to him. I believe your second point concerned political animosity against the innkeeper arising from the strong Christian Democratic persuasion of the populace."

Brace gave an impatient wave of dismissal. "That's a contributing factor, perhaps, but not a very important one, when compared with the first."

"I'm inclined to agree," said the Secretary, "not the least of my reasons being that I myself have always been the only Socialist in town. So we can certainly pass over your second point in favor of the first, and even, perhaps, the third."

"We don't have to go into the third point," Brace replied quickly. "Your meaning is becoming clear to me, Herr Sekretär. In fact, I'm willing to concede that Weber may well have painted his slogans as a gesture directed solely against me."

Caught off guard, Secretary Vogt started to shake his head, which set up an equilibrium with its previous motion that resulted in a series of small, flustered rotations. "Too strong, Herr Brace, too strong! I was merely trying to point out the possible ambivalence of the innkeeper's motives."

"You've succeeded splendidly," said Brace, with a wry smile. "Let's go on to the shepherd."

"The last of the outsiders," the Secretary observed.

"The last . . . ?"

"Well, we musn't forget the fox."

"Yes, I should've killed him to begin with," Brace said softly.

The Secretary appeared not to have heard this. "The fox, the shepherd, the innkeeper, and the townspeople pose a tangle," he said. "For example, which exerted the first influence on our story?"

"The fox, of course, especially when word got out that he might be rabid."

The Secretary mulled this over a few moments; then he reflected, "So first the people were apprehensive about the fox, and secondly about the shepherd, but only after the fox was dead."

"And after I had given the shepherd refuge at the training area," Brace said bitterly.

"Yes, after you had become his ally," the Secretary agreed. "And I, too, but that wasn't apparent, of course."

"What does it matter? The point is, after the third day, everybody began substituting the old man for the fox!"

"But the timing is important, Herr Brace, especially since it indicates the *Gänseriche* had nothing against the shepherd to begin with."

"All right," said Brace with a laugh. "I'm willing to exonerate the comitatus prior to the third day. That leaves the innkeeper, who seized the opportunity to play on everybody's fear by killing a few chickens."

"And that, too, if it really happened, was after the third day," the Secretary replied, "when it had become apparent that you were determined to protect the shepherd."

"So you want me to assume the entire responsibility for Weber!"

The Secretary shook his head sadly. "No one is ever *entirely* responsible," he said. "Remember that the innkeeper was a paranoiac."

"And that the fox finally proved to be rabid," Brace added, "but if I had killed him in the first place . . ."

"You've said that before, Herr Brace, yet I think we mustn't draw sweeping conclusions, or look for easy solutions, especially when they are no longer possible. Still, since you've mentioned it, why *didn't* you kill the fox?"

"I'm neither gamekeeper, veterinarian, nor sooth-sayer," Brace answered testily. "How was I to know? I was simply out for a quiet afternoon's fishing."

"Yet . . . you thought of it?"

"Sure I thought of it," Brace said, shrugging. "So did the shepherd for that matter. He was going to kill it himself, but he waited too long."

"The commendable failing in us all," Secretary Vogt observed. "Otherwise, there would be too many victims."

"There are enough as it is," said Brace.

"Well, the fox is dead, along with an unfortunate number of his domestic confrères, but his alter ego, our unhappy innkeeper" — here the Secretary pulled a large gold watch from the pocket of his vest — "must surely be at the border by now. At the very least, let's wish him Godspeed and a safe crossing."

The poor sonofabitch, Brace thought. Maybe the fog will help him, too . . . He was looking out the window again, thinking of Weber making his way past the last stone markers, and then crawling nakedly out across a plowed strip, between gun towers, perhaps, toward the first line of trees. Abruptly, he wondered if the fog was thick at the sheepfold on the hilltop.

"There's still the shepherd," he said, almost to himself.

"But certainly *he's* out of harm's way, Herr Brace. Legally, he scarcely even exists! Who has jurisdiction over him, except you, perhaps, his friend? Protected by the extraterritorial rights of the military establishment, isolated by virtue of my own edict of quarantine — why he might as well be in some Latin embassy!" The Secretary spread his arms in an immense shrug. "The only one who could trouble him in his asylum is yourself, and surely —"

Brace had got to his feet and was standing above the

Secretary, holding out his hand. "You're right, Herr Sekretär," he said. "The only one who can trouble the old man is me, and I intend to see that he remains quite safe where he is. You might remember I said that."

"I will, indeed!" replied the Secretary as, half rising, he pumped Brace's hand. Now he settled heavily again in his chair, and nodded vigorously. "My own inclinations toward him are quite the same as your own, Herr Brace — yes, also protective, and even . . ."

Brace was already at the door, impelled by a dreadful hurry to be gone, and a terrible anxiety about the fog. Even so, he suddenly remembered something, and turned again toward the Secretary, whose head was already beginning to drop toward his chest.

"How did you find the castle?" he asked gently. "The walls, I mean."

The Secretary came up with surprising speed, beaming. "Clean as a whistle, Herr Brace, thank you!"

Brace smiled, hesitated, and then, unaccountably, he said, "I haven't forgotten about the excavation you wish to make at the *Kaserne*. I'll tend to it today. There's a good chance, I think. Next week, perhaps. The parade field might make a good starting point."

"I'm very grateful, Herr Brace. It would really be quite a find, wouldn't it — if we could locate the tunnel? Still, with the centuries of erosion, it's hardly likely, I suppose. We're probably too late."

"There's a chance, anyway," Brace said.

The Secretary smiled sadly. "Yes, there's always a chance, even though the wearing process is inexorable. Yes, I'm certain there's a chance, but one must never be too hopeful. I remember telling you the other day about the erosion I detected after the war in my former pupils. Later, I decided I was wrong. I even wrote about it in my journal." Secretary Vogt reached for a large, bound notebook on the desk, and leafed slowly through it. "*Only man endures*," he read, "*only he does not erode.*" But now I've changed my mind again. Man erodes like every other substance, only his dreams remain intact, and even they —" The Secretary closed the journal and lifted his hand in a weary salute. "*Auf Wiedersehen,* Herr Brace."

"Good-by," Brace said, and closed the door behind him. Outside, the fog continued to immobilize all movement in the square, and for several minutes he stood on the steps before the Secretary's office, listening with the fearful relief born of amazement to the sound of Zabern's comitatus shuffling in place before the trough.

18

HALFWAY ACROSS THE SQUARE, he realized that he was sauntering as if he didn't have a care in the world, strolling through swirls of fog, with his hands in the pockets of his raincoat, and barely able to restrain himself from whistling. In this mood of detachment, alternatives clicked through his mind in an order that seemed facile and full of logic. He had, of course, missed the chance to obtain the Secretary's intervention, but that scarcely mattered now; in fact, his omission filled him with a sense of relief. Even were he to go back, burst in upon the old man's meditations, and somehow tell the whole story — Greta and all — but he stopped imagining it even before composing the words that would complete the possibility. He could already see the Secretary's sad, stricken expression. Let the Secretary be historical, he thought with a smile. Let him be mellow about the castle, he's already melancholy enough about the erosion of man. Yes, better to have the old fellow mellow and melancholy than sad and stricken. But without Vogt's intervention, whom could he count on? Surely, if worst came to worst, the Wachtmeister would be duty-bound to maintain a certain "law and order," and the irony of placing Brausch in this position was even appealing; Brace considered it happily as, reaching the jeep, he fished out a rag from beneath the front seat, and wiped the fog's foamy distillation from the windshield. It might prove to be the climactic move of the game in which he and the policeman had always indulged themselves. But would it be any easier to "own up" to Wachtmeister Brausch than to Secretary Vogt, and, in any case, wouldn't Brausch be certain to plead the pressures of his latest role? Even now he must be conferring with his superiors in the first of a succession of harried phone calls — Weiersheim to Gerberstadt, Gerberstadt to Alzey, Alzey to Mainz — Brace saw a chain of them leaping fitfully toward the border like the arbitrary arrows that cut across maps on televised newcasts.

He climbed into the jeep and sat for a few moments, drumming his fingers on the wheel and weighing the last alternatives with the absorption of a man in a queue before a pari-mutuel window. Soon he was lost in dreamy contemplation of the fog. It was murk made to order; it was working for him. Don't forget that, he thought, and also that the Secretary's theory of erosion applies to the comitatus. They're a far cry from the Visigoths, and Zabern is no Ataulf. Without mounts, on foot, in the fog — it would take them at least half an hour to reach the forest. Still, if he went directly to the sheepfold, he would be forced to await whatever might happen alone, with only the old man for company. A decidedly unattractive prospect. Was he afraid, then, of Zabern? Smiling, he started up the engine of the jeep. "It's a simple question of strategy," he told himself aloud, and with the assurance of a laugh. "Besides, you should have the

grace to warn your compatriots that the Secretary's coming down to dig up their parade field."

But as he reached the outskirts of the village and
started the long descent toward the *Kaserne*, he was assailed by a depression that tugged at him as rawly as the
damp chill sifting through cracks and crevices, where
the canvas top joined the frame of the jeep. He felt the
world — his district — slipping away from him, dissolv-
ing in the fog, withdrawing with an almost military calculation. Lisl's scorn, the Secretary's sad disapproval,
Zabern's certain discovery of his affair with Greta, and
even Weber's flight conspired to provoke in him a feeling of enormous deprivation. He had a nagging, yet
only vaguely defined wish to hold on to everyone,
everything. Surely it was possible, like the prospect of
the tunnel — he could still make a retrieve, it merely
depended on his making the right moves. "Take them
with your hands!" the shepherd had scoffed, when he
had held up the trout, and now, remembering it, Brace
smiled a grim smile.

He tried to think about Greta — it was with a pang
that he realized the extent to which he had excluded her
— yet he found he could scarcely conjure up her face
except through the reflection of Zabern's presence in
the square. He forced himself to think about her, but it
was no use. Then he fastened on to the dream in which
she had stood beside him at the top of the mountain, surveying the snowscape below, but even this image was
remote for, as in the dream, they stood apart, each one
absorbed in his own vision. ". . . to look down upon
themselves," the Secretary had said. Brace felt again the
quiet, lonely exhilaration of his first serpentine descent

on skis through the trees, and, tangled in the uncertainties of recollection, was surprised to see that he had drawn abreast of the *Kaserne*. It, too, seemed alien — this granite-walled protuberance looming suddenly out of a mist that had given a strange substance to the otherwise naked surroundings. He no longer enjoyed a complicity with its safe enclosure, and, more than that, he was appalled to be able to discern the shapes of the stone barracks buildings within. Was the fog already clearing? As he drove past the sentry, he had a terrible sense of its being dispelled by strong sunlight, and glanced up with all the fear of a man whose roof is burning overhead.

In the sergeant-major's office adjoining the battalion message center, everyone looked glum, which Brace quickly ascribed to the oppressive weather. Presenting himself at a counter-window, he pursed his lips, breathed a whistle of presentiment, and shook his head as if he had just returned from the scene of a disaster.

"How's it out there?" the sergeant-major asked.

"Bad," Brace said. "Really bad."

The sergeant-major glanced sourly at a stack of mimeographed orders lying on his desk. "Think we might get a truck or two out to the Site?"

"I'd hold off awhile. Wait'll it clears."

"Soups like this lift quick, don't they?" the sergeant asked hopefully.

"I wouldn't bet on that today," Brace said, and walked to the adjutant's office.

The adjutant — the same captain who had been in the bowels of Alpha Site the morning before — glanced with disapproval at his unshaven face. "The colonel

left for Stuttgart last night," he said. "Won't be back until late this afternoon."

"Then I'd like to see the Exec."

"He went with the colonel."

"Then you must be in command," Brace said.

The adjutant nodded somberly, as if the mantle were
an abhorrence to him, but his eyes flickered, betraying
a secret satisfaction.

"I've got an idea there may be a little trouble brew-
ing up at the training area," Brace went on. "I'd like
you to spare me a few men — just for an hour or two."

"What kind of trouble?" The adjutant was frowning
a command-responsibility frown.

"Nothing serious," Brace replied casually. "A few
troops and it'll blow over quick."

"Well, it must be serious if you need a show of force."

Brace shook his head and forced a smile. "I'm not certain I need anything," he said, "but some of the villagers
seem restless, and a soldier or two up there will probably settle 'em down."

"Well, the colonel didn't leave me any instructions
about sending troops to settle anything. I'd be exceed-
ing my authority. I'd have to get permission first."

"Okay, let's call him."

The adjutant shook his head. "He's in a special weapons staff meeting with all kinds of Pentagon brass. Why,
the balloon would have to go up before I'd dare haul
him out of there."

"Suppose I go upstairs and write out a formal request to you," Brace said patiently. "That way, if there's
any playback, I'll be the one who'll get rapped."

The adjutant flushed. "D'you think I'm afraid of being rapped?"

"Of course not. I just want you to know that I consider the matter important enough to take full responsibility."

"Another thing" — the adjutant was pointing out the window — "how'm I going to send a squad up there, when I can't even get a truck out to the Site?"

"Sure," said Brace, who was suddenly amused. "It's a tough day for soldiering."

"You forget the rest of us here are under orders," the adjutant replied bitterly. "Theorize all you want about the Site, but we have to follow a daily work schedule even if the place turns out to be made of cardboard!"

Everything's come back to haunt me, Brace thought ruefully. I shouldn't have joked about the authenticity of the captain's underground playpen. "I was just kidding yesterday," he said. "What I really think about Alpha Site is it's so full of snap, crackle, and pop that when the lid flies off, it'll pull the sea all the way in from Holland."

"Very funny," replied the adjutant. "I'll tell the colonel you dropped in."

"By the way, how's he coming back?"

"Helicopter," the adjutant said, "if the weather clears."

"Better not have him land on the parade field. He may wind up in a hole with Adolph of Nassau."

"Adolph who?"

"It's a long story, but the short of it is the parade field's about to be excavated for reasons of archaeology."

"Listen now, kidding aside —"

"Honest to God! All this time we may have been drilling troops on top of old Adolph's bones."

"Well, what am *I* supposed to do about it?"

"Stick with Napoleon's dictum," said Brace with a shrug. "When in doubt, do nothing."

He took the steps leading up to his office two at a time. Inside, the shabby furniture, the dirty windows, the reassuring wall map — everything combined to buoy his spirits. For a while he swung jubilantly in his swivel chair, reveling in his independence, and plotting for the wildest eventualities. Who needs troops, anyway? he thought happily. It's up to me. I'm really alone now . . .

But he could not sustain the mood, and a moment later he was overcome by a profound lassitude as he watched the fog breaking off the peak of a slate-roofed barracks building. When the whole roof is visible, he told himself, it'll be time to go. He repeated this several times in the manner of a superstition, but when the fog had rolled away to show the patinous green copper drains that hung out over the courtyard, he was still sitting in the chair. You've got to go now, he thought. Got to go . . .

Strange that he could remember almost nothing of his conversation with Secretary Vogt. It was as if the fog were some kind of anesthetic, and his subsequent exposure to it had blotted out any sequential patterns of the story they had so painstakingly reviewed together. In spite of this, he sensed a substance of intent and meaning — a design that was still indistinct, yet inexorably emerging, like the land from beneath its shroud of vapor. For a time, he continued to sift for clues in the few snatches of their talk that came to mind; then, abruptly, he gave up. It'll be apparent soon enough, he thought, sitting up to rouse himself from his befuddlement. "And remember," he added aloud, "it was you who chose to be obscure about the most important point."

Suddenly, he heard trucks roaring to life in the Motor Pool on the far side of the *Kaserne*. The reverberation of their engines set up an immediate clatter in his windowpanes. Everything had its echoes in this part of the world, he reflected morosely. Even the fog was a tenuous muffle. Now the engines were being alternately idled and raced as if by drivers restlessly awaiting a signal to move out. *Waiting to move out* — the idea and the continuing noise depressed him. Life seemed to be starting up again, just when he hoped it would somehow subside, but perhaps the trucks were merely the adjutant bent on proving he could make decisions. For that matter, perhaps Weber had not seen Greta at the sheepfold to begin with; perhaps he had gone to Zabern with nothing more in mind than the borrowing of a car, in which case the truck drivers might see nothing more extraordinary on their foggy way to Alpha Site than a phalanx of hunters dimly outlined in a field. But at least the signal to move out would have been given . . .

The engines stopped as suddenly as they had begun, and Brace found himself smiling at the notion that the adjutant had chosen to remain in character, after all. Perhaps, looking out his window, the adjutant had also been struck into inaction by the fog's bemusing smear, and was contemplating a world of scenographic fabrication. But would he be able to sustain such a reverie with assurance only an arm's length away? Even a cardboard house has substance when its telephone is answered, Brace reflected. In any case, the adjutant could not be expected to play spectator at a private skit in which the backdrops had been conjured up in the mind's eye of another man. Yes, when everything was said and done, Brace thought, all the mirages were his own. He had been living with too much disbelief suspended. For a time, it had worked wonders — this arbitrary wand that had even transformed the prisoner-of-war compound into a shepherd's refuge, and the harsh trees of Zabern's grove into soft, romantic props — but now it had ceased to function. He looked at the wall map of his district. It wasn't mine at all, he thought. Yet he had come close to making it so; he had merely stayed too long. Wasn't that what Secretary Vogt had tried to tell him in the end?

All at once he was hungry. Perhaps he could stay long enough to have another cup of coffee with the doctor — ah, but the doctor was surely back in bed by now, having immunized himself against croup by removing the phone from its cradle. Besides, Brace had no real desire to see him; the doctor's cynicism — a remedy he dispensed even without examination — merely masked certain symptoms to afford, like pills for toothaches, a temporary relief. It was too late for tranquilizers of any sort, Brace reflected. His own life — even a part of his desire for it — seemed to be already submerged in this fog behind the moon. He was truly alone. Besieged. The route to the sheepfold unraveled before him now in intricate detail — a passage as shrouded and foreboding as the tunnel that might be mouldering beneath the crumbled castle. Yet did it not afford the same last desperate hope?

He moved quickly across the room, and knelt before the cabinet safe. As he turned the combination dial, it occurred to him that the shepherd might also be besieged — even now at the very moment he was diddling with the knob — and this idea, that he was passively toying with another's destiny, filled him with a strange exhilaration. When he had opened the door of the safe, he pulled out the bottommost drawer, and withdrew from it a small, short-barreled revolver. As he broke the weapon open to inspect the chambers of the cylinder, he noticed that his fingertips left tiny moisture stains on the bluish side plates. Nerves, he told himself. Or the humidity, perhaps . . . Now he searched for the honeycombed box of cartridges, which, since the revolver was not a standard army issue, bore the green and red label that one often saw in sporting goods stores. Brace considered the label a good omen. There should be nothing too military about this little venture, he thought.

When he had inserted cartridges into the five chambers of the cylinder, he snapped the action shut, put the revolver in the right-hand pocket of his raincoat, and stood up, vaguely reassured by the sudden weight of it tugging at his shoulder seam. Then, as an afterthought, he reached down and pulled out a few extra shells, which he dropped into his other pocket. A moment later, he was slumped in his chair again, watching the fog; it was on the move now, coursing over the hills, changing by the instant like wash applied to a watercolor.

For a time, he considered putting through a call to his

chief, Moran, but he rejected the idea even as he reached for the telephone. It seemed hardly practical to involve a man who felt everything was "abstract" to begin with, and especially a man who, only the day before, had offered him the chance to withdraw. Besides, in this weather, Moran was at least two hours away. Abruptly, Brace picked up the receiver and asked the military operator for a civilian line. There was a considerable wait, during which he could hear a series of loud crackles as a connection was made with the *Deutsche Bundespost* switchboard in Gerberstadt. Then a woman's voice said, *"Bitte?"*

"The residence of Herr Konrad Zabern," Brace replied, wondering if his accent betrayed his nationality.

"Seven-five-seven-seven," said the operator, commencing the ring.

"Thanks."

"You're welcome."

The phone rang twice.

Then: "Hallo?"

Brace was startled to hear the voice of an old woman. He took a deep breath and leaned on the desktop. "May I speak with Frau Zabern, please?"

"Frau Zabern is not at home. Who is —"

"When do you expect her?"

"She's away. Who's calling?"

"A friend," Brace replied. "Perhaps you can tell me where she's gone. It's quite important."

"Who's calling, please?" — a strident demand, insistent, shrill, forewarned . . .

Brace replaced the receiver in its cradle, and turned once again to the window. Away — at this time of morn-

[272]

ing, or was she simply not at home to callers? Had Zabern sent her away? Had she gone off on her own? Would she try, or be able, to get in touch with him? He wondered if, when Zabern had confronted her, she had been afraid, if the eyes of her grave child's face had shown fear . . .

For a moment longer, he continued to stare through the window. Then, brushing the dead and dying flies off the sill with a sweep of his sleeve, he got to his feet and hurried out of the office.

19

〽〽〽〽〽〽

TO SAVE TIME and to avoid the village, Brace took the shortest possible cut, traversing shrouded farmyards and then skirting the beet fields until he reached the road that led to the training area and the forest. Here on the open plateau, he was overtaken by soft, buoyant swells of mist which seemed to lift the jeep and even to pulse it forward, but when he arrived at the sheepfold and shut off the engine, he had a sudden sensation of sinking, of the fog settling over him, deep as water, soundless as the snow of his dream. For a minute or two, he sat behind the wheel, listening to the faint, metallic tick of some contraction in the engine's throat; then he climbed out and groped his way to the shack. It was empty but still warmed by embers that flickered in the bottom of the stove. He made a quick inspection, noting the old man's binoculars hanging from a peg beside the door, and a plate containing a crust of bread and the bones of some bird which had surely been filched from the preserve. "Poached grouse on toast," he murmured with a smile.

Now he went out to the stable, parted one of the tarpaulin flaps, and peered into a gloomy interior. When his eyes became accustomed to the darkness, he made out

[274]

the big ram and a dozen ewes feeding quietly at stands which the shepherd had built against the far wall of each pen. I wonder why the mongrels aren't barking, he thought.

He returned to his jeep with the intention of signaling on the horn, but after a moment's reflection he decided against it. The old man was probably off in the woods and would not recognize the sound even if, in spite of the fog and his deafness, he should hear it. And, more important, the horn might serve to alert the comitatus. You're assuming the worst, he told himself grimly. You've been assuming the worst ever since you learned that the innkeeper had gone to see Zabern . . .

Abruptly, he struck out across the field toward the prisoner-of-war compound. The broken gate — now partially mended with saplings — loomed up sooner than he expected, and for a while he stood tentatively before it in the very spot where, under the clear sky of the previous afternoon, the shepherd had grasped his shoulder to urge upon him that most immediate of possibilities. A hand of benediction, Brace reflected. Only it came a day too early. We should have waited, Greta and I. We should have made love in the fog . . .

He pushed open the gate, and then pulled it shut behind him. "A cowboy always secures the corral," he muttered, as if to lift his spirits, but when he moved across the compound, he was unable to resist the temptation to reach inside the pocket of his coat, and close his fingers around the grooved cylinder of the gun.

The rest of the sheep were bunched together close to the wire on the far side. One animal on the edge of the flock looked up at him without interest; the others stood motionless, seeking only warmth. Even sheep keep still in fog, Brace thought. They must know by instinct that it's safer to be quiet. But shouldn't the dogs at least be barking?

He made a tour of the perimeter fence, and then sought out the water tank — a shadow supported on frail stilts that were soaked with slime. Gingerly, he tested one of the stilts with his hand, thinking that the whole rotten edifice might come crashing down on him at any moment. The possibility filled him with a vague exultation, and for a time he stood beneath the tank as if with the idea of tempting fate.

The fog was clearing, or perhaps it was being stirred by some faint current. In any case, he could make out the shape of a guard tower at one corner of the compound. Now a strand of wire became visible, and another parallel strand beneath it — both disappearing into the mist as if part of a diagram promising juncture at infinity. Soon the strands were dissected by posts; then another guard tower swam into view, and, turning his head, Brace watched the geometry of his prison unfold around him. Abruptly, the fog closed in again, blotting out everything and filling him with an irresistible urge to slip away. What a Godforsaken spot! he thought, starting for the gate.

When he reached the jeep, he leaned against a fender and lit a cigarette. The mist that cloaked him seemed thicker than ever — a luxurious mantle from which he derived a sense of welcome anonymity. Brausch had been right, of course — by obscuring vision and muffling sound, the fog rendered all evidence circumstantial. The policeman had merely neglected to mention that it also stifled scent, which provided a perfect explanation for the silence of the mongrels. As for the binoculars, their limitations on such a day were only too apparent. You've been worrying for nothing, Brace told himself. In a little while, the sun will break through, the birds will begin to chirp, and Mathias will come back with a rabbit beneath his coat to find you sitting here, pistol in pocket, like a sleepwalker waiting for ghosts . . .

When, half an hour later, he heard several sharp clicking sounds, he thought it might be some additional settling in the radiator of his jeep. But the mist was on the move again, confounding all the senses, and though the sounds persisted at fairly regular intervals, he could only guess at their origin and direction. Finally, they ceased altogether, and he was left to ponder the screen of vapor which hung like an illusion before him, eddying this way and that, drifting on and on, leading nowhere.

He would remember, afterwards, that the fog had suddenly seemed to bulge, even to burst, but now he saw only a strange billowing which masked a soft commotion. Then the mist parted to reveal a corner of the compound and the figure of a man who was running just inside the barbed wire fence. Like someone shaken from sleep, Brace was instantly awake, yet incapable of acting. A moment later, he heard the sheep in full cry, stampeding toward the forest. The wire! he thought with a gasp of astonishment. They've cut the wire!

The sound of his first shot died quickly in the fog. He had fired into the air, but with the revolver too close to his head, and his ears were ringing. Now, holding the gun at arm's length, he squeezed the trigger twice again. Then he dropped to his knees beside the jeep. Slapstick! he thought. Real slapstick . . .

Suddenly a terrific tumult broke upon him. He could hear men shouting, dogs barking, and the sheep bleating in terror. From all around him came the noises of a furious assault. He jumped to his feet and took steps in several directions.

"Mathias!" he shouted.

Whirling in fright, he nearly fired at a sheep that staggered past him, gushing blood from a wound in its neck. "Mathias!"

He sent two more shots into the air, emptying the revolver, and wincing as smoke from the barrel hit his nostrils.

"Mathias!"

He returned to the jeep, knelt down again, and reloaded. His fingers were trembling uncontrollably, and he dropped several of the cartridges in the grass as he tried to insert them into the cylinder. The woods continued to resound with a terrible racket that was augmented now by what he recognized to be the furious, outraged yapping of the mongrels, and the pitiful moaning of dying animals. They're killing the sheep, he thought helplessly.

He realized that he was shaking with fear. Forcing himself to stand up, he grasped a fender for support, and kicked first one foot and then the other against a tire in order to stop the shuddering in his knees. The temptation to jump into the jeep and race away was almost overwhelming. "God damn you," he told himself. "God damn you . . ."

He knew it would be foolish to shout for Mathias

again — the old man was bound to be out there, some-where, in the woods. Under the circumstances, the only sensible thing was to stay by the sheds and protect the remaining sheep — yes, the only sensible thing was to stay put. He looked about him for a place to hide, and quickly decided that the jeep afforded no freedom of movement, and that both the shack and the sheds were traps. For a terrible moment, he felt absolutely vulner-able; then he remembered the corrugated tin roof that covered the stable.

When he had climbed up on it, he found that it pro-vided an even better vantage point than he had hoped. The roof had been built on a single plane, and pitched slightly downward in the direction of the preserve so that rainwater would not fall over the entrances to the vehicle bays. By hugging it closely, Brace could look over the peak toward the prisoner-of-war compound and yet be completely hidden by the slant. The cold, wet tin revived him, and now, putting his cheek against it, he clutched the edge with one hand and his revolver in the other, and listened to the sounds of slaughter as he lay in wait for the first figure to emerge from the fog.

The fog was lifting. This time there was no doubt about it. He could even make out the water tank. The fog came swirling along the ground, dividing as it passed the knoll on which the shed was built, and merging again as it coursed toward the forest behind him. It went quickly — just as the sergeant-major had hoped it might — like a cloth whisked off a table.

Brace was breathing in short gasps — not so much out of fear now as because of the astounding tableau that unfolded before his eyes. All of a sudden he could see the outline of trees at the edge of the forest and the figures of a dozen men strung out along the logging road that skirted the clearing. The last tendrils of mist curled off the wet grass, revealing the carcasses of sheep that had tried to reach the woods. A few survivors milled uncertainly near the compound; others, impaled on the barbed wire, struggled to free themselves. Except for this writhing — a silent fluttering of debris — there was no movement. Somehow the scene was incredibly pastoral. The dead sheep might well have been asleep. The men stood on the road in frozen immobility. Everything appeared smaller than life, as if the fog had uncovered some dreamy nineteenth-century mural.

Brace turned his head very slowly, and took in the complete circumference of his surroundings. Off to his right, he could see the Jäger sitting alone in a tall *Hochsitz* at the edge of the ravine, and holding a rifle across his knees. The jeep must be sticking out like a sore thumb, he thought. I should have hidden it in the stable . . . Now he heard a commotion in the forest on the other side of the field, and saw the shepherd emerge from a screen of trees, flanked by two men who pinioned his arms, and followed by Konrad Zabern who was carrying a shotgun. Brace shifted his position slightly for a better look, crossing his arms in front of him, and resting the hand that held the revolver against the roof. He could not tell whether the old man had been hurt or merely cowed, but he was obviously a prisoner, and this realization filled him with despair. Squinting along the barrel of his gun, he placed the sight squarely on the figure of Zabern. The distance was impossible — at least two hundred yards — but even so he could barely restrain himself from squeezing the trigger.

At this point, the stillness was broken by the mongrels who came running into the field from the woods. One of them commenced to round up the remaining sheep; the other yapped in shrill confusion at the animals caught in the barbed wire of the compound. Brace was afraid at first that the diversion might bring attention upon himself, but then he saw that Zabern and the men stationed along the roadway were looking into the forest. They're looking for *me!* he thought with amazement. They must be afraid I've circled behind them.

He nearly laughed out loud. He had an insane desire to shout defiance, to goad them into range by revealing his position. If he had only brought the Thompson! Flattening himself against the tin roof, he thought about the havoc he could have raised with the machine gun. He imagined himself sweeping the whole perimeter of the clearing, chopping limbs and leaves from the trees above their heads, and chewing up the dirt and grass at their feet . . .

But as the minutes passed the men merely continued their watchful stand, and even the dogs, having brought the remnants of the flock together, fell silent. The curtain has risen and the actors are awaiting a cue, Brace thought. Someone should step out and deliver a prologue . . . His reverie was shattered abruptly by the Jäger's rifle — one shot followed by two more. Peering over the edge of the roof, he saw the nearest mongrel being tossed in the air by the enormous impact of the slugs. The sheep were bolting in all directions, and the second dog, circling and barking furiously, was trying vainly to stem their flight. Brace rolled over on his side, and, stunned by the senselessness of it, watched helplessly as the Jäger sighted on the darting target, fired, and missed.

A wild cry mingled with the echo of the shot — a cry of rage and grief that brought him up like a bolt. For a second, Brace thought dazedly that he had uttered it himself; then he saw the shepherd struggling with his captors at the edge of the clearing. Now the old man broke loose and came running across the field toward the *Hochsitz*, waving his arms and still shouting — an unintelligible, almost inhuman bellow.

On hands and knees, Brace wheeled and aimed his weapon at the Jäger, but the Jäger was looking in another direction, his rifle swerving implacably as he fired at the mongrel again and again.

The shepherd was racing through the field.

Behind him came Zabern, inserting cartridges into his shotgun on the run, and angling toward the shed so as not to be in alignment with the old man and the Jäger's rifle.

Brace had been on the verge of shouting a warning to Mathias, but now he turned his attention to Zabern, who had stopped running and was moving cautiously toward the jeep. He could hear Zabern's heavy breathing and a click as he snapped shut the action of his gun. Take a good look, Herr Chef, he thought. All the tires have tread . . .

The shepherd had reached the base of the *Hochsitz*, where the fir sapling legs that supported the chair were stuck into the ground. Twenty feet above him, the Jäger peered briefly over the edge of his perch, and then, as if confident that the old man would not try to climb the ladder, went on shooting at the dog.

Brace watched Zabern enter the shack; then he stole a glance at the men standing in the road at the edge of the clearing. None of them were stirring. They're waiting for the chief to give the all-clear signal, he thought. Brave old comitatus! When Zabern emerged from the shack, he passed out of sight beneath the edge of the stable roof. The stable is the last hiding place, Brace reflected with a smile. If Wachtmeister Brausch were here, he could write up a report stating that a search of the premises revealed nothing, and that all the evidence remained circumstantial . . . As he waited for Zabern to reappear, Brace tried to decide on a course of action. So long as Zabern stayed within range, he could be used to guarantee the safety of Mathias and the continued good sense of the comitatus, but what was the old man up to below the Jäger? Brace cast an uneasy glance in the direction of the *Hochsitz* and saw the shepherd leaning against one of the fir trunk legs, and just then Zabern came out of the stable. One thing at a time, he told himself.

Zabern was standing below him, looking first toward the roadway and then toward the *Hochsitz* as if he were unable to make up his mind. Suddenly, unaccountably, he turned and stared directly up at Brace.

"Drop the gun," Brace said softly.

Gaping, Zabern complied, and backed off several steps.

Brace swung his legs over the edge of the roof, and set himself to jump. The whine of a bullet overhead and the report of the Jäger's rifle hurried his leap. He landed heavily on the ground and rolled over on his shoulder;

then, scrambling forward on his hands and knees, he picked up Zabern's shotgun.

Zabern stood perfectly still, but he had recovered himself sufficiently to smile.

"You sonofabitch," said Brace, quietly.

"Needless to mention, perhaps, but the Jäger's a crack shot," Zabern replied.

"At this range so am I," said Brace, who remained crouching on the ground.

"Your jokes are in bad taste, my friend. The game is over."

"Is it?" said Brace, stretching out his arm and aiming carefully and deliberately at Zabern's head.

Never before had he had occasion to put a man in fear of his life, and now, seeing the flash of panic on Zabern's face, he felt close to nausea. "Listen to me," he said. "I want you to understand one thing very clearly. I'm holding you as a hostage for the old man's safety. Now turn around and tell that to the game warden."

Zabern did as he was told. "Herr Jäger!" he began, cupping his hands to his mouth, but that was as far as he got. The *Hochsitz* had begun to sway crazily against the backdrop of trees; back and forth it swayed, with the Jäger grasping the sides of his chair and struggling to maintain his balance on the teetering platform.

Brace stood up just in time to see the old man bulling his weight against the supports, throwing himself at them again and again, until the entire structure began to topple.

At the moment of collapse, the Jäger tried to jump, but before he could the platform had slipped away beneath him, and instead of pushing off, he merely fell, arms outflung, into the pile that came crashing down.

"Good God!" Zabern exclaimed.

Brace gave him a shove between the shoulder blades that nearly sent him sprawling. Then, glancing at the roadway to assure himself that the comitatus was still inactive, he pushed Zabern ahead of him, and started across the field toward the wreckage of the *Hochsitz.* As he drew close, he saw the shepherd disentangle himself from the debris, and pick up a heavy piece of beam.

"Mathias!" he shouted. "Mathias, wait for me!"

The old man was standing above the Jäger, who was pinned beneath one of the sapling legs; now he turned and watched Brace and Zabern approach.

"I was afraid you were going to kill him," said Brace, who arrived panting for lack of breath, and also with relief.

"Yes, I was going to kill him," the shepherd replied bitterly. "But I have just remembered the fox." He gave Brace a cold, hostile stare, and, turning away, hurried back across the field toward the stable.

"Mathias, wait a minute . . . Mathias!"

Brace was about to call again, but all at once he was overcome by a strange lethargy — a mixture of fatigue and despair. He glanced at Zabern, who had pulled the Jäger from the wreckage and propped him up in a sitting position.

"A broken shoulder," Zabern observed. "Perhaps the arm as well."

"Too bad," Brace replied. "Too bad it's not his neck." A feeling of rage and frustration revived him as he spoke, and he pointed the revolver directly at Zabern.

"Neither one of you moves until I say so. D'you un-derstand me? Not a move."

"This man must see a doctor," Zabern said calmly.

"Shut up!" Brace shouted. It was nearly a scream, and for a moment he struggled to bring himself under con-trol, astounded at the violence of his feelings.

The shepherd had fetched a shovel from the stable, and was dispatching the seriously wounded sheep with its blade. For a time, the men standing on the road watched him in silence; then they began to drift away, in twos and threes, in the direction of the village. As he listened to the shovel's sickening thud, Brace was re-minded of certain wartime photographs showing the aftermath of mass executions in which the victims of firing squads, already slumped and shapeless, were sub-jected to the final, pitiless indignity of the *coup de grâce*. Ah Mathias, he thought, if anyone had told me that I would see you killing your sheep . . .

Waving the revolver, he turned back to Zabern, "Well, there go the warriors back to town," he said scornfully. "You're being deserted, Herr Chef. They're leaving you in the lurch."

Zabern took a few steps away from the Jäger, and looked carefully at Brace and then at the revolver. "My wife was here yesterday," he said, speaking the words slowly and evenly as if he felt the need to make some rejoinder to Brace's mockery.

"So what?" Brace replied, but in spite of himself and the gun in his hand, he felt that his authority had sud-denly diminished.

"You and she —"

"The old man was here, too," Brace interrupted.

[286]

The shepherd had finished off the last of the wounded sheep and returned to the shack. Now, from the corner of his eye, Brace saw him emerge with his belongings. The old man plucked at the folds of his cape as he adjusted the rucksack on his shoulders; then, very carefully, as if he were laying the pallium over priestly vestments, he pulled the straps of the binoculars over his head. Afterwards, he took up his staff and went to the stable.

"My wife has admitted everything," Zabern said, moving out of the Jäger's hearing as he spoke.

He's lying, Brace thought. He only suspects everything. Greta's merely admitted that she was here. For a second, he conjured up her grave child's face, and imagined her coolly denying everything.

"Everything?" he heard himself saying. "I don't understand you."

The old man brought out the sheep that had been penned up in the stable, and whistled a command to the mongrel, who rejoined them with the animals that had survived the morning's holocaust.

"So you deny it," Zabern said. His voice had become aggressive, and he was searching Brace's face as if he hoped to find some flicker of deception that would reinforce his suspicion.

"There's nothing to deny," Brace said steadily. "Whatever you've been thinking was a mistake." He stared back, wholly detached, knowing that he had regained control.

The shepherd had driven what remained of his flock to the forester's road that descended to the meadow and the stream. Now he turned and looked in Brace's direction, and lifted his staff high above his head, holding it high and crossways as if he were brandishing a weapon in some formal gesture of defiance, until all the sheep had disappeared down the path and into the forest.

"The game is over," Brace said quietly. He pointed at the Jäger with his gun. "Now take this bastard out of here as fast as you know how, and remember that the old man goes in peace. Remember not to make any mistake about that because if I hear one hair of his head is touched I am going to blow your brains out."

Brace was shaking with anger as he finished saying this, but once Zabern and the Jäger had gone the anger left him, and he found himself standing alone in an empty field, swaying slightly, with his arms hanging limply at his sides, like a man asleep on his feet. Overcome by a profound torpor and a feeling of complete disorientation, he glanced listlessly at the compound and the sheds, almost ready to believe that nothing had happened, and that he had perhaps imagined, or dreamed, the whole affair. The sun was breaking through the overcast and flooding the training area with a moist, sultry heat. Brace had a sudden urge to shed his raincoat and find a spot in which to curl up and take a nap. The idea was strangely appealing, and for some moments he considered it with the hopeful complacency of a man who has been handed a cure for his hangover, but who knows that only time will ease the pain in his head. Then he bent down to massage his ankle, which — perhaps as a result of his hurried leap from the roof — had begun to throb, and started off across the field to his jeep.

20

THE DUTY CLERK in the battalion message center hailed
him with familiar gaiety as he came through the door of
the Headquarters Building. "Call for you about an hour
ago, Mr. Brace. Some German gal who wouldn't leave
her name." The clerk fell silent at Brace's frown of annoyance, and then continued in a voice that was both
contrite and confidential. "She said she was returning
your call, sir, and that she'd be at the tennis club in
Grünkirchen at noontime. Seemed sure you'd know her."

"I know her," Brace replied. He took the message
from the clerk's hand, crumpled it into a ball, and put it
into his pocket. Then he left the Headquarters Building
and crossed the courtyard to the Bachelor Officers Quarters. As he climbed the stairs to his room, his mind was
racing wildly, weighing the meaning of Greta's caution,
but deriving from it only the most hopeful conclusions.
Obviously he had been right to assume that Zabern knew
nothing for certain. If Greta was sufficiently at liberty
to return his call and to arrange a meeting, there could
be nothing seriously amiss — some embarrassment, perhaps, but no real trouble . . .

Brace had showered and was halfway through shaving himself, when he suddenly became aware of his re-

flection in the mirror above the washstand, and realized
that he was razoring the lather from his face in a series
of hasty and disjointed swaths. Glancing at his watch,
he saw that it was only ten-thirty. Time to spare, he
decided, and forced himself to proceed at a slower pace.
When he had finished shaving, he selected underwear, a
shirt, and a tie from his bureau drawer, but his new de-
liberation had set him thinking again, and as he was but-
toning the shirt he found himself wondering why Greta
had chosen Grünkirchen. It was a large town about
twenty miles to the southeast, on the road to Mannheim.
Brace had passed through it several times, but it was
not in his district and he had never stopped there. Neutral ground, he reflected morosely, and sat on the edge
of his bed to tie his shoelaces. A moment later, he was
standing before the mirror, whistling to himself as he
contrived to wind the tie into a suitably large, German-
styled knot. "Nothing too American," he murmured,
stepping back to appraise the result. Now he pulled on a
jacket — a bulky affair with overly wide lapels which he
had purchased in Gerberstadt — and left the room. On
the way downstairs, his ankle gave a sharp twinge, and
when he reached the courtyard he glanced again at his
watch, saw that it was still too early to leave for Grün-
kirchen, and decided to stop by the dispensary.

The doctor had just finished up with the morning
sick call from Alpha Site. As Brace entered his office, he
lit a cigarette, moved to the window, and looked into
the courtyard where the soldiers he had examined were
climbing into a camion for the return trip. "Not an ail-
ment among the lot," he said grimly. "Nothing but fake
headaches and fake groin pulls. The stupid ones are

bored, and the smart ones are both bored and scared to death. Know how I know?" The doctor gave a harsh laugh, turned from the window, and touched his crotch. "Sly questions about testicles — that's how. They don't miss a chance to get one in. Somebody must've started a rumor about radiation and impotence."

"You can't blame them," Brace said.

"I don't blame them! I give 'em reassurance, aspirin, and a warning not to bother me again. If they try it a second time, I send the following coded message to their sergeant on the back of the sick slip." The doctor turned to the window, and, with the tip of a finger, inscribed a circle around a figure eight on the grimy pane.

"You're the last of the humanists," Brace observed dryly.

"Listen," said the doctor, "what's needed at this post is a therapist, not a general practitioner. I tried to tell that to the adjutant this morning when he called up and asked me if I'd take sick call out at the Site. He claimed he was behind schedule and short of trucks on account of the fog. I told him I wouldn't mind except I'd need a lead suit and a Geiger counter. Funny thing, he didn't seem to get the joke."

"The adjutant has command responsibilities today," said Brace with a smile. "He's lost his sense of humor."

"He's lost his mind if he thinks he'll ever get *me* out there. I'd rather make a house call in hell."

The doctor's cynicism is like cellophane wrapping, Brace thought. It protects him from contact and, therefore, contagion. "I've come to have you take a look at my ankle," he said. "I took a fall this morning and I'm having a bit of trouble putting weight on it."

[291]

The doctor gave his best professional grimace and waited, arms akimbo, while Brace took off his shoe and stocking, and climbed up on the edge of the examining table. Then he began manipulating the foot and pressing his fingers at various spots around the anklebone.

"That hurt?"

"No," said Brace.

"That?"

"A little — not much."

The doctor shook his head. "I don't think there's anything very wrong," he said, cupping Brace's arch in his hand. "A slight sprain, perhaps. Actually, it's a splendid foot. Anyone should be proud to own such a foot."

"That's very reassuring," Brace said.

"Reassurance and aspirin," the doctor replied, "is what I've got a medicine chest full of. In your case, I'll throw in an ace bandage, but it's a waste of government money. What I ought to do is toss you out with the other eight balls. You've got some nerve bothering me for nothing."

Brace climbed off the table and pulled on his sock and shoe. "You think I'm imagining things, eh?"

"No," said the doctor. "Like everybody else around here you're probably trying to escape from something. You wouldn't know it, of course, but that's because you've been stuck away in the boondocks too long."

"You should write a paper," Brace replied.

"I'm going to," the doctor said affably. "I'm going to call it 'Psychasthenia Behind the Moon Compounded by Nuclear Anxiety,' and I'm going to take your case as a prime example."

"What's the remedy?" Brace asked. He had gone to the window and was staring out at the treeless escarpments that rolled off toward the Rhine. "Transfer," the doctor replied, but Brace, who had glanced at his watch and realized that he must be going, had barely heard him. "Look," he said, "how about letting me borrow your car for a couple of hours?"

"Why not?" the doctor said. He was grinning broadly. "So the ankle was just a ruse, after all."

"I've got to run an errand."

"What's the matter with that jeep you're always tooling around in?"

"It's a bit too —" Brace hesitated, searching for the exact word — "A bit too conspicuous," he replied.

"Aha! Some undercover deal, hey?"

"No, no," said Brace with a rueful smile. "Nothing like that."

"Don't kid me, young fellow. Why the kraut-type get-up?"

"All right," Brace said wearily. "But keep it under your hat, will you?" People are always happy when you tell them what they want to hear, he thought.

"You can count on me," the doctor was saying. "I'll be mum as a cadaver in formaldehyde." He had moved to Brace's side and was looking into the courtyard where his car was parked. It was a pre-war Borgward — a long, narrow-styled, and distinctly obsolete vehicle which he treasured because of its obsolescence. "Just the kind of buggy to conduct a surveillance with, hey?"

"None better," Brace replied. He was amused at the shrouded salience of the conversation and at the barely concealed wistfulness in the doctor's voice. Perhaps the doctor's cynicism masks a romantic heart, he thought. "I appreciate your loaning it to me," he said.

"Well, try not to bring it back full of bullet holes."

"No bullet holes," Brace replied, and started for the door.

The doctor seemed disappointed to see him go. "Say, don't you want the keys?"

Brace halted abruptly in the doorway, and smiled a flustered smile.

"They're in the ignition," said the doctor with a triumphant laugh. He was looking carefully at Brace as if he were searching for some obscure and elusive symptom. "You in any kind of jam, young fellow?"

"Nothing serious," Brace answered.

"How are things in 'Sleepy Hollow'?"

"Back to normal. How are your croup patients?"

"Coughing," the doctor replied.

Brace forced himself to grin. The doctor was still frowning at him, and, sensing a scrutiny that was sure to breed further questions, he was anxious to be gone.

The doctor nodded his head in somber fashion. "Look, if it's the ankle that's worrying you —"

Brace interrupted with a hasty, deprecating wave of his hand.

"Well, if it's still giving you trouble tomorrow, I'll send you down to the hospital at Ramstein for an X-ray. Of course, under the circumstances, I don't recommend it. I mean —" the doctor was suddenly beaming — "the less radiation the better, hey?"

Brace felt strangely diminished by his visit to the dispensary, which seemed somehow to have reduced him to the dilemma of a patient who, fearing an adverse diagnosis and distracted by hypochondria, glumly refuses to derive hope from even the most enigmatic verdict. Now, as he traversed the highlands toward Grün-kirchen, the memory of his ambivalent banter with the doctor, the consciously disproportionate knot at his throat, and the borrowed Borgward — all conspired together to make him acutely aware of the clandestine nature of his journey, and to put him on the defensive. Like a man whom fortune has contrived to make a fugitive in his own fief, he had the sensation of being absurdly and unjustly hunted. Even his district no longer seemed familiar and reassuring to him. The towns with their narrow, cobblestoned streets and archways, which he had always found charming, now seemed oppressively confining, and from the rolling, patterned fields between them there suddenly emanated the patchwork confusion of an alien landscape. The faces of the villagers who stepped aside to let him pass, and of the farmers who stared at him from the roadside did not reflect the usual dull, peasant curiosity, but appeared to be full of the furtive cunning with which peasants recognize intruders. In this mood, Brace was scarcely able to contemplate his meeting with Greta, and soon found himself thinking of the shepherd. He imagined the old man wandering through the hills, seeking barns for his sheep. I should be out looking for him, he thought.

It was exactly noon when he drove into the yard of the tennis club, which was deserted except for Greta's blue Volkswagen. In spite of the early morning fog it had turned out to be a hot day, and the sun, shining through the clear, autumnal sky, cast a particularly harsh and unpleasant glare on everything. There was an almost Mediterranean quality in the stillness and the lack of shadow surrounding the clubhouse and the half-dozen adjacent courts. Brace parked the doctor's Borgward at a discreet distance from the Volkswagen and the fence, and sat behind the wheel, watching Greta who was practicing her service on one of the center courts. She was wearing the short pleated skirt and jersey she had worn for her match with Frau Kemp, and she was throwing the balls above and slightly to one side, and then twisting gracefully as she stroked them across the net. How effortless her movements were. How at home she looked even on this strange clay! "Out there everything is bare," she had whispered to him, only yesterday, from the confines of that grove which Zabern had since repossessed, and now, at the sight of her standing alone in the brilliant sunshine, Brace felt a terrible pang of deprivation, and fought off the urge to leave the car and join her.

Greta had seen him and was coming off the court, picking her way through a galaxy of tennis balls that lay strewn in her path. As always, she seemed absorbed by what was closest at hand; she was carefully avoiding the balls by sidestepping, skipping, and shifting her feet as if she were playing one of those awesomely deft games that children endow with fantasy. Brace searched her face for some sign of recognition, but not until she had come through the gate in the fence, crossed the yard to the car, and climbed in through the door which he held open for her did Greta acknowledge him.

"I was afraid you wouldn't get my message, yet here you are," she said gravely.

"There are some appointments for which one is never late," he replied.

Her laughter was a sudden conspiracy that lifted his spirits, for, sensing its acceptance of things past, he also found in it a promise for the future.

"You have a new car," she said. "I prefer it to the other."

"Not mine," Brace answered. "A vehicle of antiquity borrowed for the occasion." He looked directly into her eyes, challenging her to remember the sequence of their sojourn in the grove, and hoping to evoke from her another admission, a fresh commitment, renewed desire . . . But even as she turned away, he realized the desperation and futility of the design. Was it possible that he had ever pulled her, protesting with laughter, through the forest, and then awakened to find needles of time already filling her outstretched palm? One can never awake from the same dream twice, he thought.

"How quickly things change and we are left behind," she murmured. "I didn't really understand until this morning, when you telephoned. It was you, wasn't it?"

"Yes, I was afraid he might have . . . mistreated you." Brace faltered over the words, struck by the absurdity of the fact that twice in the space of a few hours he had had occasion to express the same apprehension to two different women.

"No," said Greta, giving herself a tiny shake. "As you can see —"

"He believes you, then?"

"Yes, in a strange way, though he remains suspicious. For his own sake he must believe me and not the innkeeper — a question of position, you see. It's also fortunate, I suppose, that the innkeeper told a rambling tale — one that in the light of his strange predicament and of your own relation to his wife could easily be discredited upon reflection."

Everything's come back to haunt me, Brace reflected disconsolately. He saw Greta regarding him with an expression of grave candor, and nearly flinched. "It wasn't my intention to conceal that," he said. "I would have told you."

"There was hardly time," she replied, smiling at him sadly. "Besides, I've mentioned it only in another context. You mustn't feel that I am asking for explanations."

"But I'm ready to give them. I want you to know everything."

"Please —" Greta had closed her eyes and placed her hand on his wrist, exerting upon it that same exquisite and almost unbearably anticipative pressure that had accompanied the rising of yesterday's desire. "There isn't time," she said. "You must understand that I can't possibly see you again. The risk, even today . . ."

"You're going to stay with him?"

Her answer was a slight shrug — a tremor that could have been a sigh.

"Leave him," Brace said hoarsely. He said it with a rapidity that surprised him, but the husky desperation in his throat gave the words such an agonized earnestness that he suddenly saw his going and her following as an inexorable result — the only solution. "Leave him and come away with me."

Now Greta opened her eyes, and he saw that they were filled with tears.

"Where?" she asked. "Where should I come?"

"I'll apply for transfer," Brace said quickly. "I can get one today or tomorrow. I'll send for you as soon as I know my next post. I'll write — we'll have to arrange an address so I can write you." Even as he spoke, he was filled with dread at the hastiness of his improvisations, but the need to speak had fallen upon him like a chill, and for some moments longer he rambled on enthusiastically about the lovely scenery in Baden-Württemberg and the possibilities of where he could expect to be stationed.

Greta was shaking her head. "I couldn't bear a military place like Kaiserslautern," she said. "All those women and stores so close together."

"We won't have to live on post. We'll live in some small town." He paused, and when she made no reply he took her silence hopefully. "I'll rent a lovely house and then I'll write to you," he went on.

"In the forest everything was simple," she replied. "We never realized."

"It will be again," Brace said.

"No." Her voice was hushed. "No," she repeated. "Not simple."

Now, studying the grave child's face that was always so engrossed with each successive moment, he understood that she had no facility to foresee happily beyond an interim which might be painful, and, realizing that because of this her pain was greater than his, he wanted desperately to bridge the gap and carry her along with him into the future, any future, even the most illusory of futures. He put his arm around her. "I'll be leaving the army in the spring," he said. "We'll go to Paris!" The road unfolded before him in immense detail.

He imagined them driving through the hilly Saarland, the poplar corridors of Champagne, the grim fortress towns of Metz, Verdun, Châlons-sur-Marne . . .

"In the spring," she echoed, hugging her bare knees with a shiver. "But it isn't even winter."

She was weeping silently.

Brace leaned back in his seat and stared at the roof. Why am I doing this? he wondered. Why am I tearing her up this way? Do I want assurance — a souvenir? "I'm going to give you the address of a man named Moran who lives in Kaiserslautern," he heard himself saying. "He's a friend of mine and you can write me in care of him. When I've arranged things, I'll contact him and have him get in touch with you. He'll do it in a very —" Brace broke off and, not wishing to involve her in a scheme that, as yet unplanned, seemed overly complex, lapsed into silence. Now he looked at her again, hoping for some response, but saw only tears coursing down the tiny ravine between her cheek and nostril. Somehow he managed to pull a piece of paper and a pencil from his pocket, and when he had written out Moran's address, he folded the paper and pressed it firmly into her hand; then he got out of the car, went around to her side, and opened the door.

She emerged misty-eyed but no longer crying, and walked into his arms, which he held outstretched, tilting her face toward his. A moment later, he was gazing past her hair at the sun-drenched courts, thinking over and over, I'm leaving, I'm saying good-by . . .

Then she was walking toward the fence.

"Good-by," he called.

He saw her slow as if she were going to turn around,

but without looking back she went on through the gate and across the courts.

I'll wait until she serves a ball, he thought, but long after the first initially taut and then smoothly unfurling arc of body, wrist, and racket had been repeated — even after the point at which he felt himself excluded by the fierceness of her concentration — he stood rooted on the spot, keeping time with the tempo of her motion, and listening, as if to half-forgotten music, to the soft, percussive sounds that broke the stillness.

Then he climbed into the doctor's car and drove away.

Brace spent the afternoon tidying up his office, checking the contents of his safe against the notations in his documents logbook, and collecting his personal belongings — some books, several pens, and a pocketknife — from recesses in the drawers of his desk. He did all this very slowly and methodically and when he had finished, he sat down in his swivel chair, reached for the telephone, and dialed the field office at Area Command. Instantly, much sooner than he was ready for it, a connection was made, and Moran's voice broke in on him from the other end.

"I've changed my mind," Brace said abruptly.

"Hullo . . . Harry?"

"Yes," replied Brace. "Look, Moran, I've changed my mind about that offer you made. I'd like a transfer, after all."

"You would . . . ? Well, okay, I'll see what I can do." Moran spoke with the puzzled calculation of a man who has been taken by surprise.

"When can you get me out?"

"Well, give me a minute to think. You in any trouble up there, Harry?" Moran's voice had suddenly become familiar, fatherly, solicitous . . .

"I've got a few personal problems," Brace answered shortly, "but there's nothing wrong professionally, if that's what you mean."

Moran coughed. "How soon d'you want to leave?"

"As soon as you can dig up a replacement."

"You don't even have to wait for that," Moran said. "I can have Coolidge cover your district until a new man arrives. Of course it would be better if you could stay to break him in yourself, but under the circumstances —"

"What circumstances?" said Brace with a laugh.

"Yeah, well — you're playing it rather close to the vest, aren't you?" Moran responded with an embarrassed chuckle. "What I can't figure, Harry, is — I mean why didn't you let me know when I was up there yesterday? Why the sudden change of heart?"

"One of those things," Brace replied. "I suddenly got fed up." He tipped back his chair and closed his eyes as he remembered that he had used those same words to describe the fox to the doctor on the morning of the second day.

There was a long pause at Moran's end of the wire. "Tell you what, Harry. Suppose I send someone up tomorrow to sign over your gear and the documents. As soon as that's done, you can come down here for a few days and get yourself debriefed while I see what I can do about getting you another berth."

"Fine," Brace said. "I appreciate it a lot."

There was another pause; then Moran's voice again, hesitant and apologetic. "You sure there isn't anything I should tip off Coolidge about?"

"All's quiet," said Brace. "Oh, one thing — we finally found out who's been smearing the K.P.D. signs around. An innkeeper by the name of Weber from Weiersheim. There's a repatriated-prisoner-report on him in the files. He took off for the border last night and I've got a suspicion he made it, but you might have Coolidge check with the local policeman."

"Was he in a position to know anything . . . about the Site?"

"No more than anyone else in town. He was a —"

"Hold on a minute, Harry. There's a call coming in from headquarters on another line."

Brace heard a loud clatter as Moran dropped the receiver on his desk, and then a faint clicking of typewriters in the background. Suddenly, he was overcome with impatience — a sense of sedentary impotence. I should be out looking for Mathias, he thought again. For some moments, he gazed through the window, realizing the hopelessness of such a quest, yet savoring the bittersweet prospect of combing the wrinkled terrain of his district forever. Then, all at once, he saw a huge shadow sweep across the courtyard, climb the wall of the BOQ, and brush the slate roof of the dispensary. A strange turbulence followed, which set up a tempest in the windowpanes, and hard on the heels of this came a racket as awesome as the engines of doomsday. With a supreme effort, Brace looked up, expecting to receive a stunning blow, and saw a helicopter darting skyward, tilting against the horizon's edge, and then spinning off on a wide circuit of the *Kaserne* — the helicopter bearing the colonel back from Stuttgart. He found himself shaking with relief. So there was nothing overhead except the colonel! And what was *he* thinking of as he looked down upon this land behind the moon — this profound sea with its myriad roiling contours? The helicopter was hovering like a darning needle above the parade field; then it descended slowly out of sight behind a rooftop. Brace imagined the colonel stepping out and planting his feet with proprietary pride upon ground that covered a tunnel which appeared on no one's map. The idea filled him with a savage and anarchistic frustration. He saw himself setting fire to the documents in his safe, to his maps, to the buildings of the *Kaserne*, even to the forest! — ah, but he could not sustain the vision of this private *Götterdämmerung*, this scorching twilight fantasy that would leave nothing but ashes for his successors, and once again everything seemed to recede before him. Now, as if with the advent of sleep, he saw Greta's sweet, grave face bending over him in a forest of cardboard trees; the Town Secretary peering sadly up at him from a trench filled with water; and the shepherd wending his way through the folds and crevices of an empty world . . .

Moran's voice — detached and professional — brought him back.

"Now this innkeeper, Harry. You're sure he can't tell them anything over there?"

"Yes, I'm sure," Brace replied wearily. "I'll see you tomorrow or the day after." I'll have to go back to the training area tonight and bury the sheep, he thought.

Moran's voice was full of insistence and caution. "Nothing compromised, then?"

Brace wanted to laugh, but found that he could not.

"Nothing compromised," he said, and hung up the phone.